The Children of Mapu Street

The Children of Mapu Street

a novel by

Sarah Neshamit

translated from the Hebrew by David S. Segal

The Jewish Publication Society of America
Philadelphia 5730 · 1970

Prologue

Dirt roads meander through fields of rye and endless meadows. The standing grain sways to and fro, the golden ears of corn bow down. Wild red poppies stare boldly up to the sky and shy cornflowers droop their deep blue heads.

A bone-tired mare plods down an unpaved road, dragging a buckboard wagon. On the wagon seat sits a broad-shouldered farmer, half asleep. Big-bellied cows spot the meadows, some brownish-red, some black flecked with white, lazily munching grass. Woolly sheep look about in fear.

Fish-filled ponds mirror groves of pines, firs, and maples, ash and willows. Wheat fields gleam in flowery whiteness and patches of blue flax flowers rise from the plain.

A land of fields and hamlets. An old wooden cross, covered with moss and half rotted, thrusts upward at a crossroads, amid small wooden cottages, scattered and alone. The huts' tiny windows look out on small flower plots where the rue is turning green and mints and mignonettes give off sweet odors. Trees sagging with cherries glow red in the sunlight.

1

Factories and smokestacks are rare here. No tractors chug through these broad fields, no combines gladden the workers' hearts. Here the farmer slowly trails behind the plow, flicking his whip lazily over his wretched nag. At harvest time the farmer wields a scythe and his wife stoops over behind him, binding the sheaves.

A cross above the tower of a church flashes gold in the sunlight.

A small town. The streets converge on the marketplace, where stall is jammed upon stall. Jewish merchants move about swiftly to serve their customers, the region's farmers.

The town is cloaked in twilight. Dim lights emerge from the windows. Behind a closed door a Jew adds up the day's earnings and hurries off to afternoon and evening prayers. Children, hunched over their notebooks, are preparing their lessons.

Such is the land of Lithuania.

And the capital of Lithuania is Kovno.

Long ago it was merely a tiny fishermen's village. Over the years, it grew and prospered, and under the Russian czars became a fortress. Remnants of the fortifications surround the city to this day.

The year 1941. About forty thousand Jews live in Kovno—merchants and scholars, artisans and writers, doctors and teachers, lawyers and workers. They have expanded the city and beautified it; they have built the new Kovno.

Kovno is indeed a Jewish city, teeming with elementary schools, high schools, and all kinds of institutions; Hebrew rolls off the children's tongues.

The city is situated where the Viliya River spills into the Niemen.

How lovely the Niemen is and how grand the Viliya. Their tall banks are decked with rich green forests. On the Sabbath Kovnites leave the city to swim in the river and lounge in the shade of the trees. Many Jews have even built summer homes in the forests.

At night, anyone who goes up the mountain adjoining the rivers can see the whole dazzling city spread before him. On one of these hills Abraham Mapu sat and wrote his famous novel, *Love of Zion*. Here, on the banks of the Niemen, his mind's eye saw the banks of the Jordan and the Sea of Galilee.

Kovno boasts a Mapu Street—an old thoroughfare, with gray buildings one, two, and three stories high. The houses have courtyards flanked on three sides by the living quarters and on the fourth side by a gate that opens onto the street. Almost none of these courts have gardens or grass, only paving stones, and wherever they sink into the ground the rain gathers in puddles.

This is a tale about one of the courtyards in Mapu Street.

The Children of Mapu Street

By the Birch Tree

It was a courtyard somewhat larger than usual. The house wasn't very big, leaving all the more room for the yard. There were a few apartments on the second and third stories. The ground floor was taken up by a small grocery store, a garage, and a warehouse.

The courtyard held a treasure that was unique in the immediate vicinity—a small garden and a birch tree with bright green leaves and bark as white as snow. Thanks to the tree, all the children of the court knew each other; they would often meet in its shade and peel off the white bark in the very thinnest strips.

These were the youngsters of the court: Rivka and David, the Wilensky children, whose family lived in a small apartment on the second floor, over their grocery store. Shula, thirteen years old, the only daughter of Dr. Weiss, lived on the second floor at the entrance to the left. The children of the bank clerk Levine—Yisraelik, thirteen-and-a-half, and Yankel, four years old—also lived on the second floor but to the right. Four children of Cohen the tailor lived on the third floor: Hanna, five; Etta, eight; Shmulik, twelve; and Reuven, a university student. Below, alongside the warehouse, lived the Lithuanian janitor. He had three children: Jonas, who was army age; Biruté, who had just completed elementary school and was learning how to sew from Mrs. Cohen; and the youngest, Juozas, ten years old.

It was early June. After the heavy rains it had been hard to play in the garden. The earth was mucky and stuck to one's shoes, making walking a chore. The wet even got to the bench next to the birch tree and its paint began to peel. Only the tree itself flourished, its small leaves turning green and glistening in the sun.

Etta Cohen and her brother Shmulik were in the garden.

"Come here, Etta, let's write our names on the birch tree," said Shmulik. "A birch tree is like paper."

"Why do you want to?" asked Etta.

"Because when we grow up we'll move away from here," answered Shmulik.

"Where'll we go?"

"Don't you know where? To Eretz Yisrael!"

"So what if we go there?"

"So then we won't be here anymore; other kids will. They'll read our names and know we lived here."

"Good, let's write! I'll get a pen and some ink," she teased.

"C'mon, you know the rain will wash it away. We'll carve our names." Shmulik unsheathed the shiny new penknife he had just received for his birthday the day before and set to work.

"Say," asked Etta with concern, "whose name are you writing first?"

"Mine."

8

"That's not right. Aunt Miriam says ladies should always go first."

Shmulik hesitated. He had heard that argument too, but he was itching to see his name engraved on the birch bark.

"Oh, it doesn't matter," he said. "I'll carve my name and then put yours on top so it will look like I wrote mine second."

"Hey, what you doing there! Stop ruining that tree!"

"Shmulik," said Etta in fright, "the janitor's yelling. Let's get out of here."

Eleven-year-old Rivka Wilensky entered the garden, paying no attention to the two Cohen children.

"Why don't you say hello when you see people?" asked Etta.

"My mother says you don't have to 'hello' everybody in the court."

In walked Yisraelik Levine with Shula Weiss behind him. Catching the last exchange, he volunteered, "You girls are just nincompoops. You're supposed to say hello to everybody you know. But you're not even people yet," he preached.

"Kids *are* people, too," pouted Etta.

"My mother says that well-mannered children always say hello," Shula gravely observed.

Yisraelik puffed out his cheeks scornfully. "What do you know, little girls?"

"If we're little girls, why did you come over here? Who asked you?"

"I didn't come to see you, I came over to the garden. The garden belongs to everybody."

9

"The garden is *not* everybody's. It belongs to the janitor. He just bawled us out for starting to carve our names on the tree."

"You mustn't do that," Shula said. "Only a ninny writes her name everywhere."

"Who says so?" retorted Etta, blushing furiously.

"Our teacher, that's who."

"Well, he's not right." Shmulik chimed. "Adults write their names all over. I saw a whole bunch of names on the benches in the park."

"So what, do you think all grownups are smart?"

"Ha, ha, ha!" laughed Rivka. "Yisraelik's the oldest here but he's sure not the smartest!"

"Don't laugh so hard, smarty-pants," Yisraelik blurted, "you're just a scaredy-cat. You're so scared, you can't even cross the street at night without your mother."

The conversation was turning heated just as Mrs. Levine came back from the park with Yankel. She called to Yisraelik. "Go do your lessons, son. This afternoon I'm taking you to the forest."

Yisraelik gladly tore himself away, bounded up the stairs three at a time, and dove into the house.

Even doing homework was fine if it meant going to the forest. Yisraelik loved the forest—and the river, too. He had even learned how to swim. The year before, his mother had rented a room in a forest lodge and they had spent the whole summer vacation on the beach by the Niemen. Yankel had been with them too, but their father came up only on Saturdays. They were going to spend the coming summer at the same resort. He meant to work hard on his swimming so that by the following year he would be able to enter the student swimming contests. Yisraelik was best in his class in language and arithmetic but there were better swimmers than he and he did not want to lag behind them.

How glorious that there was such a thing as summer and forests and the Niemen!

War

Yisraelik bolted awake. Time to get up already? *Today there will be a test in literature for sure,* he thought. But he was not afraid. All of his last compositions had been marked VERY GOOD in big red letters. Suddenly, however, he remembered that summer vacation had begun a week before. He pushed his cheek into the soft pillow and drew his knees up to his stomach. What a pleasure to be able to lounge around in bed. It had to be early; the sky was still gray. Yisraelik cast a glance at the opposite wall. Yankel slumbered on peacefully, his right fist clenched beneath his head.

Why had he awakened so early? Yisraelik wondered. Then he heard the long, thunderlike rumble. But it was not thunder. It was low-flying planes.

Their airplanes again!

11

True, it was exciting to watch airplanes zoom about the sky, flip over, and work all sorts of wonders. But nighttime was for sleeping. For a whole week now the planes had been spreading terror.

After a few minutes the rumbling quieted down and Yisraelik drifted back to sleep.

"Get up! Hurry, get up!"

Before him stood his mother, ready to go out into the street, her shopping basket on her arm.

"Get dressed, Yisraelik, and take care of Yankel. Don't let him into the street. This is a war. I want to get some food." Then she was gone.

War! More than once he had seen battles in the movies. But movies were not real life. Even so, war was terrifying enough on the screen. Houses collapsed with people inside them, there were fires, corpses. . . . Yisraelik recalled Mr. Feld, a refugee from Warsaw, who had boarded in their house the year before. What horrible things he had told them of the Germans!

What would happen if the Germans were to come to Kovno? *They won't reach us*, he comforted himself. *The Red Army has been in Lithuania for a year, a powerful army. The Russian tanks are as large as this house.*

Suddenly he remembered that he had to look after his little brother. Where was Yankel?

Yisraelik leaped out of bed and searched for his brother in his parents' room, in the guest room, in the kitchen. Yankel was nowhere to be found. Yisraelik dressed in a frenzy and dashed down the steps to the courtyard. Yankel was not there either. Yisraelik sped out the gate.

The once quiet street was unrecognizable.

The doors to the dry-goods warehouse were flung wide open. Automobiles kept coming and going. People were dashing about in all directions. Wilensky's grocery store was jam-packed, with an enormous line spilling out into the street.

"Hey, kid," someone shouted, "get out from between my legs!"

Yisraelik wanted to get back into the courtyard, but he could not free himself from the mad tangle of people. The line outside the grocery had become a wild mob. Everyone was surging onto the sidewalk, crushing against each other and screaming. A truck weighed down with trunks emerged from the courtyard of the warehouse, but its path was blocked. The driver honked and honked but the people kept pushing forward frantically, refusing to clear a path.

"Ho, officer!" shouted the driver. "Officer!"

"These Yids are blocking the way!" Yisraelik heard the wife of their janitor exclaim. "No matter what they've got, it's not enough."

"They'd swallow the whole world," another voice broke out. "Hey, driver, run 'em over, no pity—there'll be more than enough Yids left in Kovno." The man guffawed hoarsely.

"Wise words, by God's life, wise words," murmured the janitor's wife.

Yisraelik was stunned. Never had he heard the woman say such things. Looking about him he discovered Shula by his side, as confused as he was.

Where was Yankel? God forbid, could he have been run over by the cars? He begged Shula to help him find his

13

brother. The two of them forced their way through the packed crowd. Curses showered down on them, but they paid no attention.

"Yankel!" cried Shula with joy, sighting the little boy. She grabbed his sleeve and pulled him aside.

"Why did you leave the house without permission?" Yisraelik demanded angrily, imitating his father's voice. "I'll teach you! You realize there's a war on?"

"A war! A war!" cried Yankel gleefully.

"What are you so happy about? You don't even know what a war is!" chided Shula. "Why did you go out?"

" 'Cause there were so many cars and it looked like fun."

"Dumbbell!" fumed Yisraelik. "They kill people in wars. You can't go outside."

It took an hour for the street to empty. Mr. Wilensky closed the store. A police officer arrived and ordered the crowd to disperse. Back home, the children took in the scene from the windows.

Yisraelik, unable to restrain his curiosity, went outside again. Down the street leading to the bridge streamed column after column of Russian army troops in full battle dress. They marched silently with tight lips.

They're headed for the front, Yisraelik thought. *Maybe some of them will never see their families again.*

That day Yisraelik and Yankel had a cold lunch. Their mother and father whispered at great length and their faces were drawn.

Everything was topsy-turvy in the home of Shula's parents. No one rang the doorbell and there were no calls for

14

the doctor. The waiting room was empty, the receiving room closed. The family maid, Ursula, who had worked for them for twelve years, had not shown up that day. Shula's mother was enraged. She wandered about the rooms as though she had forgotten something, went over to the piano, opened it and closed it again.

If I were to do that, thought Shula, *she'd sure give it to me. But adults can do anything.*

Her mother was telling her father that according to what she had heard, the Germans had already crossed the border and were approaching Kovno; the Russians were retreating. Mrs. Weiss's eyes were filled with fear. Her husband tried to calm her, maintaining that the Russian retreat was merely a tactical maneuver. He lit a cigarette, and Shula saw that his hands were shaking.

Finding the atmosphere unbearable, Shula slipped into the court. There in the garden by the birch tree, the gang had already assembled.

Five-year-old Hanna Cohen, the tailor's daughter, had come down with her doll Rina. Rina had long blond braids, blue eyes, and a red dress.

"We have lots 'n' lots of rags at home," Hanna was explaining, "'cause my Mommy is a seamstress. When I get big I'm going to be a seamstress, too. Then I'll sew Rina lots 'n' lots of dresses. I'll sew new dresses for all your dolls, too."

"My parents are very upset," Shula reported.

"It's lots of fun at our house. Lots of people are coming today," Etta said proudly. "They're all coming to take the clothes they gave my mother to sew."

"Why?" asked Rivka.

15

" 'Why?' She always asks why," thundered Shmulik. "It's war today, you can't leave clothes anywhere."

"My daddy says we'll have to run away from here," piped David, " 'cause the Germans are coming."

"Run away now?" said Shmulik disdainfully. "We can't run away. We have to give it to them first."

Being one of the oldest of the group, Shmulik considered himself an authority on every question. Shula, however, objected that the Germans were too powerful.

"Uh-uh," interrupted David, "the Russians are the most strongest. They got great big tanks. Daddy says we have to go to Russia."

"Go on, Jews, go on to Russia. There shouldn't be one Jew left here!" The voice was that of Jonas, the eldest son of the janitor, who seemed to have sprung up from the earth. His hands were in his pockets, his eyes full of hatred and contempt.

The children looked at him in amazement. What brought that remark on? What had they ever done to him to deserve such abuse? A blind fear gripped them.

It was Shmulik who broke the silence. "We'll go wherever we want and live wherever we want."

"Ha, look at this hero! We'll see you tomorrow, when Hitler gets here. Jews *kaput!*" cried Jonas, passing his hand across his throat like a butcher and turning his back to them.

The children were dumfounded. Never had Jonas said such things to them. They had always considered him their friend. His younger brother, Juozas, had played with them regularly in the garden. More than once Jonas had made them toys. Both the little table and the pale green bench

16

were his handiwork. They always greeted him with candy. What had happened to Jonas? Where had all that hatred suddenly come from?

The day was drawing to a close, the sun flickered weakly behind the clouds. The last rays touched the roof of the house opposite, the birch leaves in the garden turned gray and the trunk, purplish. Behind the garden fence stood Juozas, the janitor's youngest son, observing the children silently.

"Juozas, c'mon over," shouted Etta.

But Juozas did not stir. He simply looked at the children silently. Only a low wooden fence separated Juozas from the rest, but all of them knew that never again would the janitor's boy jump over that fence, never again would he enter the garden to play with them.

The Canceled Birthday Party

"I've got a birthday, I've got a birthday—I'm eleven," Rivka gaily announced to the children. "Everybody's invited to my party."

"Do we get treats?" asked Etta.

"There'll be a chocolate cake—I'm baking it myself."

"You know how to bake?" asked Shula.

"Today I'll learn how. My mother said that when I turned eleven she'd teach me how to bake and cook. 'A young lady has to know everything.' That's what my mother says."

"And my mother says it just doesn't matter," Shula rejoined. "Cooking you can learn afterwards, when you get married. Now we have to study."

"That's not right," Shmulik shook his head. "A girl has to learn how to cook before she gets married."

"It's not necessary at all," Shula insisted stubbornly. "My mother still doesn't know how to cook and she's married."

"And who cooks for you and your father?" asked Etta.

"Ursula makes our meals."

"And when you don't have Ursula?"

"Why should that ever happen? She'll always be——"

"You're talking like little children," interjected Shmulik, agitated. "A girl has to know how to cook and bake and sew. But she doesn't have to do everything. She can even be a lady doctor, like our lady doctor in school."

"A boy has to know how to sew too," Shula said, after some reflection.

"Why?" asked little David. "A lady sews for a man."

"Well, suppose he's ugly and doesn't have a wife?"

"Then, then"—David groped for an answer—"everybody's got a wife. If he's ugly, he's got an ugly wife!"

"I'm going to bake the cake now," said Rivka as she raced up the steps.

"Cookies, too?" Etta called after her.

"Cookies, too."

"And candy?"

"Yes. And you all bring me presents."

"It's not nice to ask for presents," Shula shouted.

Rivka stopped short in amazement at the threshold of the apartment she had left two hours before. The rooms were full of bundles, sacks, and suitcases which her father and mother were energetically tying and untying, yanking items from one container to stuff into another.

"Close the door and stop wandering around!" her mother snapped.

"Mother, I came to bake the cake."

"What cake? Don't give me any headaches now."

"But Mommy, it's my birthday."

"Yes, but leave me alone right now. I don't have the time today."

"But Mommy, you promised that today I could bake the cake myself."

"You're not baking any cakes, you hear?" her father shouted. "Don't you realize what's happening? A girl of eleven should understand these things."

"I . . . I . . . want to celebrate a little," Rivka replied and burst into tears.

"What are you yelling at the child for, Meir? She's not to blame for this accursed war."

"So what did I say? I didn't say anything," her father mumbled.

Rivka's mother gave her a handful of candies and honey wafers and coaxed her to go out to the court.

"Mommy, I don't want any candies," whispered Rivka with trembling lips, "I want a birthday."

"Go, daughter, go. We'll celebrate your birthday when it's quieter—after the war, if we live. We're terribly busy now. We have to save some goods, so they don't take everything away from us."

Rivka still could not grasp it all. Hurriedly her parents kept filling sack after sack, dragging each one to the open cellar door where her father would carry them down. Sweat was pouring from him, and her mother's breathing was heavy.

"Mommy, why are you taking everything down to the cellar? I'll help you," offered the girl, suddenly aware of her mother's fatigue.

"No, child, you'd only get in our way. You take the candy and go outside."

"Mommy, I'll celebrate my birthday in the garden. A birthday like . . . well, just like that. I'll give out nice things to the kids, O.K.?"

"Fine, fine. Go dear, go."

"Here you go," called her father, tossing her a small blue paper bag filled with nuts. "Make yourself a party in the garden."

"And let's hope we'll be able to celebrate your birthday next year, daughter, in peace and quiet," added her mother with a sigh as she closed the door behind her.

Shula bounded up the steps and pushed twice on the buzzer, long and hard. *Father will think it's a patient,* she thought with a smile.

But something was wrong. No one was opening the door. Impatiently she rang again, this time sharply. Shula heard her father's footsteps approaching. He merely opened the door and at once returned to the reception room.

Why did Father open the door, not Ursula? pondered

Shula, as she entered the dining room. Not a soul was there, or in the bedroom or the kitchen. Her mother's angry voice erupted from the reception room.

"So what should we do then? You tell me."

"I suggest that we pack what we can in two small valises and leave immediately."

"Become hobos? Leave the house, everything, like refugees?"

"Leave everything. The government has already fled."

"Oh, Max, what will become of us?" Shula heard her mother sob.

"The Russians will be back soon. In the meantime we must get out of here. There's not much time."

The door opened and her mother emerged, her eyes swollen with weeping. Her father's face was grim.

"Mother . . . ," said Shula.

"Yes, daughter?"

"I . . . wanted you to buy a present."

Her mother looked at her distractedly.

"*Nu*, a present for Rivka, Mother, she has a birthday today."

Shula's father laughed bitterly.

"Come here, child, I want to tell you something." Her father sat her down beside him on the sofa. His voice had changed over the last two days.

"Do you know what war is, my daughter? It's a terrible thing. Men become wild beasts, ready to tear their neighbors apart. And this war is worse than any that has ever been. In this war it will be mostly Jews who get killed. Understand? And now, child, help your mother pack your belongings."

21

Shula sat there gaping. It was still beyond her.

"Why, Father?"

"Because we're leaving here. We have to save ourselves."

"Leaving now? Right now?"

"Right now. We haven't got a minute to lose."

It was all too horrible. Shula refused to understand.

"You mean I can't go to the birthday party? And I can't buy Rivka a present?"

"You can give her this whole apartment for a present," snapped her father with sudden impatience, leaving the room and closing the door behind him.

Shula stood rooted to the spot, staring at the closed door.

"Shula, come here," she heard her mother call.

Shula ran to the bedroom. It was in utter turmoil. The closet was open, the dresser drawers had been pulled out and emptied. Socks, undershirts, blouses, all kinds of clothing lay strewn about the floor, the chairs, and the beds. From time to time her mother would take an article, throw it into the valise, then take it out, tears streaming down her cheeks the while. Dr. Weiss returned.

"You want to take all this? Impossible!"

"But how can we go without it? I'm leaving my piano, your instruments, the furniture, and the rugs. At least let me take the silver and the clothes."

"Impossible, there are no more trains."

"How did that happen?" Mrs. Weiss demanded.

"The last train has already pulled out."

"God in heaven! What shall we do? What are the neighbors doing? What is Mr. Levine doing?"

Leaving her packing, Mrs. Weiss paced to and fro, at an utter loss for ideas. "What shall we do? What shall we do?"

"We'll go on foot," her husband calmly replied.

Unable to control herself any longer, Shula's mother burst into tears. "Max, I won't go. Go by yourself. You're a man. You have to go. I'll stay. They won't touch women, I'm sure they won't."

"We all go or we all stay," her husband replied, his face pulling taut.

"To leave everything and run with just the clothes on our backs and then throw ourselves on people's mercy? No, no. . . . What will happen, will happen. I'm staying."

"Do as you like." He turned and stalked into the reception room.

Shula looked at her mother sobbing, unable to understand her refusal to leave Kovno. Father was right. They had to escape. After all, Father was a doctor. There would be sick people everywhere needing his help.

Then again, maybe it would be better to stay. The Germans would need doctors, too; they had sick people. And even if they took everything, they would have to pay her father for his help.

Shula wondered where the Levine family had gone. How lonely that apartment had become. Where were Yisraelik and Yankel? Too bad. Yisraelik was the oldest one in the gang. Who would she play with now?

BOOM, BOOM, BOOM—the thunder of canons.

"Shooting again. They never stop shooting."

Shula went to the window to have a look. To the south a smoke column twisted upward, poking gray fingers across the sky. *There must be a fire*, she thought.

23

She was out the door before her mother could shout "Shula, don't leave."

A few leaps brought her to the court, but there was nothing to be seen there—the houses were in the way. Shula dashed to the gate. The street, too, was empty. In the gate across the way, however, stood a group of men. After a moment's hesitation she was in the street.

"Hey, girlie, get back home quick. Don't you hear the shooting?" someone scolded.

The street was truly deserted. Only one man was in sight, walking with measured steps, addressing everyone who so much as poked his head outside a gate. Shula recognized him. He was the mailman. Every morning, on her way to school, she would meet him hurrying to his job.

Shula returned to the court. She had no desire to go back inside the house, but walking around by herself was no fun either. From the hallway emerged the wife of the janitor and Ursula, the maid. What was Ursula doing there? Why hadn't she come to work?

Shula started to walk toward Ursula and ask her, but there was an odd, hateful look in Ursula's eyes. Shula froze, speechless.

The sound of weeping rose from the garden.

"Rivka, why are you crying?" asked Shula, embracing her friend.

"I wanted a birthday party. I brought candy and honey cakes and nuts. And no one came." Rivka's narrow shoulders shook.

"Don't cry, Rivka. We'll make you a party right away. We'll call the kids and play in the garden," said Shula.

24

"Uh-uh, we can't."

"Why?"

"Uh-uh," Rivka sobbed brokenly. "No children, no Yisraelik, no Yankel. . . ."

"Then let's get Etta, Hanna, and Shmulik."

"Not there," sniffed Rivka.

"Don't cry, Rivka, you just hold on."

Shula scooted up the steps to the Cohen apartment. She knocked but there was no answer. Hesitating just a moment, she pushed the door open with both hands and walked in. All was still. Shula ran to the children's bedroom. Empty. The beds were not made. Pillows and quilts lay jumbled together, linens were strewn all over the floor and chairs, and red socks hung from the small night table —Etta's socks. Steps seemed to resound from the tailor's room. *They're back*, thought Shula joyfully.

There, too, however, as in the bedroom, half-sewn clothes and linens were all over, as well as dishes with bits of food on them.

"What are you doing here?"

Shula was startled. Before her stood Biruté, the janitor's daughter, whom Mrs. Cohen had taught how to sew.

"What are *you* doing here?" retorted Shula angrily.

"None of your business. The Jews ran away. Now I'm the owner."

Shula stared at the girl, hardly recognizing her. The janitor's daughter was wearing a blue dress of Mrs. Cohen's which was far too long and wide for her.

"It doesn't matter, I'll fix it," said Biruté arrogantly, as though reading Shula's mind. "I'll alter all Mrs. Cohen's dresses."

"But they're not yours!"

25

"Now everything's mine," laughed Biruté. "And we'll take everything you've got, too."

"We won't give it to you. We won't," gasped Shula.

"You Yids. . . . All the Yids are *kaput!*" she taunted, drawing her hand across her throat.

To prove to Shula she meant just what she said, Biruté opened wide the doors of the closet and randomly tossed out dresses, blouses, and other clothes onto the table, the chairs, the floor. Finally she took a red garment and flung it scornfully at Shula's feet.

"Don't touch that, that's Hanna's!" The cry leaped of itself from Shula's throat.

"Ha, ha, ha. What Hanna?" Biruté snickered as she scooped up an armful of children's clothes and dumped them over Shula. On the floor lay Rina, Hanna's favorite doll, her head split in two and her red dress gleaming like a ribbon of blood on the scattered white garments.

Shula wrenched herself away.

Back in the garden, she did not see Rivka. On the table and bench lay the small bags of candy and honey cakes her friend had brought down for her birthday party.

Father Is Taken

The shooting went on uninterruptedly an entire day. The walls of the house trembled, the windows shattered, chunks of glass littered the floor. Shula and her parents took refuge in the cellar. There they found Rivka and her little brother, David. It was dark and damp in the cellar and smelled of mold. The waiting seemed endless. Shula lost all track of time.

On and on went the shooting. The house shook, horses pounded over the streets, a shriek cut through the air, then died away.

Shula's eyes grew accustomed to the dark. She saw her mother leaning against the wall, half asleep. Rivka Wilensky was drowsing too, her head on her mother's knees. Mr. Wilensky and the doctor were whispering together. David tried to climb up on a trunk and sneak a look through the latticed cellar window, but his father rebuked him angrily. The boy sat down on the floor again, alongside Shula.

Shula looked at him anxiously. "Why are there wars?" she asked in a whisper, as though thinking out loud.

Suddenly her father ended his conversation with Mr. Wilensky, got up, and touched his wife's shoulder. Mrs. Weiss opened her eyes.

"I'm going to see what's up," he said, and left.

"Max, don't stay away long," her mother called after him in a tremulous voice.

Half an hour passed and still Shula's father had not returned. Hours, it seemed, went by. Shula's mother kept glancing worriedly at the door or window. After an hour, the cellar door finally opened.

"Father!" Shula cried, running to greet him. But the word froze on her lips. White-faced, Dr. Weiss stood against the wall, his right palm cupping his left elbow. Two dull streaks showed on his white shirt.

"M-Max," stammered Mrs. Weiss, "what happened? You're wounded!"

"Hush, don't raise your voices. They nicked my arm. It's nothing. There aren't any Russians left in the city; the Lithuanians are killing Jews in the streets."

"Oh, my God, my God! We're lost, we're lost!" sobbed Mrs. Wilensky.

"Quiet!" rapped the doctor. "The Shauliai* are going from house to house looking for Jews."

All fell silent, even the children. They realized that the danger was great. That night they all stayed in the cellar. Hunger began to gnaw at them. The little food they had brought from the house had run out earlier in the day. The water, too, had been used up and more was needed from upstairs. But to go to the apartment was out of the question. Anyone might discover them and inform the Shauliai. Shula's head ached as though it were weighted down with bricks, but she held her tongue, not wanting to worry her parents. Suddenly, however, her head dropped onto her mother's bosom.

"What's the matter, child?" She pressed her palm against her daughter's forehead. "Why, you're burning up!" Her father touched her forehead, too, and checked her pulse.

"Come on, Esther" he said, "Let's go upstairs. The child is sick."

Dr. Weiss picked Shula up and, half supporting her, led her up from the cellar.

* The name given by the Jews to the organization of Lithuanian Nazis that went around murdering Jews.

Shula had a fever. Her father paced back and forth across the room, his arm bandaged. He approached her bed, looked at her wordlessly and went back to the window.

Her mother entered the room. "Max, let me go down to the storekeeper. Maybe I can get some flour from him."

"Not now, don't go anywhere now. Quiet! Someone's ringing!"

Shula's parents looked at each other questioningly. Mrs. Weiss approached the threshold but her hand remained suspended in the air. Dr. Weiss opened the door.

"Ursula!"

She was not alone. Two armed men in gray uniforms entered the room with her. Mrs. Weiss emitted a frightened cry.

Her husband, leaning against the wall, addressed Ursula calmly. "Hello, Ursula. Who are these gentlemen and what do they wish?"

Ursula only glared.

"Who are we? None of your business, Yid," hissed one of the two. "And why we came—you'll find out real soon. Let's go!"

"Max!" Mrs. Weiss clung to her husband protectively with every ounce of her strength. "Where are you taking him? What harm did he ever do you? He's only a doctor, leave him alone."

"We don't need no Jew doctors," the same man answered, his eyes narrowing.

"Move out!" barked the second soldier, a cloddish, broad-shouldered fellow, striking Dr. Weiss with his rifle butt.

29

"Ursula, help us! Why have you done this? We never hurt you."

"So you won't be the big bosses now, that's why. We've had enough of your lording it over us in Lithuania. Not a single Yid will stay here." Ursula all but spat at Mrs. Weiss, raising her hand as though to hit her.

"What are you waiting for? Move!" One of the soldiers kicked Dr. Weiss in the direction of the door.

"Max, Max!" Mrs. Weiss shrieked after them.

"Daddy, Daddy!" cried Shula from her bed.

"Ursula, what have you done to us? When did we ever hurt you?" Shula's mother asked again.

"Look, go with him if you want to. Don't think you're going to stay in your apartment."

"Ursula," she begged. "take the apartment, the clothes, the furniture, everything—just save him."

"Too late for that," shot back Ursula as she left, slamming the door behind her.

"Daddy, where did Daddy go?" Shula raced to the door in her nightgown, feverish, barefoot, and pathetic.

"Hush, child," her mother tried to quiet her. "Go to bed, your father will be back. He's a doctor and he never hurt anyone."

But Shula's father was not to return.

Flight

Shula was toiling up an enormous mountain. Streams of sweat ran down her forehead onto her lips, and she was panting heavily; there was a long way to go. Her legs were gashed and running with blood. She had almost reached the crest when an awesome black chasm gaped before her. No path remained, only that yawning pit.

All at once someone seized her and dashed her forward. Screaming, she plunged headlong into darkness—and awoke.

Standing alongside her bed was her mother, pressing her shoulder. "Get up, child; hurry, we have to get out of here."

Shula was still half asleep. She pressed her cheek against her mother's soft, smooth hand. Ah, it had only been a dream. Any minute her father would come in and kiss her on the forehead.

"Get dressed, child, we have to leave the apartment," her mother urged.

With that, the last few days' horrors all came back to her. The day before, her fever had gone down a little. Her face was still pale, though, and there were blue circles around her eyes.

"Where will we go, Mommy?"

"I don't know myself, child."

Mrs. Weiss's eyes were red with weeping. Dressed in

her gray suit, with her raincoat slung over her arm, she was ready to travel.

"You take this package, Shula," said her mother, handing her a small bundle and hiding another beneath her raincoat.

Shula stayed behind in the hallway while Mrs. Weiss cautiously slipped down into the court, looked around and signaled her daughter to follow. The morning sky was a pale gray streaked faintly with pink and purple on the eastern horizon. The court was empty. The street seemed wrapped in slumber. Mrs. Weiss swiftly crossed to the other side and entered the first alley.

"Quiet, Shula, and be careful," she whispered, her voice unsteady.

After a fifteen-minute walk Shula's mother stopped before a gray four-story house with a small placard hanging over the doorway: DR. VYTAS, EYE DISEASES.

Mrs. Weiss pressed down on the door latch. "Thank God, it's open," she sighed in relief.

They climbed to Dr. Vytas's office on the third floor and Shula's mother pressed the buzzer. No answer. Again she rang. This time they heard steps.

"Who's there?" a woman inquired.

"Dr. Weiss's wife," came the muffled answer. "I have something to talk about with Dr. Vytas."

"The doctor is still sleeping," the woman replied in annoyance.

"Please tell him that Dr. Max Weiss's wife is waiting. It's very urgent."

"Stay there," came the answer.

After a long wait in the gloomy stairway, the door

finally opened. A girl in a white apron ushered them into the waiting room and disappeared through one of the doorways.

Shula took in her surroundings. She recognized this room with its wicker furniture and the strange picture on the wall—a dead man encircled by a group of people wearing odd-looking headwear.

Shula had been there twice before. First, after the children at school had thrown dirt into her eyes, inflaming them. Dr. Vytas had refused to take any money from her father for that visit. The second time she had come with her mother on Algirdas's birthday—he was the Vytases' oldest boy. She had brought him a picture book. After that, Dr. Vytas and his wife had come to visit them. Her father said that he and Dr. Vytas were friends, that Dr. Vytas was a cultured man and a progressive.

The door on the left squeaked on its hinge, and Mrs. Vytas entered the room, wearing a gray-green dressing gown.

"Good morning," she said in a chipper tone. "Forgive me for having kept you waiting."

Shula's mother rose in greeting. "Oh, no, please forgive me, Mrs. Vytas, for having woke you at such an early hour. But . . . I couldn't wait."

"Yes . . . yes. . . . What does bring you here at such an early hour?" said Mrs. Vytas, extending a white hand with long, pink-lacquered fingernails to indicate that they should sit down. "It's dangerous to be wandering about the streets now—I mean for you people," she added, looking knowingly at Mrs. Weiss.

"Yes, that is just the problem," answered Mrs. Weiss

33

going on to relate all that had happened to them during the preceding few days—how they lived in their cellar, how Shula fell sick, how Dr. Weiss had been taken from them, and what their maid Ursula had done. Then she disclosed why she had come. Fearful of remaining with Shula in their apartment in Mapu Street, she wanted Mrs. Vytas to give her and her daughter refuge for a time. After a few days, she trusted, the city would return to normal and they would be able to go back to their apartment.

Mrs. Vytas listened very attentively.

"I am terribly sorry," she said finally, "but I can't take you into my apartment. My husband is not home. He's gone on a trip and won't be back for the longest time. You must understand, Mrs. Weiss, I'm a woman and I'm simply afraid. You know that the new law forbids any Christian to house a Jew. I'm very sorry, but I cannot endanger my family."

Mrs. Weiss turned white. Wordlessly she turned to the door.

Mrs. Vytas blocked her path. "Mrs. Weiss, that doesn't mean you have to leave right away. You can't be roaming about the streets at this hour. I suggest that you wait an hour or two. I'll make some tea . . . then you can go."

Shula's mother fixed Mrs. Vytas with a look of contempt. "Thank you very much. But we will drink tea, my daughter and I, elsewhere, with people who haven't forgotten that there is another law that says one should give refuge to the hunted and the innocent, even if they are Jews. Good-bye, Mrs. Vytas."

When they got outside, day had already dawned. A

glorious summer sun lifted from behind the roof of the gray house from which they had just emerged. Some people were hurrying along the street, others were still standing in the gateways of their courtyards, yawning. Among these passersby Shula did not notice one person she knew; it seemed that the street, which had once buzzed with Jews, was a different road entirely.

"Where can we go now, Mommy?" she asked, frightened.

"I don't know, daughter. Perhaps we should go back to our apartment."

"No, no, I don't want to go home!" she pleaded.

"All right, dear, we'll go to Mr. Kubilius, the engineer. Maybe he will take us in."

A buggy stood at the end of the street. Mrs. Weiss approached the driver. "Take us to Prospect Vytautas, Number——"

The driver examined her face and smiled. "I don't take Jews, but if you pay me enough. . . . I'll have to raise the carriage cover so no one sees me driving Jews around the streets."

"Fine, fine, just go!"

"What are you in such a rush for?" laughed the driver. "There are Germans in Prospect Vytautas too. They'll find you."

The coachman pulled his carriage hood up, and Shula and her mother leaned back, hiding their faces.

When they arrived at Mr. Kubilius's home, Mrs. Weiss entered the hallway and rang. The door opened at once, revealing in the entranceway a tall man wearing a shiny raincoat and a felt hat.

35

"Good morning, Mr. Kubilius," said Mrs. Weiss.

"H'llo," he replied, tipping his hat slightly, "Come to see me, Mrs. Weiss?" He did not motion them in.

"Yes," the woman sighed. "I've come . . . to ask you . . . to take us in for a few days."

"Hm-m, yes. . . . Well, I'm afraid that's impossible. I'm a government engineer. I'd gladly help you out but it would be very ticklish, you see. Maybe you need money? I can lend you some."

"Thank you," Mrs. Weiss replied, "I don't need a loan." She hurried down the stairs so the engineer would not see her eyes fill with tears.

"Mommy, Mommy, where will we live now?"

"We must go back to our apartment, Shula." Mrs. Weiss had discovered that, in her frantic haste, she had taken only a few coins with her.

They made their way back to Mapu Street on foot and slowly climbed the steps. Shula's legs ached and her head was throbbing. Her mother took the key out of her purse only to discover that the door was open. From the guest room burst gales of laughter and chaotic notes from the piano. Someone was banging on the keys.

"Hey, don't break it"—it was Ursula speaking—"it's better to sell it."

"Stupid, who's gonna buy a piano off you nowadays?" a coarse voice jibed. "Anybody needs a piano can just go inside some Yid's apartment and grab one."

"Come, child, hurry." Mrs. Weiss yanked Shula after her. They reached the gate at a run, almost bumping into a man dressed in workman's clothing headed toward them. He blocked their path.

36

"Excuse me, ma'am," he said, "aren't you Dr. Weiss's wife?"

"No, no," she shot back, terrified, attempting to go around him.

This is the end, thought Shula, *Ursula must have planted him here to catch us.* She began to cry.

"What are you crying for, little girl?" the man asked kindly. "I'm headed for Dr. Weiss. He saved my sick daughter; she's just your age, too. If it hadn't been for the doctor, who knows if she would have pulled through. I thought that now, at a time like this, maybe I could help you out."

Mrs. Weiss began to feel hope. The man looked like the carpenter who lived on the outskirts of the city. Her husband had indeed spent a good bit of time tending the young patient at his house.

"You are Paulauskas?" Mrs. Weiss asked timidly.

"Yes, ma'am," he replied happily. "So, now you remember me. But I spotted you right off. We haven't forgotten what Dr. Weiss did for us."

"The doctor is gone," Mrs. Weiss said brokenly. "They took him away."

"They took the doctor!" the carpenter repeated, shaking his head in disbelief. "Then I got here too late. . . . And the two of you, where are you going?"

"I don't know. Wherever the wind takes us."

"Mrs. Weiss, please come home with me. I may not be rich but whatever my family and I eat, you'll eat, too."

Paulauskas led the way carrying their packages for them. After a long walk they arrived at a narrow alley on

37

the outskirts of the city and entered a modest wooden cottage set in a small garden. The carpenter knocked on the door.

"Maré, I've brought guests."

To the doorway came a big-boned woman in a frilled dress, with a bright kerchief on her head. She looked over the new arrivals and said, "Please come inside, you must be exhausted. Sit yourselves down at the table, rest a little, and eat your fill."

"Veronica," she called, poking her head into the adjacent room, "go down the cellar and bring up milk."

Before many moments had passed a tall, slender girl of twelve had entered the room. Her hair was golden and tied in two slender braids with red cord. She placed an earthen jug on the table and stood to the side, eyeing the guests curiously.

"This is my daughter, Veronica," said the lady of the house to Mrs. Weiss. "If it hadn't been for your husband, the doctor, she would have been an invalid for life, for sure. Please come to the table. We're not rich enough to serve you a meal like you're used to, but whatever God has given us we'll share with you. Oh, now don't cry," she added, seeing the tears well up in Mrs. Weiss's eyes. "Good God will return your husband to you. My husband runs around the city all day, maybe he'll be able to bring you some good news. Now eat, then you can lie down and rest."

Never in her life did Shula find a meal as tasty as the potatoes and the cup of milk served her by Paulauskas's wife.

After eating she lay in bed wrapped in a colorful quilt

38

and pressed against her mother. "Mommy, there still are good people in the world, aren't there?" But Mrs. Weiss did not answer her. She was already asleep.

Outside the Law

When Yisraelik entered the room he found his mother cutting strips of yellow cloth. He recognized the doily that used to be under the radio.

"Ah, Mom, why did you cut the doily up?"

"Jews don't need radios or doilies anymore, son; what we need at this point are yellow patches," noted Mr. Levine with a wry smile.

Yisraelik looked into his mother's sad eyes and said nothing. They had returned to their apartment in Mapu Street only the day before. They had attempted to cross the border and reach the Soviet Union, but in vain. When they had come back utterly exhausted, having made most of the journey on foot, they found their apartment broken into and ransacked, their clothing and good dishes all gone. Mrs. Levine had always been a hardworking and spirited woman, but now she was deeply depressed. Blue circles ringed her eyes, which were swollen from weeping.

"Finished, finished, finished," Yisraelik heard his father say forlornly from the hallway. All that morning Mr. Levine had not been home. Only now he had returned from his "stroll," as he called his visits to the neighbors to hear news.

Yisraelik was about to ask his father what was happening, but on seeing his grim expression, thought better of it.

"*Nu*, Rachel," Mr. Levine turned to his wife. "I see you're making us a royal badge . . . yes indeed, a royal badge. . . ."

Mr. Levine's head was bowed; he paced to and fro monotonously.

"What do people say?" his wife asked. "What do they intend to do to us?"

"What people say doesn't matter; what logic says, does. It's going to be very ugly. They aren't marking Jews for nothing."

"Moshe," pleaded Mrs. Levine, "maybe you can get hold of a wagon and we'll get away from here."

"Where will we go? The Germans are everywhere."

"Moshe, there are Jews who've escaped to the villages in the area. They say we're going to be locked inside a ghetto."

"Then they'll bring all the Jews from the villages to the ghetto too," said Mr. Levine in a choked voice.

"I don't know what's going to happen, but we've got to leave here."

"Mommy, Daddy," Yankel burst into the room. "Guess who's here? Etta and Shmulik and their daddy."

Yisraelik dashed outside. For weeks the tailor's family had not been about. He knew the Cohens had fled to the countryside. Why had they come back now? In any event, he was very glad Shmulik was home; the two of them had always been close.

The door to the Cohen apartment was open and voices poured out from inside. No sooner had Yisraelik entered than he wanted to leave, but someone thrust him against the wall and blocked his exit.

Shmulik's father, white as chalk, was pressed against the table clutching a package to his side, while Shmulik stood next to him, holding Etta's hand. In the doorway opposite them stood the janitor's wife and her daughter, Birutė.

"If you don't clear out right now I'm calling the Shauliai," shrieked the older woman, shaking her fist at Mr. Cohen.

"At least give me back my sewing machine," he pleaded. "My machine is my bread."

"We're not giving anything back," the woman yelled.

"Now I'm the seamstress," shouted Birutė. "I'll sew yellow patches for all the Yids." She shook with laughter.

"Get out, get out of here, you damn Yids!"

Yisraelik was frightened out of his wits. He had to tell his parents; they would take in the Cohens.

"Dad, Mom, come on down. The Cohens don't have an apartment anymore, they can't get in."

"Go on, Rachel, see what's happening," Mr. Levine told his wife.

Mrs. Levine found Mr. Cohen sitting on the steps with his package on his knees. Alongside him stood Shmulik and Etta, the latter wracked with sobs.

"I can't really say 'Come in peace,' Mr. Cohen," said Mrs. Levine. "Now, Jews do not come home in peace. But

41

it's good to see that you're alive and well. Where are your wife and little Hanna?"

"I left them in the village for the time being. And it's a good thing—we don't even have a roof over our heads here."

"Don't worry, Mr. Cohen, come in with us, our apartment can do for two families. Let's only hope that they leave us in peace there."

So that was how the two families came to live together.

The Yellow Patch

Before there were any Germans or hints of war in Kovno, when Jewish children were not afraid to go out in the streets, every morning on his way to school Yisraelik would come across a black puppy with a long chin and short, pointed ears. He was a scroungy skin-and-bones affair with his tail always getting tangled in his legs. The first day he saw the dog it was so sad and hungry looking that Yisraelik quickly offered him some of the bread his mother had packed for lunch. But the boy's moving hand frightened the pup away. The next day Yisraelik found him by the gate of the court and again tossed him some bread. The dog eyed him suspiciously, but no longer ran off. After Yisraelik drew slightly away from the gate the puppy hurriedly snatched up the morsel and swallowed it. Thereafter he no longer feared Yisraelik, but wagged his tail when he met the boy as though he were a good friend.

After one week, the puppy began to accompany Yisraelik to school and to enter the court with him. Every day the boy would bring him leftovers from meals—crumbs, bones, a little cereal or soup. No longer was the puppy sad. His tail curled upward in a semicircle and at the sight of Yisraelik, he would bound up with glee.

"Hear that, Yankel? The pooch is saying hello to me." The dog became a fixture in the court. Even the janitor could not chase him away.

"What's his name?" the other children in the court asked, having themselves begun to bring him food.

"Let's call him Pickup, because I picked him up off the street."

Yisraelik took care of Pickup lovingly, washing and grooming him. Finally he brought him into the Levine apartment and made him a full-fledged member of the family. The dog grew and fattened out into a fine-looking animal with a coat as black and shiny as velvet. Everybody liked Pickup, but he was a one-man hound. Wherever Yisraelik went, he went, too. Little Yankel said that Pickup would kiss Yisraelik; so Yankel would pick the dog up and try to coax a kiss out of him, too.

But all that was before the war.

When the Levine family came back from their attempted flight to Russia, they found Pickup gaunt, mangy, and limping on his hind leg.

43

"Pickup, Pickup, what's happened to you?" Yisraelik groaned, lovingly patting his dog's head.

Pickup replied with two weak barks and licked the boy's hand. When the Cohen family moved into the apartment, Mrs. Levine wanted to put Pickup out but Yisraelik and Yankel begged for mercy. While this went on, the dog lay stretched on the floor, his emaciated body glued to Yisraelik's legs, making short whimpering sounds and looking up alternately at his master and Mrs. Levine.

"Pickup already knows you want to kick him out, so he's crying," said Yankel.

Their mother sighed. The dog stayed.

"Yisraelik," said Mrs. Levine, "put your coat on and hurry over to Klimas. Maybe you can get us some milk."

Yisraelik took his coat and put it on with a grimace. It was new and smart, sewn for his bar mitzvah. Light gray, it had two rectangular pockets and four shiny buttons. "A real man," family acquaintances used to say when he sported it. But now the coat embittered him, with its two huge yellow patches sewn on the front and back, each as big as his fist.

I'll go out without the coat, Yisraelik thought, but recalled at once that he would then have to sew the patch onto his shirt. Yisraelik left, trailing Pickup behind him. The boy walked along the paving stones, next to the street's gutter, and Pickup ran alongside him on the sidewalk.

From the alleyway opposite them two big Gentile boys emerged, one of them holding a rifle.

"Hey, Yid," called the rifleman, spotting Yisraelik.

"You wear a coat and let your dog go naked? You didn't even sew him a yellow patch."

Yisraelik said nothing and quickened his pace, his heart pounding furiously. Only fifty yards more and he would be at his destination. If only those two would let him pass through. But they were heading straight for him, descending from the raised sidewalk and blocking his path.

"Aha, trying to run away from us, Jewboy? That's a pretty coat you got, but it belongs to your dog. Give it here, double quick!"

Yisraelik was confused. To flee was impossible, and to stand up to them was beyond him.

"Strip it off him!" the one with the rifle cried to his buddy, chuckling. "We'll dress the mutt." The tough grabbed Yisraelik and began undoing his coat buttons.

"Lay off," cried Yisraelik, struggling to free his sleeve from the hoodlum's grip.

"Try this on, you damn Jewboy!" A hard punch landed on Yisraelik's shoulder.

Pickup, hair bristling and teeth bared, growled menacingly from deep in his throat.

"You against us, too, you dumb mutt?" jeered the hoodlum. "It's easy to see you're a Jew dog. You stay out of this—we're doing it for you. You'll be the master and your owner'll be your dog."

Pickup growled, tensed and opened his mouth wider.

Forcibly, Yisraelik's assailant began to pull the coat off; the boy struggled ineffectively.

"Pickup, Pickup!" Yisraelik shouted in desperation.

The dog sprang forward and sank his teeth into the attacker's leg.

45

"Ay, ay!" yelled the tough, letting go of Yisraelik and clutching at his leg.

"So—sic a dog on Lithuanians, eh?" hissed the rifle owner.

Two shots split the air.

"What happened? What happened?" shrieked a stout woman, elbowing and punching her way into the crowd that had materialized.

"Nothing," somebody answered with a laugh, "they just shot a dog and a Yid."

In the Ghetto

For weeks and then months the Cohen family lived in the attic of a rickety, wooden two-story house in the ghetto, not far from the fence surrounding it. The walls of the cottage were moldy and grew moss.

Their room was very small, without even enough space for two beds, so Hanna and Etta slept together with their mother in the one bed, while their father and Shmulik slept on benches.

Mr. Cohen was absent from the house for days at a time. He would come back only at night, exhausted, and go to sleep at once. Mrs. Cohen told the children that their father had to work a great deal so that the Germans would not kill him. Shmulik, too, went out to work often. He was already considered an adult. During the previous week Mrs. Cohen, too, had begun to work, leaving only Etta and Hanna in the house. All day long they stayed in the room; very rarely were they able to go into the courtyard. Their mother said that in the ghetto there were bad men who snatched children.

When they had first come to live in the old house Hanna had cried. She did not want to stay in such a narrow, dark room where the sun never shone except just before night. Very slowly, though, she grew used to her new surroundings. At dusk she would watch the sunlight streak the gray wall with a broad strip of gold that would dance toward the door and disappear long before her father and mother returned.

Frequently Hanna would try to catch the band of gold. The light would spill over her tiny hands and slip through her fingers every time she drew back from the wall.

The girls found it very dreary in the gloomy room. Through the window they could see only a blue or gray strip of sky, depending on the weather. At times they would pull the stool over to the window, get up on it, and look outside. Even then, however, they couldn't manage to see much. The walls of the adjoining houses blocked any view they might have had.

At times birds landed on the rooftop opposite their window to chirp and twitter. Little Hanna would clap her hands for joy. "A swallow, a swallow, that means good luck!"

Occasionally the windows across the way would open and eyes would peer from behind a curtain.

"Mommy, Mommy, there are children there too," Hanna would exclaim delightedly.

"Yes, little one, there are many children in the ghetto," her mother would sigh.

The girls could not understand what their mother was sighing about. What was wrong with children being there?

Hanna would have liked to ask question after question, but Mrs. Cohen never had time. She had to prepare food for their father, launder clothes, run off to get their ration of flour or grits, patch Shmulik's pants, bring water from the well at the end of the street, and go out every morning to work.

Hanna wished that she were grown up already, that one morning she would wake up as big as her mother, so she could help out. Eight-year-old Etta already knew how to do lots of things, like washing dishes or sweeping the room, but she couldn't cook or wash clothes.

Their mother was so very tired! Often she would complain of headaches. At times Hanna would wake up at night and grope for her mother in bed, only to discover her sitting up and sewing by the light of the oil lamp.

Mrs. Cohen had no sewing machine and so had to do everything by hand. Hanna wanted to get out of bed, run over, and hug her mother. But her eyes would close of themselves and she would sink off to sleep. In the morning the room would be empty except for herself and Etta.

Always their mother was pale. Etta was too. One day their father looked at her worriedly and said, "I'm afraid Etta is sick. She's gotten very thin lately."

"The ghetto will eat up the children," whispered their mother tearfully.

48

Hanna could not understand how the ghetto could eat children. What was it—a wolf?

At first she had no understanding of the ghetto whatsoever. During their first week there Hanna had asked her mother, "Mommy, is it the Sabbath tomorrow?"

"Yes, my daughter."

"Mommy, let's take a walk to the Niemen."

"We can't do that, child, we live in a ghetto. You can't leave the ghetto."

And on another occasion, "Mommy, you remember Shula?"

"Yes."

"Why doesn't she come visit us?"

"Shula isn't in the ghetto."

"Let's write and ask her to come."

"You can't send letters from the ghetto, and people can't come into the ghetto."

Another time the little girl had asked, "Mommy, when are we going to the park?"

"There is no park in the ghetto, child."

"Well, when are you going to bring flowers home for the Sabbath, like you used to do when we lived on Mapu Street?"

"Hanna dear, there aren't any flowers in the ghetto."

"So what is there in the ghetto?" the child burst out crying. "I don't want to live in the ghetto. I want there to be flowers, at least one flower. Let's leave here, Mommy, let's leave."

So it had been those first few days. After a while, though, Hanna came to understand. No Jew wanted to

49

live in the ghetto. Only Hitler wanted that. He was a very bad man. And Germans and Lithuanians beat up Jews. And all around the ghetto there was a fence, so no one could get out. There was mud in the ghetto and it was dark at night. And they didn't give Jews anything to eat in the ghetto.

Hanna was always asking for bread. Sometimes she would wake up at night and couldn't fall asleep again.

Once she woke up smiling, but after one look about her she burst into tears.

"Why you crying, Hanna?" asked Etta.

"Where's my cake? You took my cake!"

"What cake, Hanna? There aren't any cakes in the ghetto."

"There was so," the child whimpered. "Right here on the bed there was a cake."

She had had a dream.

Hanna and Etta were still little, but Shmulik was practically an adult. After his older brother, Reuven, did not return from the airfield one day, Shmulik became the big boy of the family and had to help out his parents.

Shmulik missed his older brother terribly. He had always looked up to Reuven and modeled himself after him. When the war broke out Reuven had already been at the university for two years. Their mother had insisted that the older boy study medicine; nothing was better for a Jew than to be a doctor. Even the worst anti-Semite might need a Jewish doctor. Furthermore, a doctor didn't have to depend on anyone to assign him work, had no one over him, and made a fine living.

Reuven was the best student in his class, but the medical

department did not accept him because he had been graduated from a Jewish institution. The university informed him that there was no more room, that priority was being given to holders of certificates from Lithuanian high schools (called gymnasiums). Reuven then decided to study law and began poring over stacks of books and newspapers.

When the war broke out Reuven tried to escape to the east but returned, finding that he was unable to endure separation from his family.

Even in the ghetto Reuven managed to read a great deal—how, Shmulik never could figure out. After all, the government had confiscated all books in the ghetto. Moreover, where did Reuven find the strength to read? He worked night shifts at the airstrip at a backbreaking job—shoveling and hauling dirt and stones in ice and snow.

No one worked at the airfield willingly. Everyone tried to get out of it, looking for softer jobs, especially where you could get a little food. No one was paid for the grueling labor at the strip. The workers weren't even given food, and it was also impossible to exchange any objects for food among themselves. In addition, people were beaten murderously. Anyone who had money hired workingmen to take his place, and people whose friends were on good terms with ghetto authorities avoided service that way. But Reuven was in neither of those two categories. He was his family's representative at the strip, freeing his father and mother to find other jobs and earn food.

One morning Reuven did not come back from work. Mrs. Cohen wept a great deal and her husband ran about

all day, from the police to the *Judenrat** to the Work
Council and back. Only that night did they learn that the
Germans had made a sweep of the streets that morning,
arresting workers heading home from the airfield and
loading them onto trucks, destined for points unknown.
Reuven must have been among them.

His father replaced Reuven at the airfield, and it fell
upon Shmulik to win food for the hungry family.

To Greener Pastures

A cold rain mixed with snow lashed the windowpanes. The
wind whistled through cracks in the wall, and the oil lamp,
flickering on the window sill, was at the point of going out.
The single drops of rain that had been pattering on the
rickety roof turned into a thin stream of water pouring
relentlessly from the ceiling onto Hanna and Etta's bed.
Their mother moved it aside and put a bucket on the floor.
The water spattered into it loudly.

No one spoke. Their father had gone to work hours
before. Mrs. Cohen finally dozed off at the table, a sock in
her hand. Shmulik lay listening to the wind roaring

* The *Judenrat*, the Jewish Council or Jewish authority, was
organized by the Germans in ghettos to administer the occupied
Jewish community.

through the chimney and looking at the ghetto fence opposite their window.

Suddenly the door opened, revealing a figure in rags, dripping water, a thin red line running across his pale face.

"Reuven!" Shmulik cried.

The youth stepped into the room unsteadily and sank to the floor. With difficulty Shmulik and his mother stripped off his wet, muddy clothing and laid him down. His body was covered with sores.

For days Reuven lay in bed speechless. Finally he told how he had managed to flee the work camp to which the Germans had transferred him and his fellow workers. Nineteen men had been taken there; seven survived. Every night, after the prisoners spent a hellish day's work in peat bogs up to their waists in water, the Lithuanians would torment them, running them around for hour after hour, making them leap over taut ropes. Laggards were clubbed to death.

After weeks passed, Reuven got out of bed. Then one day a messenger of the *Judenrat* arrived with an order for him to report for work—at the airfield.

"You can tell them I have no intention of working for them," said Reuven coldly.

"You're not working for 'them,' you're working for the Germans and the Lithuanians!"

"It's all the same," snapped Reuven, turning his back.

His mother looked at him plaintively. "Reuven, your father's not young anymore. He doesn't have the strength."

"Dad should stop working there, too."

"They'll send police over, they'll force you to go."

"The police can jump in the lake."

53

His mother sighed and said nothing else.

After a few hours Reuven disappeared from the room. A week later he came back, then disappeared again. Shmulik was aware of the change that had taken place in his brother. His brother's eyes shone intensely. His face was pale and gaunt but his stride was swifter and surer. At times some young men would turn up at the room, asking for Reuven. They would speak with him in hushed tones and quickly leave. Shmulik recognized one of them, a former classmate of his brother's. Their paths had parted after high school; Reuven had gone on to the university and his friend to a trade school. At times Shmulik would pass his brother's friend on the street. Once Shmulik asked about Reuven, who had disappeared again. The young man glared at him. "I don't know a thing," he growled, "and my advice, genius, is not to mention him to anyone. Get it?"

Shmulik noticed how distressed his mother had become, and how angry his father, since Reuven's return. Mr. Cohen was growing weaker day by day. Often he could not get out of bed.

Then Reuven stayed away from home for ten days. When he returned Shmulik was sleeping. Loud voices woke him. The voices died down, then rose again. His eyes shut, Shmulik listened closely.

"If you had any way of being sure you would meet these partisans, then I wouldn't say a word," he heard his father argue.

"Do you want guarantees in a war like this?" Reuven countered impatiently.

"You're out to get killed!"

"As if you're safe from death in the ghetto!"

"Hush, hush! Don't shout so, for God's sake. The walls are made of paper, they'll hear every word," his mother pleaded. "Reuven, if you don't care about yourself, at least have pity on your little sisters. Your father can't work anymore."

"I can't, Mom, I can't go on. You're all making a terrible mistake. I made mine when I did what you wanted the first time. I begged you. 'The Germans are coming,' I said, 'let's escape to Russia.' But you wouldn't listen."

"Who could have known? Who?"

"Well, at least don't hold me up this time."

Shmulik strained so as not to lose a single word his brother was saying. He was right. They couldn't stay in the ghetto any longer, but where did Reuven want to go? To the partisans? Fatigue overcame the boy and he sank into sleep.

One night Shmulik sensed that someone was leaning over him. He opened his eyes and saw Reuven standing by his bed, dressed in a brown sheepskin coat and a leather hat pulled down over his forehead and ears.

"Look out for yourself, Shmulik, and take care of the girls," he whispered, kissing him on the cheek.

Before Shmulik could even answer, the door had closed and Reuven was gone forever.

Etta adored Shmulik. He was a hero to her, practically grown up. Daily he would work outside the ghetto and on occasion bring back real treats—an egg, potatoes, even a chunk of sugar or a piece of candy.

Once he brought home a little bag of pea pods.

"Today we will feast like kings," Mrs. Cohen announced.

"Mommy, give me a few pods," Hanna begged. "I want to play."

"I'm sorry, dear, but a pea isn't a plaything. Peas are precious. I'll bring you some smooth stones from the courtyard to play with."

Little Hanna, however, continued to implore her mother until finally she was given a few. The girls climbed onto the broad window sill and began to play. Suddenly one seed slipped out of someone's hand and rolled into the crevice between the window and the roof beneath and two others followed. Etta took a stick and poked about inside the crack but could not manage to extract the peas. There they stayed and eventually the girls forgot all about them.

One evening their father came home white with anger and whispered something to his wife. Neither of them went to sleep that night. The next morning, when the girls awoke, they found two long, weatherbeaten boards leaning against the wall.

56

"Mommy, what are these for?"

"Hush, girls, don't even talk about them."

From that day on Mrs. Cohen forbade her daughters to go out at all or even poke their heads outside the window.

When their parents returned the next evening they brought back additional boards. All night they hammered away. Shmulik, too, did not sleep, but worked along with them. The next morning when the girls awoke the room had become even tinier and narrower. Covering the entire length of the wall opposite the window was a new wall built of old boards. Their mother removed one board to reveal a narrow space between the two walls.

That night, before going to bed, their father lectured to them. "Listen, girls! There are evil men in the ghetto who kidnap little children and hand them over to the Germans. When Mother and I aren't in the room and you hear any footsteps in the courtyard, you must get right into the hiding place between the walls and close up the board very carefully behind you. You'll have to stay there without making a peep. Not a word, not a laugh; you can't even cough."

Their father showed them a few times how to hide quickly and then had them go through the motions on their own. When they had done so perfectly, he let them go to sleep.

Life became even more difficult for the sisters. They had to spend all their days, and even nights, between the walls. It was painful: their legs ached from so much standing, for there wasn't enough room to sit down. Breathing was difficult because of the lack of air and the dampness of the boards. More than once they heard, from their hiding place, the tramp of hobnailed boots from the courtyards, then shouting and cursing and the sound of women and children screaming. At times their very room was filled with the noise of heavy steps. Someone would search the corners, kick the walls and furniture, rummage through the closet, curse and leave, while the girls hugged each other tightly, holding their breath.

A few weeks of this went by, then they were allowed to pass their days outside the hiding place once more. But going outdoors or looking out the window during the day was forbidden. The neighbors were not to see them.

"Why can't they?" Etta asked. "Our neighbors are Jews, so they wouldn't hurt us."

Winter passed and spring arrived. The girls would not have known it in their dark room except for the fact that it grew less cold. Then the days got longer and the sun's rays began to come calling again.

One day the girls were waiting, as usual, for their brother to come home. The strip of gold on the wall had almost stretched to the other end of the room and very soon would disappear. Shmulik always walked in when the band of light reached the door. That day, though, the light passed that boundary and Shmulik still had not arrived. Their mother had returned a good while before and had gone to the street to get bread.

"C'mon, let's go to the window," little Hanna urged. Impatient at having waited so long, they sat on the window sill.

"Ooh, look there," cried Hanna.

From the crack alongside the window a slender, light green stalk stared them in the face.

"A flower's growing from the wall, a flower!" Etta

clapped her hands. "We have to water it. It must be thirsty."

"What does a flower eat?" Hanna asked.

Etta knotted her brows. "Dirt," she concluded.

"But there isn't any dirt here."

"It must have found a little drop in the crack, only we don't see it," Etta answered in the grave tones of an expert. She jumped down from the sill, ran over to the water bucket, and scooped out a cupful.

"That must be a pea plant," their mother explained when she came in, "from the peas you played with by the window. Now they are growing in the crevice."

From that day on it seemed as though new life had entered the dark, narrow room.

Every evening, when the sun set, the girls hurried over to the window to view the stalk and water it. In the twilight the thin stem looked like a gray thread spun out of a ball of yarn, but the girls saw a rainbow of colors in it. The tender plant, grateful for their concern, prospered from day to day, clad in light green with pale shoots and bright, delicate leaves sprouting from its sides.

One night a downpour drenched the house and lightning split the sky. In the morning the girls rushed to the window and found their flower lying flat on the roof as though it had fainted.

"It is sick," said Hanna fearfully. Etta, too, was very worried. When Mrs. Cohen came back that evening she soothed her daughters.

"The stem is tender and weak and can't lift all that weight. We have to support it." She drove a few nails into the wall and tied the stem to it with strings.

After two weeks the girls saw minute buds wrapped in

tiny leaves at the top of the stem. It was not long before the buds opened and the stalk was crowned with light purple blossoms.

"We have flowers in the ghetto, our own flowers," the girls exulted.

The pea blossoms peered through the window into the dark room and waved their shoots. Joy spread through the apartment.

"Look, Mommy, it's not pale anymore," exclaimed Etta one evening. "And its head doesn't hurt either. Isn't it wonderful there are such things as flowers?"

The Death of Etta

Days passed. The pea blossoms on the window sill quivered with every light breeze. They were beautiful flowers, delicate and purple.

Etta, however, grew progressively paler. Very rarely did she get out of bed. Usually she sat up, her back propped against the wall, her eyes sunken, staring at the tender stalk while beads of sweat glistened on her forehead.

Occasionally her cough grew very deep, shaking her wasted body. Hanna would become terrified and plead,

"Sh-h-h, Etta, sh-h-h. They'll hear us and come up."

Months passed. One day their father did not return. Mrs. Cohen said that he had been taken to a work camp. At first the girls kept asking, "When will Daddy come back?" but after awhile they stopped.

Shmulik alone knew that his father would not return. Only three men had come back from that camp. From their report it was learned that all the Jewish workers, ninety men, had been shot.

At times Shmulik would close his eyes and think about his father and his friends from Mapu Street. The Wilensky family had disappeared before Shmulik and his family had moved into the ghetto. Where had the Wilenskys gone? Shmulik had heard from neighbors that they had left for Vilna; a Polish friend, a man with an estate, was supposed to have taken them there. Had they arrived safely? And were the children, Rivka and David, alive? No one was left of the Levine family. Mr. Levine, Yisraelik's father, had been taken to the camp together with Shmulik's father. Yisraelik had been shot in the street by thugs. His mother and little Yankel had been arrested in the last "action."

Action, action—what a horrible word! Before the war he had never heard it and now it was on everyone's lips. Shmulik recalled the details of the roundup as it had been described to him by witnesses. Germans and Lithuanians fanned out in the ghetto alleys to ferret out Jews in hiding. They entered the Levine apartment where Mrs. Levine and her son were hiding beneath the big baking stove. Yankel was very sick and could not stop coughing. They heard him and dragged him out. He began to cry and scream. "Mommy, Mommy, I'm scared!" Mrs. Levine burst out of concealment and clawed the face and hands of the Lithuanian policeman who had grabbed the child. The officer, however, easily subdued her, beating her on the head and face with a rubber truncheon. The two never came back to the ghetto.

One day when Shmulik came back from work Etta was lying quieter than usual. Mrs. Cohen was seated on the edge of the sick girl's bed with tears running down her cheeks. Etta's eyes were closed and her breathing was labored and irregular.

"We've got to get her something to give her some life, a drop of milk at least," whispered the mother in desperation.

Shmulik slung his pack off his back and took out a few potatoes and some slivers of wood he had brought home to kindle a fire. Then he looked at Etta and turned toward the door.

"Where are you going?" asked his mother worriedly.

"Out. Maybe I'll get something."

The street was deserted. Here and there a dim light would suddenly appear in a window and as quickly go out. Shmulik advanced with caution, his heart pounding in his ears. Could he evade capture? And if he were caught, what would become of his mother, Hanna, and the sick Etta?

The day before he had seen a gap in the fence. It must be a passageway to the outside world. He approached the end of the alley, turned left, and fifty paces brought him to the spot.

Thank God! No one had stopped him. There stood the fence before him, with two boards pulled out. Shmulik stuck his head and arms into the gap and wriggled his skinny body through to the other side. He was on the outskirts of the city looking at Lithuanian homes, beyond which lay broad expanses of meadowlands.

He paused, wiped the cold sweat from his forehead, and filled his lungs with air.

A starry sky arched overhead. Shmulik lifted up his eyes. A tiny star winked at him, but too slyly, thought Shmulik, as though some crafty scheme lay behind the gesture.

The street was desolate. Where to now? Should he knock on one of the doors near the ghetto? What if he were to be captured and turned over to the authorities?

No! Better to cover some ground first. The farther he got from the city, the less the danger. Villagers were better than city dwellers, he thought, even though he remembered what happened following the first major "action." Farmers of the nearby villages brought their wagons into the ghetto, broke into the houses whose residents had just been driven out, and filled their sacks with everything they could lay their hands on. Even blood-soaked articles they took. . . . Still, villagers were better than city dwellers —a truly bloody bunch.

At the end of the road lay a lone house encircled by a fence. A small gate led into a courtyard that contained a few fruit-laden cherry trees. Softly he crept into the garden, approached the rear door and, holding his breath, knocked.

"Hello, who's there?"

Shmulik was taken aback. Before him stood a broad-shouldered woman wearing an embroidered cotton blouse

63

and a bulky homemade skirt. In her hands she carried a pail of steaming milk. She must have just come back from night milking.

"What do you want, little Jewboy? You can't stand here, we're right on the road."

Shmulik stared openmouthed, at a complete loss for words.

"You're hungry, right?" she asked warmly.

"My little sister is dying," he whispered, gathering courage. "I need a little milk for her."

"Wait a minute. Not here. Come into the hallway and stand in the corner so no one sees you."

The woman disappeared into the house and came back with a bottle of milk and half a loaf of bread.

"Here, take this and hurry on out of here." She thrust the bread and milk into his hands, pushed him out of the hallway, and slammed the door behind him.

Shmulik pressed his treasure to his chest and began running. Once again he stood by the hole in the ghetto fence, his throat dry as he trembled from fatigue and tension. For a moment he was almost overpowered by the desire to taste some of the milk to revive his strength. All he had had since morning had been a dry crust of bread and a bowlful of a diluted, foul-tasting dish called grits soup.

"Ho there, halt!" thundered someone in Lithuanian.

Shmulik did not hesitate an instant or even look in the direction of the voice. He quickly slipped through the fence and began to run.

"Halt or I shoot!"

On he ran with all his might.

A shot rang out behind him.

Something hot pinched his left thigh. He reached down and felt a sticky substance.

I'm wounded, he thought, but continued running.

After he outdistanced his pursuer, he stopped and sucked in air. Only then did he feel the full agony of the pain searing his thigh. Trembling, he wiped the sweat from his face and pressed his palm against his heart. Breathing was torturous, he had no strength left; in another instant he would collapse.

But then he thought of his sister Etta whose life depended on the bottle of milk in his hands.

For a moment he leaned against the wall of the nearest house and filled his lungs with air. Only three hundred yards separated him from his home, but walking was excruciating. With his last strength he dragged himself along, leaning against the walls of the houses until he arrived at the gate to his yard.

Upstairs, he found his mother dozing at the foot of Etta's bed.

"Mom, I've brought milk!"

Mrs. Cohen opened her eyes and a cry of terror escaped her lips. "Shmulik!"

"I'm wounded a little in the leg, Mom, but . . . it's not too bad."

His mother pressed him to her. Then she swiftly tore a fresh piece of linen, made a dressing, and washed and bandaged his wound. Shmulik lay down and his mother gave Etta some milk. The girl sank to sleep with a smile hovering over her bluish lips. Shmulik, too, was shortly asleep.

65

He awoke to the sound of crying.

It was Hanna. The child was sitting on the edge of her bed, her skin showing through her torn nightgown. "What happened, little one?" he asked, his chest tightening. Turning his head toward Etta he saw his mother seated on the floor alongside the bed, her head in her hands. His sister's face was white and wondrously relaxed. Her eyes were shut.

"Mom," whispered Shmulik. "Mom."

He struggled to get down from his bed, but was unable to move his wounded leg. His mother twisted her head toward him. "Rest, Shmulik, Etta doesn't need us anymore."

Hanna Leaves the Ghetto

Three weeks passed and Shmulik's wound began to heal. In the meantime he had to remain at home and become Hanna's protector. For entire days they had to stay wedged between the double walls. Often Hanna would cry from hunger and thirst. Then Shmulik would have to crawl across the floor, dragging his aching leg behind him, and bring her some water or a crust of bread his mother had denied herself.

66

One night their mother came home more exhausted than ever, her eyes red.

"Something's going to happen again," she said in a choked voice.

That night Shmulik got up, wrapped up his leg, and began to get dressed.

"Where are you going?"

"Out, to see what's up."

"There's nothing to see. Tonight Stasé Giriené is coming to the ghetto fence. You remember her; she worked for us once, when Hanna was born. She and her husband have bought a farm on the banks of the Viliya. I'm going to try to talk her into taking Hanna home with her."

"I'll go with you."

It was almost midnight. Shmulik had fallen asleep sitting up, leaning against the wall. The creak of the door awakened him. He rose quickly and hobbled after his mother, catching up with her at the end of the alley. They walked on in silence, hugging the sides of the buildings.

Walking the streets of the ghetto at that hour was, of course, forbidden. Fortunately, the skies were cloudy and all was cloaked in darkness. No one observed them and they arrived safely at the designated spot by the ghetto fence.

On the other side a shadowy figure arose.

"Cohen?" it whispered.

"Yes, Stasé."

"Who's that with you?"

"Don't you recognize him? My son Shmulik."

"A person has to be very careful, times like these."

For an instant they were all silent. Then the Lithuanian stretched her hand out. "I've brought you a loaf of bread."

"Thank you so much, Stasé."

Again, silence.

"Stasé, do you want to save a human life? You are a believing Catholic, aren't you? Your God Jesus commanded you to have mercy, even on your enemies."

"Mrs. Cohen, what can I do? The Germans have taken over this country."

"Ah, but you can . . . you can save someone, if only you want to. Take my little Hanna home with you!"

Stasé started as though bitten by a snake.

"Jesus Maria! What are you saying? A Jewish child? I want to live!"

"Stasé, we all want to live. You've just bought a farm; you've done very well for yourselves during the war. God has helped you. Please help me. You're going to move far away from here. No one will know you or your family. You can tell people that Hanna is your daughter, your niece, an orphan, anything you like."

"No, no! Jesus Maria! I'm afraid, I know they'll find out. The Germans know everything, nothing's kept secret from them."

"Stasé, listen, you won't be taking my daughter for nothing. We still have a gold watch and a gold chain. I'll give you my fur coat, too. And if we live, you'll be paid handsomely. The war can't last forever."

Evidently Stasé was thinking it over.

"I'll have to talk to my husband. I'll give you an answer tomorrow. It's not so simple. Someone could inform on us."

68

"Say she's your daughter."

"Tomorrow, tomorrow."

Stasé vanished into the night.

Two weeks later Stasé reappeared by the fence. She agreed to take Hanna.

A week of horror engulfed the ghetto. Yellow posters plastered onto the walls screamed the news: residents of specified streets were to assemble at a given hour in the square by the ghetto gate to be transported from there to another locale. Anyone who disobeyed would be executed, together with his family.

To be transported. . . . The meaning was too clear. All that week the Cohens stayed in hiding.

One night they thought they were lost. From behind the false wall they heard the stomping of hobnailed boots in their room, the pounding of walls with clubs and fists, the overturning of benches and the table, and the vile outbursts in Lithuanian.

Through a hole in the real wall that he had punched with a nail sometime before Shmulik saw the ghetto police together with two of the Šauliai take their neighbors away.

Every time their mother had tried to explain to Hanna that she would have to go to Stasé, the little girl burst out crying. However, after that night of terror, at long last she no longer refused. Her mother dressed her in the last wool clothing they had, wrapped her in a warm shawl, bundled some underwear for her, and the three of them left for the rendezvous. Shmulik stood lookout. Jonas Girius, Stasé's husband, awaited them by the fence. Dressed in a short sheepskin coat and a brown hat pulled down over his eyes, he looked like a thief in the shadows.

At the last moment Hanna dug her tiny fingers into her mother's kerchief, unwilling to part. The farmer, losing patience with the girl, tore her trembling hands loose and disappeared with her into the darkness.

Between the Fences

For over a month Shula and her mother had lived at the Paulauskas home. Daily the carpenter would go into the city to hear the news, and daily he would return looking glummer than before he had set out. Jews were being taken from their homes or were being seized on the streets and sent to unknown destinations.

One day he brought back new information. All the Jews of Kovno had been ordered to leave the city and gather in the Slobodka neighborhood, where a ghetto would be erected. Mrs. Weiss wondered. Could it be for the best? Perhaps in the ghetto the Jews would be left alone.

"Maybe," Maré Paulauskas sighed. "God alone knows."

Mrs. Weiss decided to chance going.

Their hostess bundled some food up for them: bread, cheese, butter, and eggs, as well as two linen shirts, and accompanied them to the gate. "God keep you!" she exclaimed, wiping away her tears.

Mrs. Weiss embraced and kissed her. Tears shone in her own eyes, too.

"I hope and pray I will be able to repay you two someday for all the kindness you have shown us."

Paulauskas squeezed her hands in reply and said, "If you find yourself in need, my house is always open to you. We'll find a bit of bread for everyone."

Shula and her mother entered the ghetto. Hard days came. The two sank rapidly into poverty.

Nothing remained to them of their apartment on Mapu Street. Paulauskas, who had gone there on their behalf to salvage whatever was left of their possessions, found the rooms occupied by a German official and was afraid to go inside. It seemed they would have nothing to cover themselves with in the face of the approaching winter. For the first time in her life Mrs. Weiss stood in need of charity. She and Shula were forced to wear torn clothing obtained through relief agencies. Ghetto life had its effect but Mrs. Weiss adjusted.

Snow covered the earth. Onto the low roofs of the ghetto settled choruses of cawing crows. As Mrs. Weiss hurried off to work every morning through the ghetto streets, the screeching of the birds seemed to pursue her.

As a doctor's wife, she had been given a nurse's job, whereby she barely managed to sustain herself and Shula. Ghetto life changed her appearance. Silver threads appeared in her hair. Her eyes were sunken and her brow was heavily creased. She even began to stoop. At first she had had some hope for her husband, but month followed month and nothing whatsoever was heard of the doctor.

After a grueling day's work Mrs. Weiss would hurry to her room at the edge of the ghetto, completely exhausted, prepare some food for her daughter, and then wash and patch their clothes. Frequently she would be wakened in the night: once a baby was sick, then a wounded man was brought into the ghetto; another time a woman was convulsed with birth pains. Mrs. Weiss would put her own discomfort and fatigue aside and rush out to be of assistance.

Over the year Shula matured a great deal. Her eyes grew more reflective. She learned how to keep a room in order, how to launder, even how to cook. Frequently she relieved her mother of all household duties. She even began to work outside the house; sometimes she would serve at her mother's clinic, washing floors and dishes or laundering bandages.

At night whenever she managed to get home before her mother, she would light the fire in the stove, but often there wasn't a sliver of wood in the room. Then she would sweep, climb onto their one bed, curl up her legs, and sink into reverie.

Shula loved to dream and fantasize. She saw herself accompanying her mother on a visit to a sick man, the two of them binding his wounds, feeding him, cleaning his apartment. This patient was old. You didn't see old people in the ghetto anymore; he alone had been miraculously saved.

All at once the old man got out of bed and started to

expand before Shula's amazed eyes. His head reached the ceiling. Then the ceiling itself opened, revealing a blue, star-strewn sky. The wondrous old man was holding a ring out to her. In a voice that she sensed more than heard, he said to Shula, "The ring is black; it has no sparkle or beauty, but don't mind that, my dear. It is a magic ring and with it you will conquer all your enemies." So spoke the old man and vanished.

Fascinated, Shula tried the ring on her finger. Her mother noticed nothing; she was busy gathering her things together preparing to leave for home. Shula walked after her, smiling.

"Mother, dear, you have no idea what's going to happen in just a few minutes."

They entered their apartment, Shula twisted the ring and lo and behold, the table was piled high with choice food. Her mother was astounded. She did not dare to draw near, afraid to believe her eyes. Shula was laughing and crying for joy as she served her mother the delicacies: fresh rolls, milk, butter, eggs.

"Now I'll go outside and feed everyone who is hungry."

Swiftly Shula descended to the ghetto streets and ran from house to house. Soon the Jews were eating and drinking their fill. Joy spread through the ghetto.

No, no, that's not enough, thought Shula, *they're still in the ghetto. How can anyone be happy in the ghetto? Just a little while*, she thought, *and the ghetto walls will fall.*

Morning, between five and six. The Jewish brigades—ghetto labor squads—were lined up by the exit gate in twos and threes. All around them scurried the Jewish

73

ghetto police and the Lithuanian officers. The enemy talked among themselves, pointed to individual Jews, leered and laughed.

"That's fat cat Finkelstein—he had the biggest factory in Kovno. I worked there as a janitor. Now he comes to me every day to sweep my yard. Every morning I spill the slop around on purpose to make sure he's got plenty to do. Ha, ha, ha! And that's the engineer Lewinstein—he cleans toilets now."

"That tall one, the one in the gray dress, she's an artist. Every week after her work in the brigade she does my wife's laundry, and she's happy to get a loaf of bread for the job."

Shula pressed her ringed finger to her heart. *Just wait, just wait. We'll see who laughs last.*

A commotion broke out by the gate. The brigades were beginning to move out when a Lithuanian policeman spotted, in their ranks, a small boy.

He was about ten years old. The officer stopped him with a kick. The boy's father insisted that the lad was thirteen, that he had been assigned to the brigade and went out to work every day. But the Lithuanian stood firm. He took his rubber truncheon and began beating both father and son about the head.

Shula darted from her place and ran toward him.

"What are you doing, you animal? Trying to kill the boy?"

All regarded her with amazement. "Who is that girl? What courage!"

The policeman's face turned beet red. He pivoted to seize Shula, but she simply spun the ring about her finger.

A mighty rumble was heard; the fence about the ghetto crumbled and the gate vanished. The officer lay dead at her feet, his whip at his side. The Jews stood rooted in fear and confusion.

"Jews, our hour has come!" Shula cried. "First we will avenge ourselves on our torturers, and then we will leave this cursed land!"

"Where will we go?" she heard voices call out.

"To the Land of Israel! All of us. Not one Jew will stay here."

She led the way. Every German, every Lithuanian policeman fell dead before her. She walked from house to house, from street to street, entering every apartment where Jews lived. And woe to any non-Jew whose hands had shed innocent blood! All the Jews boarded a train headed for the port. Shula recognized the city—more than once she had visited it with her relatives. There too she rendered judgment upon the enemies of the Jews. Not a German remained alive in the city. The Jews who had been driven out returned and set fire to their homes. "We will not leave them to our enemies!" they cried.

Then they all boarded the ship and, singing, sailed for the Land of Israel. . . .

The creak of the door awakened Shula from her visions. Her mother had come home.

Mrs. Weiss lay down alongside her daughter; they held each other and fell asleep.

Summer passed and the cold autumn rains filled the ghetto streets with muck. Their second autumn in the ghetto.

The population had shrunk. Some had died of illness, some had left for work and never came back, others just "disappeared." Mainly, though, it was the "actions" that took the heaviest tolls.

Then one day, the butchery came to a halt. The ghetto prisoners tried to believe the government's assurances that no more Jews would be taken out to be killed. They only had to do their jobs well.

Rarely did Shula see any of her friends from Mapu Street in the ghetto. At times she would run into Shmulik. They would smile at each other, wave, and go their separate ways. Occasionally, Shmulik would come see her in her room. He told her of Etta's death and that they had handed his sister Hanna over to the Giriuses and he had heard nothing of her.

At times Paulauskas would come to the fence, always laden with gifts: flour, bread, grits, potatoes, even butter and meat. Shula would set aside a portion of these treats for her friend Shmulik. After receiving such treasures she would get up early and run to the gate where he left for work and invite him over.

Shmulik would accept these invitations only rarely; he was embarrassed to eat at his friend's house. Mrs. Weiss would remember him nevertheless, wrapping up food and sending Shula to his apartment with it. At times Mrs. Cohen visited too; they didn't live very far apart. Mrs. Weiss, who in the past had kept some distance from her neighbors, enjoyed the visits of Shmulik's mother, who was modest and pleasant. They both had suffered the same fate—losing a husband. They chatted together and at times that gave them some relief.

With the reduction of the ghetto's size, after the many "actions," the two families moved in together.

Shmulik would manage to bring back pieces of wood from his place of work and light the stove. Mrs. Weiss and Shula went out to work and Mrs. Cohen took care of the small household's affairs, cooking, cleaning, and laundering.

Shula's health became a matter of grave concern. The girl grew very thin as she grew taller. She had frequent attacks of headaches and coughed a great deal. Etta's fate kept haunting Shmulik. After witnessing one particularly acute bout of coughing, he resolved to get Shula out of the ghetto, no matter what.

Mrs. Weiss decided that her daughter should go live with Mr. Paulauskas and his wife, but Shula was adamant. She would not stir without her mother, she would not leave her mother alone. Mrs. Weiss's own strength had waned steadily under the burden of caring for her daughter. Shula felt responsible for her mother. No, she would not abandon her. They would leave only together.

Mrs. Weiss did not want to flee. She was tired of life; she lacked the will power to put forth the effort. To get to Paulauskas it would be necessary to escape from the ghetto, pass through the packed city streets for a distance of a mile and a half, shiver at the sight of every Lithuanian brat—it was all too much for her. She only wanted to save Shula. But what was there to do? The child would not give an inch; without her mother she would not budge!

Mrs. Weiss surrendered, already grown accustomed to backing down before her daughter's demands. Still, how could they contact Paulauskas? Could he have moved? For three months he had not come to the fence, nor had they received any messages from him.

Consequently Shula mapped out a new plan; she would go to Paulauskas alone and would send him to fetch her mother. If her mother refused to come, Shula would return to the ghetto.

The crucial problem was getting the uniform of a Lithuanian high school student—that was the only way she could disguise herself. But where were a brown wool skirt and black apron to be had in the ghetto?

One night Shmulik and Shula sat up very late. The fire in the stove had long since died out and only a few embers still glowed, but they were enough for the youngsters to warm their hands by. A bright moon poured through the window onto the opposite wall, where their shadows swayed. The children listened to the heavy breathing of Mrs. Weiss and the sighs of Mrs. Cohen.

They came up with a plan. Every day Shula and her mother would set aside a portion of their rations and Shmulik would try to get a loaf of bread on the outside. In exchange for food one could get anything in the ghetto. With the food they saved they would obtain the uniform.

Weeks passed but the plan was not carried out. Then salvation came from an unexpected quarter.

Christmas had arrived. The windows of the Lithuanian

homes adjoining the ghetto sparkled with an abundance of gala, multicolored lights. Shmulik and Shula went out, approached the ghetto fence, and looked beyond it to the lit-up windows. Through them they could see small firs decked with chains of colored paper, ruddy apples, shining pictures of angels, and small colorful candles burning at the tips of their branches. The sound of singing spilled out of the adjacent two-story house, with the gay laughter of dancing children, the tumult of a festive celebration.

Shula recalled how once she had been invited to the fir-tree holiday at the home of a Lithuanian doctor, her father's friend. She too had danced with the young guests and received presents and in the hubbub of the celebration had forgotten that she was a stranger there, a daughter of the Jewish people—the same people now forbidden to come in contact with the Lithuanian lords of the land. It seemed to her that many years had passed since that Christmas.

Suddenly the singing ceased. Cries of terror erupted from the house along with the sound of falling chairs and women's screams. A man with disheveled hair burst forth from the doorway in a panic. His glance fell on the two children pressed against the ghetto fence. Hesitating only for an instant, he rushed toward them.

"Let's go," whispered Shmulik, tugging Shula's sleeve, but the man motioned them to remain where they were.

"Don't leave, I won't hurt you. I need a doctor. You have a doctor or a nurse anywhere? Somebody's head's split. Speak up, the man could die."

Shula's impulse was to turn and flee, leaving the Lithuanian by the fence. What did she care if the wounded man died? Let him. That would make one less Lithuanian butcher in the world. Hadn't they spilled enough Jewish blood? Nonetheless, as if by themselves, the words tumbled from Shula's lips. "My mother is a nurse."

Anxiously, the Lithuanian stretched out his hands. "Please, I beg you, come with me. My father is hurt badly." With one leap he had bounded over the ghetto fence and Shula led him to her apartment.

"Are you the nurse?" he asked Mrs. Weiss.

"I am."

"Please, I beg you, come with me. My father is hurt badly." Mrs. Weiss looked at the man. For a moment she, too, could almost taste revenge. That feeling however was immediately superseded by another: a man was in danger of dying—she had to help! Silently she took her instruments and equipment and descended to the fence. There she stopped. She was not allowed to cross over the barrier that they, the lords of the land, had erected between the Jews and themselves, the "master race." Bitterness and pain swept over her.

"You have penned us in like wild animals to keep us apart from human beings, and now you come to ask me to help your father!"

After a short while Mrs. Weiss returned, carrying a loaf of bread, a holiday cake, and a huge sausage—payment for her services. The victim, she reported, had been smashed over the head by a whiskey bottle, wielded by a drunken neighbor in the heat of argument.

The following day Shmulik took the sausage when he left the house. Upon his return, he had the uniform they

80

needed. Shula put the dress on, tied the black apron around her, and took the brown leather briefcase, almost all that remained to them of their former possessions. To avoid suspicion she wrapped a large woolen shawl about her head and upper body.

She rose early with Shmulik, left the house and mingled with the work teams heading out of the ghetto.

They approached the gate. The wintry morning lay wrapped in murky gray; a thick falling snow covered everyone, making them all look alike. The gatekeeper, counting heads automatically without looking at faces, signaled her group through. Another moment and they were outside. Shula heaved a sigh of relief.

Now she was confronted with her second major problem—slipping out of the ranks under the eyes of the Lithuanian guards.

Shula looked about. Her brigade had peeled off from the others and was headed for a side street. The houses were small, most of them one story, and the sidewalks narrow. Shula saw that only two Lithuanian guards were accompanying the group, one in front and one behind. She would have to drop back toward the last lines and wait her opportunity.

Shula began to limp. She lagged and was pushed to the rear. Some looked at her in pity, others in annoyance. Fearfully she followed the guard's movements. So far he had noticed nothing.

She reached the last row, near the guard.

What would follow? How could she escape? The guard would shoot at her and would wound members of the brigade too; any passerby would help capture her.

At that point fortune smiled on Shula. A man emerged

from the gate of one of the houses; no sooner had the guard spotted him than a huge smile formed on his lips. They hurried toward each other.

The guard plunged into conversation with his friend and for a moment disregarded his charges. The alley was almost empty. Shula stopped, the brigade drew away from her, and she promptly stepped through an open gateway into the adjoining courtyard. There she snatched off the shawl with the two yellow patches, stuffed it into her briefcase, and donned the headpiece of a Lithuanian high school student.

Shula felt that someone had seen her enter the courtyard and was lying in wait for her. She pulled herself away and went back to the street. The hour was early and traffic was very light. Shula headed toward the station, boarded a bus, and sat all the way to the rear.

The bus was soon full. Though no one paid her any attention, it seemed to Shula that they all knew who she was and were only waiting for the right moment. Any second the cry would ring out: "Get the Jewess!" and many hands would seize her. Opposite her sat a boy of fifteen or sixteen, his bright blond hair hanging down over his eyes. Alongside her sat an elderly man wearing a green felt hat. He caught her eye and smiled. "A diligent student to be off to school this early."

Attempting to look calm, Shula smiled back. "I have to take care of a few things for the house, sir, before class. My mother is not in good health."

"Ah, yes," the man nodded, "war is hard, even on the young."

The boy across the aisle eyed her with interest. Shula

almost gagged. She struggled to act natural, but the blood rushed to her cheeks. She undid the top button of her vest, revealing a small cross hanging around her neck. From her pocket she took a hand mirror, peered into it, and with feigned vanity readjusted some hairs that had slipped from under her hat. She grew somewhat easier on seeing that the boy had stopped staring at her. The bus grew more crowded, passengers entered and left. Shula turned toward the window.

Only five more minutes till her stop, only five minutes more! The bus was crawling. Until it next halted it seemed as though an hour had passed. Only three passengers remained on the vehicle. Again it seemed that they were all looking at her, that they were all waiting for her to get up. The man with the leather hat and the brown coat distressed her especially. He had boarded the bus one stop after her and still had not gotten off.

He is only pretending to read the paper, she thought, *actually, he's trailing me. There, he just wiped his nose so he could get a look at me. Those hard eyes, he's giving me the once-over. . . .*

The bus stopped. Shula's legs quaked; she could not get up. The young man with the leather hat rose, turned to the door, and descended, heedless of her.

Just as the bus was about to pull away Shula leaped from her seat and hurried off, crossed the street, and turned to the dirt road where her friends lived. How would the Paulauskas' receive her? Would she even find them?

The gate behind the house, alongside the barn, creaked. A woman wrapped in a black woolen shawl approached —it was Maré Paulauskas. The woman was dumfounded.

She saw her guest at a glance, looked about, and wordlessly motioned her to follow. Maré returned to the barn
with Shula behind her.

"Jesus Maria!" she exclaimed when she was inside,
clapping her hands as she examined Shula. "Where's your
mother? How is she doing?"

"She's still alive," Shula answered, standing in the barn
door, all but overwhelmed by the odor of manure and the
body heat of the cows. She was so confused by this
encounter that she scarcely knew what was happening.

"My poor child," Mrs. Paulauskas lamented.

"Maré," Shula blurted, afraid that at any moment she
might lose her power of speech. "I've come to you for
refuge."

"For yourself?"

"For Mother, too."

Maré fell silent. Shula did too. For an instant it seemed
that the earth was slipping from beneath her, that she was
plunging into an abyss.

"I don't know, my husband's not home. These are hard
times, they search so often. . . ."

Shula's eyes flooded with tears. Seeing the child's
anguish, the woman placed her hand on her shoulder.
"Now, now, don't cry. We'll see, we'll find a way. My man
will come home, tomorrow he'll be home. In the mean-
while, you stay here. Climb up on top of the haystack,
you'll keep warm. You can't stay in the room now—they
search there."

Shula wanted to say that she couldn't delay, that her
mother was waiting for her in the ghetto, but she remained
mute. Worn out and hungry, she climbed atop the roof-
high haystack that filled half the barn, covered her legs

84

and body, and closed her eyes. How lovely it would be if she could lie there till it was all over, without being disturbed anymore, without having to eat or drink—to lie there until the war was over or to sleep and never wake up again.

Someone was shaking her arm. She opened her eyes. There stood Maré before her, in her hand a large cup of milk, bread, and cheese.

"You fell asleep, poor thing, you must be exhausted." She looked at her compassionately. "Eat up and then sleep. Oh, do you need rest, do you need rest. . . ."

A tear dropped from Maré's eye.

Shula saw it and a rush of warmth swept over her. That tear had rolled a heavy stone from her heart.

Shula spent that day on the haystack in the barn. In the evening Maré brought her a blanket and a hot meal—a bowl of soup with bits of meat in it. After she ate, she curled up in the blanket and sank off to sleep.

The second day passed in a similar fashion. Between meals she slept as though she were making up to her sticky eyelids for all the long ghetto nights, the terror-filled nights of straining for sounds from their secret hiding place.

Paulauskas came back three days after she had arrived. In the evening he entered the barn, welcomed her, and said, "You rest here. I'll get your mother."

Only her embarrassment prevented her from embracing the good man. Instead she merely whispered, "There, by the fence."

"I know. Don't worry, I'll find her. And you just eat well and rest."

85

He wished her good night and slowly slipped down the haystack.

In the morning, when Shula opened her eyes, she felt the warmth of a body by her side. "Mother, Mother, you're here; Mommy, you're here. . . ."

Mrs. Weiss slept, one arm embracing Shula, the other beneath her own head.

The days passed, and outside the winter cold grew more severe. It drove through the stacks of hay and straw that they piled on top of themselves, and it pierced their flesh like needles. Shula and her mother would press tightly together to find warmth.

At night they would slip off the haystack and walk about the barn for exercise. Shula would go over to the cow and stroke its soft skin. The cow would regard her kindly and lick the girl's hand. Shula would press her face against the cow's head, embrace her neck, and find relief for her tortured soul.

The mother and daughter knew no want of food. Only their isolation from the world oppressed them, their living like rats in the hay, unable to keep themselves clean. Even in their difficult ghetto circumstances, in their cold room, they had heated water daily and bathed. In the barn they could not impose that much upon their hosts. Saturday night, after the Paulauskas family bathed in honor of Sunday, Maré would offer to heat them up water for a bath, if they liked.

Then in the dark the two of them would steal through the courtyard and into the house. The windows would be covered with thick dark curtains, with only the stove's fire piercing the darkness. In the middle of the room stood a big wooden tub used for laundering. Maré would fill it halfway with hot water and would give them a large chunk of laundry soap, a long linen towel, and two white gowns.

"You two get undressed and I'll scrub your backs," she would say, "I know you don't have the strength. We're only human," she would continue, "and no one knows what fate has in store. Today you need me. Tomorrow I'll need your help."

"I hope you never need our help," answered Mrs. Weiss, "but I pray that I'll be able to pay you back someday for your goodheartedness."

In the Cellar

Shots split the morning silence, wrenching Mrs. Weiss from sleep into the grayness of predawn. Her chest tightened; she feared disaster. She shook her daughter, "Wake up, child, wake up," she whispered, "they're shooting."

With trembling hands the two assembled their bedding, bundled it up, and stuffed it deep into the hay. Then they squeezed into a dark corner, burrowed into the stack, and lay deathly still, peering into the darkness.

The hail of bullets was constant, along with the crackle

of machine-gun fire heard in the distance. The ghetto was under attack.

Shula thought of her dear Shmulik and wept. Her conscience pricked her—she had saved herself and left him to his fate. Many a day she had lain for hours in the hay, thinking up plans to save him.

"Hush, Shula, hush," soothed her mother, "any louder and they'll hear us." But Shula could not contain her grief. "Shmulik, Shmulik," she whimpered.

Louder and louder came the shots. At times it seemed they were whistling over their very place of concealment. After hours went by only scattered shots were discernible. Then there was silence.

No one entered the barn, not even Maré on her daily visit to milk the cow. Their meal was not brought to them. They were not even able to tell what time it was or how long the shooting had lasted.

They both lay in the hay, ears perked for any sounds from the outside, afraid even to peek through the slits in the wall. A dog barked fiercely in the courtyard and the heavy tread of boots drew ever nearer. "Sh, Wilkas, sh!" A man's husky voice tried to quiet the hound.

"I only have one cow in the barn," they heard Paulauskas assert clearly, "only one cow."

"Open up and let's have a look," they heard the stranger say.

Bloodhounds, thought the Weisses. *It's all over*. The barn door creaked open. Shula and her mother huddled deep in the hay, holding their breath. Then the barn door closed and the steps faded into the distance.

That night Paulauskas appeared and brought them

food. He urged them to eat and stood by silently. Mrs. Weiss could hardly touch the dinner. "Tell us, what happened?"

"It's not worthwhile. . . . Butchers, bloodsuckers!" he spat angrily. "I'll have to build you a shelter. You can't stay in the haystack. They have begun searching."

All the next day they heard the sound of hammering. One night Paulauskas awakened them and led them across the courtyard into the house through the back door. The room was pleasantly warm and filled with the aroma of fresh wheat cakes. Paulauskas invited them to the table. For weeks they had not dined like human beings. Maré came in, greeted them silently, and left.

"My wife is watching so we won't have any unexpected guests," Paulauskas explained. "Last week they killed a whole family near here—found a Jew in their home."

More than ever Mrs. Weiss realized what a burden they had placed upon their rescuers. Every motion that their host made, every squeak of the door, every ring of the fork unnerved her.

Mrs. Weiss got up. "It's best that we go."

"Why?" asked Paulauskas. He approached the closet, opened the door, and bent over and lifted a board, disclosing an entrance. Then he kindled a piece of wood as a light and, leading the way, ushered them into a pit. The air was close and damp, heavy with the odor of rotten potatoes. By the light of the torch Shula saw that they were standing in an empty cellar only recently cleared out. At one end stood a bed made from a huge wooden crate, and on it a mattress made of straw.

"It's not an elegant apartment," Paulauskas apologized,

"but you'll be near us, and when things are quiet you'll be able to climb upstairs and warm up. Maybe in the meantime we'll hear some good news."

That night they slept soundly; the cellar gave them a sense of security.

In the course of time, however, Mrs. Weiss was forced to realize that Shula's cough was growing worse and worse. Frequently the child suffered from headaches. The mother's experienced eye marked well the unusual pallor of her daughter, the unhealthy gleam in her eyes. Concern for her child gripped her night and day.

Aware of her mother's worried glances, Shula tried to disguise her depression and look cheerful.

The forced inactivity weighed heavily on both of them, particularly on Shula. Mrs. Weiss slept frequently, but Shula was awake even at night. She would lie alongside her mother, her eyes closed in the dark, her ears attuned to the least noise. Sometimes she would be reminded of stories she had read of evil kings or emperors who had tortured their subjects and buried them alive.

We have been buried alive, too, she thought. *We entered this grave willingly. Strange that a person should crawl into a grave while he's still alive, even to save his life.*

The state of Shula's health grew critical. She lost her appetite; often her forehead was drenched with cold sweat. Her coughing bouts became more acute; she struggled desperately to control herself whenever she heard steps.

Mrs. Weiss began to concoct a bold scheme. Perhaps she and her daughter could pass for Christians in a different neighborhood! Their features were not particularly Jewish, and Shula had spoken Lithuanian fluently from

90

infancy. She would ask Paulauskas to find her work in a distant city, perhaps in the northern region of Lithuania, bordering Latvia.

One day Mrs. Weiss unfolded the plan to him. If she and her daughter couldn't work at nursing, she would be content to clean house. All she wanted was food and a roof above their heads.

Paulauskas looked at her with kindly eyes. "How naïve you are, Mrs. Weiss. Who would accept you without identification papers?"

Mrs. Weiss knew that papers could be forged. She had heard of such doings in the ghetto, where all kinds of documents were falsified—work cards, ration slips, and the like. Let her host procure her false papers as a Christian.

Such a document, however, would cost a great deal of money. How could she pay? She thought at once of the two gold watches she and her daughter still possessed. They would serve.

Paulauskas was hesitant. He could promise nothing. They might fall into a trap. He would see, he would try.

In the meantime the days flew by. Shula looked at the silver threads in her mother's hair and at her face, which only one year before had been so young and fresh, and was filled with foreboding. What if she should fall seriously ill? Who would take care of her mother? Stabbing pains sliced through her chest, but she struggled to conceal the agony and fear, struggled to look alert and gay. She chatted often, recalling the happy past and wove plans for the future.

"You'll see, Mother. The war will be over soon. The

Germans aren't winning anymore. We'll get out of this country and never come back. In the meantime we'll go to some city where no one knows us. I'll work and you'll rest. After all, I've grown up already, I know housework backwards and forwards."

Mrs. Weiss would let her daughter ramble on in an effort to comfort her, but inwardly she feared. *My child, my poor child, who knows what fate still has in store for you? Now I'm trying to leave our dear friends' home, our refuge, where we lack nothing. Who will guarantee our not having to go hungry, not having to sleep under the open sky?* Still, whenever she looked at Shula's face, she would decide anew that they had to get out of that cellar, come what may. The child would soon go out like a candle.

After three more weeks had passed Paulauskas announced that he could obtain the papers. A short time before, a Russian woman had died in the vicinity. Her papers were available. The only difficulty was getting identification for the girl. However, he hoped to clear that hurdle too. Again, many days of waiting. . . .

Finally the longed-for hour arrived; they were to prepare to set out. They would be leaving for the vicinity of Palanga on the shores of the Baltic Sea. The owner of an estate there, an elderly widower who was a friend of Paulauskas needed a woman to manage his household. But the Weisses dare not let him know that they were Jewish.

"Listen, child," Mrs. Weiss instructed her daughter, "learn this well: from now on your name is Onyté Dudaité, daughter of the late Jonas Duda, and I'm your stepmother, Sofia Mikhailovna Dudainé."

Mrs. Weiss spoke Lithuanian poorly. Her possessing the papers of a Russian woman who had married a Lithuanian prior to the outbreak of the war would explain her proficiency in Russian and her lack of fluency in Lithuanian. "But why should you be my stepmother?" Shula could not make peace with that idea.

Then, "Mother, will we always have to lie that we're Christians?"

Looking her daughter squarely in the eye, Mrs. Weiss answered, "Dear child, 'lie' you say? Our lives will always be truer and holier than our enemies'. Their lives are a lie, their every act is deception, and every step they take is brutality. Maybe someday we will be able to walk upright once again."

Early in the morning, while the last stars still glimmered in the sky, Shula and her mother arrived at a small station about twelve miles from Kovno. There they boarded a train heading northward to the coast. They were dressed in peasant clothing and carried wicker baskets containing their meager belongings and provisions for the way. Paulauskas had taken them to the station in a farmer's wagon.

The winter came to an end. For months little Hanna had lived in her new home, a wooden cottage plastered white and thatched with a straw roof. In front of the house lay a small flower garden where stalks of rue ripened, and behind it, in the bloom of spring, a few cherry trees waved their slender branches with every passing breeze.

Not far from the house flowed the broad Viliya. Its waters, still swollen from the melted snow, the eroded soil, and the rotted leaves and branches, surged by with awesome power.

Beyond the river lay fields of ripening rye and oats and black, plowed earth; and on the other side, forests of pine and firs strewn with birch trees.

Hanna seemed content. Slowly she had grown accustomed to her new situation and her new family.

"Listen to Stasé, do whatever she tells you, and call her Mommy." Her mother's parting words were engraved on her heart.

Besides Stasé and her husband, Jonas, the household included a widow, Jonas's sister, with her two grown sons, Jurgis and Petras, and her daughter, Aldona.

Aldona was two years older than Hanna—a slender girl, tall for her age, with smooth hair bright as flax and blue-gray eyes. She usually wore a coarse, homespun dress that fell to her ankles and a big yellow kerchief tied to her head. Barefoot she would trip through the fields, a long willow rod in her hand. Every morning she would take the geese out to graze on the banks of the Viliya and Hanna was sent with her.

In this farmers' home she was no longer called Hanna but Maryté Giriuté. Neighbors on the scattered farms in the vicinity only knew that Maryté was the youngest daughter of the Giriuses, a relative of theirs, an orphan, that they had adopted after the death of her parents, who had been poor janitors from the city.

Hanna, however, simply could not manage to call the Giriuses "Daddy" and "Mommy." When strangers were about she tried to keep away from the house, and when none were present she called Stasé "Auntie."

Hanna grew, and her face and legs turned brown in the wind and sun. She too wore a broad, peasant blouse with long sleeves, and a homespun skirt made of coarse weave. When she ran, the cloth chafed so that her legs hurt. Her head was tied round with a thick wool kerchief, and her shoes had been taken from her.

"Shoes you need only in the wintertime," they told her, "when we go to church in the city. No use wearing them out—you can run around barefoot."

"C'mon, slowpoke," Aldona would call out to her, waving her bright kerchief from afar.

It was hard for Hanna to run barefoot over the plowed soil that dried out and hardened in the spring wind and scraped the bottom of her feet until blood flowed. The going was somewhat easier beyond the plowed fields, along the river bank where the grass was turning green and there were tall birches and willows.

It was nice to sit on the bank and look at the gray-white clouds in the mirror of the water and at the stretches of blue, to close her eyes and daydream. Where was Mommy at that moment? And what was Shmulik doing?

Since she had arrived at the village she had not seen them. She had been ordered to forget she had come from the ghetto and that she was Jewish.

"You know," Aldona told her once, "yesterday they brought a hundred Jews to work. I saw them. They're terrible, those Jews. They got strange eyes. . . . Jurgis says every Jew has a devil friend. At nighttime they meet monsters, and they dance around a campfire. Lady devils give 'em Christians' blood to drink."

Hanna kept quiet as though not understanding. She was gripped with fear. What a horrid story! "That's a lie," she wanted to shout, "a lie, a lie, a lie!" But she sat petrified looking into her friend's cloudy eyes, unable to make a sound.

"Jurgis knows," Aldona went on, "he studied three years in school, he even studied with the priest. Jurgis says all Jews are cheats and crooks, but the Germans are gonna kill 'em all and there won't be any Jews left in the whole world!

"Hey, have you been to the priest yet? Boy, is his house pretty! There's a chandelier hanging from his ceiling, all made of crystal. Real crystal! And he has lots of candlesticks. The priest's guests get served with forks and spoons all made of silver! You ever see forks and spoons made of silver? Oh, course not. You're just an orphan, your folks were janitors. Your mom must have seen 'em in the Jews' houses—those Jews have everything!"

Hanna wanted to cry, the tears choked her, she wanted to scream, "Lies, lies! Everything you say is a lie! I'm not an orphan and the Jews are nice! And we had crystal candlesticks and silver forks and spoons in our house, too!" But she remained silent and tears raced down her cheeks.

"Aw, shush now, don't cry, I didn't want to make you sad. What can you do? That's the way God wanted it, so he took your mommy and daddy, but now you got a new mommy. Look, Uncle Jonas adopted you, so what are you crying for?"

Baptism

Violet lilac blossoms in the garden greeted the month of May. Slowly the branches were cloaked with green, and pink and purple blooms perfumed the air. Preparations were under way in the Girius household for the month's prayers.

"Listen here, Maryté," Stasé addressed Hanna. "Tomorrow you're coming to church with us. Now, you know, you're a little Catholic girl. We're going to go up to the priest to say hello and kiss his hand. You watch me and do just what I do."

Stasé woke the girl while it was still dark. She had her

wash and dress quickly in holiday attire—a colorful skirt with broad pleats, a blouse embroidered with flowers, a green vest, and a multicolored belt. On her neck she wore a chain of amber and a few gay ribbons. The whole family set out in a horse-drawn cart.

The outside of the church was mobbed, the church doors were open wide, and the yard was flooded with lights that blinded Hanna temporarily. With difficulty the Giriuses managed to clear a path for themselves through the throngs of women in their white silk kerchiefs carrying prayer books under their arms. Finally they pushed their way between two benches.

Hanna raised her eyes. Before her was a pulpit garlanded with wreaths of flowers and adorned with beautiful rugs. On the wall in front of the pulpit shone a huge silver cross. The portraits on the wall and the wood engravings around the ceiling resembled figures from a strange world, filling her with fear.

Then her glance met two large eyes, deep-sunken, staring out at her from a niche in the wall. The gaze was warm and heartening and stilled Hanna's fear. The eyes cast a thin shadow on a pale face crowned with long locks.

Who was that man with the long hair and kindly, sad eyes? She kept staring until she realized that the eyes belonged to a life-size statue.

A faint breeze brushed the candelabrum, washing light and shadow over the statue's face. It seemed to Hanna that the face moved, that the figure had turned its head and looked on her with great pity.

The low strains of the organ set the air astir. The congregation froze and a solemn hush settled over the church. A wave of warmth swept over Hanna.

98

The thick voice of the priest floated down from the pulpit. Hanna looked at his round, ruddy face. This was the first time she had seen a priest at work, and so close at that. His cassock was white, ornamented with embroidery and needlework. She remembered the white Sabbath dress her mother had sewn for her and tears swam before her eyes.

"Mommy, my mommy," she whimpered inaudibly.

The bass voice of the priest was chanting again. The congregation kneeled.

"On your knees!" Hanna heard Stasé's voice as the woman yanked her arm. Hanna knelt alongside her and continued crying. "Mommy, why did you send me away like this?"

Stasé saw the child's wet cheeks and her eyes seemingly fixed on the priest. She tugged at her husband's sleeve and winked in the child's direction. "See how moved she is in church? She's going to be a good Catholic."

Stasé leaned over her, wiped her face with the edge of her shawl, and whispered affectionately, "Don't cry, Maryté, our Lord Jesus saw your tears and he'll forgive your sins. Just try to love Him with all your heart. Pray every day to the Holy Mother and she'll surely spread her wings over you. Soon you'll start visiting the priest, you'll learn the principles of our holy faith, and our Lord Jesus will have mercy on you."

The service ended and the church was emptied of its congregation. Stasé led Hanna across the courtyard through the back door into a dimly lit, almost empty room. On the sides stood two long benches, and on the wall hung a small wooden cross. Beneath it, on the end of one bench, were a bucket of water and a cup.

Stasé paused for an instant alongside the crucifix to cross herself and Hanna. Then she approached the doorway at the end of the room covered with heavy brown curtains and announced loudly, "Blessed be the name of Jesus Christ!"

"Forever!" issued a voice from behind the curtain. In the doorway appeared a tall, lean woman dressed in black. Stasé greeted her respectfully, kissed her arm, then pulled her aside and whispered into her ear. The woman fixed two angry eyes on Hanna and the child felt transfixed. She tried to shrink, anything to escape that glance. Tight-lipped, the woman in black motioned to Hanna to follow her. Once again they were in a long hall of the church. The large candelabrum had already gone out, and light shone from only one corner of the room.

Hanna tiptoed on, trying to muffle the echo of her steps in the empty chamber. Their shadows danced on the wall as they proceeded, filling her with terror. She walked as close to Stasé as possible, reaching for her skirts with her fingertips. As they approached the point from which the light was emanating, the woman motioned for them to step to the side and wait.

Before them stood a square cell with a small window, behind which the priest's head was visible. Kneeling outside the window, a veiled woman moved her lips for the longest time. Finally she rose, kissed the priest's hand, and left. The woman who had accompanied them drew near the opening, whispered into the priest's ear, and motioned to Stasé to enter.

Hanna remained outside. She thought the proceedings would never end, that she would stand there all day pressed against the wall of the cell, alone and abandoned in the empty church. For a moment she was seized by a desire to flee, to run until her breath gave out.

At long last the door of the booth opened and out stepped the priest with Stasé behind, beaming for joy.

"Come, Maryté, kiss the hand of our father, the priest, for the great kindness he is about to do you—saving not only your life but your soul," said Stasé, pushing the child toward the priest. A soft, round hand extended toward her lips.

Every night Stasé taught Hanna how to pray. First she showed her how to make the sign of the cross over her chest and forehead, then how to recite "Our Father" and a few prayers in honor of the Virgin Mary. Hanna, blessed with a good memory, was an apt learner and gave Stasé no end of satisfaction.

Weeks rolled by. Once again the child was awakened before dawn. Stasé dressed her swiftly in a white dress and a thin veil and decked her head with a wreath of ruc. That done, she wrapped the girl in a large shawl so that her holiday attire would not show, and they piled into the farm wagon. Jonas flicked the reins and the wagon moved out.

A sharp tug on her arm awakened Hanna, who had fallen asleep during the journey. The eastern fringe of the sky was turning red.

When they arrived at the church Jonas hitched his horse to a fence post and the three of them went inside. Stasé knocked three times at the rear door. In a few moments it opened, revealing the tall woman dressed in black. She greeted them softly and bade them follow her.

One candelabrum was lit in the empty church. The

priest was waiting. Hanna's warm shawl was removed, and she stood in her thin white dress, weary and frightened.

Why had she been brought there? Why had she been decked out like a bride?

The priest looked at her and said in a low voice, "Recite 'Hail Mary.'"

Hanna did so in a trembling voice, but fluently and with no mistakes. She recited the other prayers Stasé had taught her. A smile of satisfaction spread over the priest's thick lips and he stroked the girl's pale cheek. "You have learned well, my daughter. You are worthy of coming under the wings of the true faith."

Stasé was about to dissolve for sheer joy. Even the grim face of the lady in black was clothed in a smile.

The priest approached the water font hanging from the wall, dipped in a bunch of brushlike twigs and sprinkled water on Hanna's head, face, and shoulders.

"Kneel, daughter, before our Lord the Redeemer!" Stasé and Jonas knelt, too.

"Henceforth your name shall be Maria Magdalena Giriuté. This day you are born anew and these are your parents." He pointed to the Giriuses. "In the name of the Father, the Son, and the Holy Ghost, I usher you into the covenant of the Roman Catholic Christian faith," he solemnly intoned.

After a moment he continued. "Forget your past as quickly as possible, for your own good. Be a true daughter to the Church which has spread its saving wings over you and to your new parents, and merciful Jesus will have mercy upon you. And perhaps you will be worthy of becoming one of his blessed brides."

The ceremony was over. The priest left. He returned shortly and gave Stasé a rolled up scroll. She bent over and kissed his hand.

"Now you kiss the hand of your benefactor, too," Stasé said, pushing Hanna forward again. "Here you have a birth certificate of a true Christian. From now on you don't need to be afraid of any Germans."

Girius patted her on the shoulder affectionately and said, "We didn't celebrate this great day in your life properly. We had to do it quietly so no one would know. But years from now when you grow up and you're ready for it, we'll arrange for a second baptism celebration, your confirmation. Then we'll do it up proper; my name isn't Jonas Girius if all the farmers in the neighborhood won't leave my house drunk that day!"

The Adopted Daughter

Time passed. Hanna grew, her face and legs showing an ever darker tan from wind and sun. No longer did she feel the piercing pain of stones and hard clods of earth. She was one of the girls of the village. Two shining braids tied with red or green ribbons jiggled over her thin shoulders as she ran. She wore a colorful kerchief and a long linen dress.

Farmers in the region recognized the youngest daughter of the Giriuses by her bell-like voice.

At Christmas time she would delight churchgoers as she sang the hymns in the children's choir.

Slowly she grew used to her changed life. She learned to do every farm task. When the adults got up early to go to work, she would take a cup of water, dip her hand in, and sprinkle every corner of the one room that served the family as kitchen, dining room, and bedroom. From the corner by the stove she would take the rush broom and sweep the floor—its unpainted boards dulled over the years by the water and dust.

The house had two wings linked by a square corridor with doors on each side. Most of the time the second wing was closed. It was a room whose meticulously plastered walls displayed pictures of the saints. In it stood a table covered with a white cloth, whose edges were embroidered with multicolored flowers. Along one wall stood a bed covered by a white linen spread, atop which lay three pillows—large, small, and very small—resting one on top of the other in white pillowcases. Along the second wall stood an unpainted wooden closet, and in the corner by the door, a chest of drawers decorated with colored paper cutouts. Generally that room would be opened on Christmas or for very important guests.

Summer mornings, Hanna loved to get up early, dress hastily, and go outside to wet her feet in the dew that covered the grass like tiny pearls.

104

She would wash her hands in the icy waters of the pump and her face, too, wipe them with the edge of her kerchief, and then run off to lead the geese out. Next she would feed the chicks and wash the pails in preparation for the morning milking.

At that point she would go inside to devour with relish a breakfast of buckwheat cakes and sour milk. Then she would wash the dishes and head out to the pasture with Aldona.

In the snowy, cold winter days Hanna loved to sit by the warm stove fixing the men's shirts and knitting socks. She especially loved to spin; her hands were gifted. Round and round whirred the wheel under her tiny foot as her fingers drew out the fine wool or flaxen yarn.

The Giriuses' turn to host the neighborhood in a traditional gathering called the *talka* came round. Women filled the house, sitting on the benches and the beds. On the floor, mats were spread and sacks full of wool were placed upon them. The women pulled the wool out of a sack, handful after handful, and combed out the fibers, chatting of local news as they worked. One by one the men trailed in. The older ones drifted off to their corner to smoke pipes and discuss matters of the day; the younger ones mingled with the women, teasing and gabbing while waiting for refreshments from the lady of the house.

The children ran about among the adults' legs, now gathering up the carded wool in empty sacks, now getting smacks on the behind.

Thick, oily wheatcakes steamed on the table, alongside chunks of sausage and meat, and neither vodka nor *midus*, a honey-based liquor, was lacking. From time to time the young people would sing.

105

Hanna actually introduced the spirit of gaiety, her bell-like voice ringing out with the singers. As soon as the neighbors heard her they did not leave her alone. Hanna entertained them with folk songs, pouring out the tunes and words as feelingly and perfectly as any native-born village girl.

The peasant women could not hear enough. Stasé, her heart overflowing, pressed Hanna to her bosom.

The conversation rolled around to Jews. One of the neighbor women said, "You know, the Jewish tailor Shmulka from hereabouts had a nine-year-old boy that played the violin something terrific. Last summer, before the war started, he lived with his mother in the village of Roda. My sister married off her daughter then. They begged him to play at the wedding. First he refused, said he didn't know how to play Lithuanian wedding songs. So they sang him some and he played. On the spot! And what playing! Me, an old lady like me—I couldn't keep my feet still. He had all the grandmothers dancing!"

"They're talented, those Jews, that's a fact," an old farmer interjected.

"They didn't get rich for nothing, you can bet your life," one of the younger men added.

"They're rich," interjected another woman, Agné, " 'cause they're all sneak thieves and businessmen."

"Oh shut up, shut up! I'm sick of all that junk," her old father snapped. "The Jews had tailors and carpenters and shoemakers and smiths, too. And they worked. They sweated for what they earned. And they had golden hands. Now, we had a tailor in our village, Pietro's son from Roda. Learned how to be a tailor three years in the city.

And what came of it all? One day he comes to me and says, 'Let me sew you a *sermega*.*' 'All right,' I say, 'go to it. Here's some material, best around, pure wool. My late missus spun it with her own two hands just before she died.' He whips out scissors and snips away. And what do you think? When it comes to putting it together, one sleeve is too long, the other too short, the pockets are on the back, the whole thing is lopsided. I wanted to smash him one. Did he think it was a joke to ruin such a piece of material? Well, then I went and called in Shmulka the tailor. He takes out his scissors, needles, and thread. One, two, three, a stitch here, a stitch there, a snip somewhere else. He had that *sermega* ready in one day. And it looked like I'd been born in it! Let me tell you, there's nobody good as a Jewish craftsman!"

"Oh, Father, you're always singing the same song! And how many of them are master craftsmen? Two or three, and the rest are cheats. Like lice on our bodies. You can't count them, there are so many of them. The villages are crawling with Jews. When you go into a Jew shop to buy three yards of cloth, you just keep your eyes on the Jew's hands—and he'll still rob you blind! You come home and you see you're four inches short!"

"Enough, enough already! So don't shop in Jews' stores!"

"And it serves 'em right. They should have been killed off long ago. Now we'll be able to breathe in the villages again. The markets stank from Jews."

A farm wife turned to Stasé. "You know what happened two days ago to Mykolas Dagys from Lazdynai? I

---

* A winter coat made of coarse, homespun fabric.

found out just today from my godfather. Germans came to his house for fresh butter. Mykolas told them he didn't have any. They saw his wife and started in on her. 'Give us some butter or we'll shoot you.' They must have been drunk. She swore she took all her butter into the city, but they began looking in all the corners. Finally they went down into the cellar. And guess what they found there!"

A hush fell over the room. All eyes were on the story-teller.

"A little Jewboy. About seven years old. Dr. Landsberg's son, people said."

"*Vay, vay!*" rose a moan from the group.

"Well, they must have paid Mykolas a big fat lump. He was rich, that Dr. Landsberg."

"So why make a long story out of it?" the woman continued. "They dragged the kid out into the courtyard and shot him right by the kitchen window."

"*Vayeh, vayeh!* And Mykolas's wife, what happened to her?"

"They burned the house down and took her away with them."

"Ah, poor thing, she'll never come back, never," the women moaned, clapping their hands in anguish.

"So don't let 'em hide Jewboys in their house! The order is to kill 'em and that's that!" a young boy said.

"Shut your mouth!" the old man raged. "They're not God's creatures? They're not human beings, too?"

"No, they're not. Maybe you're hiding Jews, too?" The boy fixed him with a cold stare.

The old man did not answer. The silence grew oppressive.

"An order is an order," the host declared with finality.

"We're just farmers and we have no business getting mixed up in politics. The people on top know much more than we do."

"They told us not to hide Jews, so we can't!" Stasé added. "But now eat, my guests, eat!"

She hurried off to bring a fresh plate of steaming wheat cakes to the table.

All that while Hanna had sat behind Stasé, her legs folded beneath her, her heart fluttering. She had heard the Giriuses' last remarks and had not dared to look up.

Why are they like that too? Why? The question rang through her brain. She wanted to run off, sink into some dark corner, become invisible, but she could not even move. She was glued to the floor.

The Test

Summer was at its height. Light clouds drifted through the deep blue sky, but the farmers looked up at them with concern. They had no need of rain now. The harvest had not yet all been gathered in. It lay about the fields, in stacks exuding a pungent odor that roused the appetites of the flocks. The grain was ripe in the fields. The stalks, unable to bear the weight of their kernels any longer, were bowing low. With every breeze golden waves surged over the countryside, one after another. All the while, the gray-green waters of the Viliya rolled on.

It was a dry season and therefore doubly pleasant for Hanna to dip her legs into the cool waters of the river, then skip about on the shore over the smooth, round pebbles.

One stone would resemble a goose, another a snail. Then there were small fishes swimming with the current —school after school of fish would draw near the shore, nipping at the little girl's feet. Another moment and she would catch them! Then forward they would dart with Hanna in pursuit. Farther and farther she would wander, without Stasé noticing, as she was busy laundering.

With all her might Stasé would whack the flax cloth spread out before her on a small, wooden, bridgelike structure made out of three boards. Drops of water would splatter about and the echo of the pounding would spring back from the other side of the river.

"Maryté, Maryté, where are you?"

"Here, Auntie."

She had to look out for the child, make sure that she did not wander too far. The preceding weeks had not been quiet. Informers and spies had been crawling about the countryside, doing their work.

As she passed through the village, Stasé would sense suspicious eyes upon her. Only the day before Agné had taken her to a corner. "Stasé, people are saying that Maryté is——" and Agné whispered in her ear.

Stasé blushed crimson. With difficulty she swallowed her feelings and burst out laughing.

"What? A Jewgirl! Their tongues should rot, damn

them! Maybe you'd like to ask the priest? Wait a minute."

Stasé hurried inside and came out with Maryté's "birth certificate" and waved it under Agné's nose.

"What do you have to say now? A Jewgirl, my daughter? Ha, a Jewgirl!" she cried triumphantly.

Agné was confused. Stasé saw that she had the upper hand.

"Well, you realize . . ." Agné apologized. "I'm not a busybody and I don't gossip either. But times like these. . . . It's a rotten trick. I came to warn you."

How had they sniffed her out, the animals? Stasé fumed inwardly. Who could have told them? Who among her neighbors was her enemy, lying in wait?

"Maryté, Maryté," she yelled at the top of her lungs. "Come here!"

By chance she looked down the road toward the village. Her knees shook. Hanna was standing alongside the clerk of the village council, who was accompanied by two policemen and a third man dressed in city clothes. The stranger was bending over the girl and stroking her hair. No doubt they were asking her her name, who her parents were. . . . Icy terror gripped Stasé's heart. She could not hear what they were saying, she only saw that the child had turned in her direction and was pointing straight at her. What was she saying?

Soon a whole squad would come, no doubt. *They will surround the house*, thought Stasé.

She had to escape quickly before it was too late! She would run along the river, hide in the tall grasses, then plunge into the forest. It wasn't that far off, only a mile or two.

111

But Stasé could not move. What would become of Jonas? And his sister and her children?

The police and the stranger, however, turned and walked off in the direction of the village.

Stasé was still rooted to the spot unable to believe her eyes. Could it be true? Maryté was at her side, looking up at her with big bright eyes.

"Maryté, what did they ask you? What did you tell them?"

"They asked me who I was, and I told them, 'Maria Magdalena Giriuté.' "

"Nothing else?"

"They asked me where Daddy was and I said, 'In the field, bringing in the hay, and Mommy is washing clothes by the river.' "

For an instant Stasé just stood there, the strength flowing back into her. Then she swept the child into her arms and pressed her to her breast.

"My poor, wise little one," she whispered, comforting herself as she wiped away her own tears.

By the Sea

Dumbliai, respectfully called The Estate by peasants in the area, was actually an ordinary tract of a well-to-do farmer. Prior to the First World War it had been part of the Count Tyshkiewicz estate, containing a palace surrounded by an exquisite garden. To this day the palace stands at the entrance to the village of Palanga, on the coast of the Baltic Sea, and serves as a rest home.

A road, ending in a courtyard paved with unhewn stone, led to an old two-story house with a porch in front. Below the windows of the second floor pieces of iron projected—the remains of a balcony. Scraggly bushes shaded the house on both sides, some bearing roses, others, lilacs in season. Behind them lay a vegetable garden.

To the left of the courtyard stood a stable, its roof half gone, housing a team of horses. In the center of the yard was a long barn, and alongside it two plows and a seeding machine. At the end of the yard lay the livestock barn, with its milk cows and a few calves.

Once the landscape had been splashed with the color of flowers and plants and fruit trees, but now it had an abandoned look. The fenceposts leaned awry, the branches on the trees grew wild—obviously no gardener's hand had touched anything for years. In the winter every wind would shake snow down from the branches, and the cawing of the crows would emphasize rather than break the heavy silence. The small brook running through the garden was locked in ice and snow.

The estate lay a few miles from the sea. Whenever a strong wind rose, it brought the roar of the ocean waves to the ears of the residents.

The owners of the property—Wladislaw Jankowsky and his sister Helena—lived on the land. Jankowsky had grown up in a poor family on the Tyshkiewicz estate. His father had served as the count's wagoner, but Wladislaw

113

felt that his father's position was demeaning, for theirs was an aristocratic family, even if they had fallen upon hard times. Never did he forget to stress that he came from noble stock and insist upon being treated with respect. In his youth he had gone to America. There he had labored in the mines until he had amassed a good bit of money. Upon returning to his homeland fifteen years later, he bought the estate and began to enjoy life as both a farmer and a landowner.

Alongside the vegetable garden rose the rambling army barrack—a long, stone house with a number of floors of one room each, built to quarter the workers on the estate and their families. Now the barrack stood empty, except for one family that lived down at the end.

Wladislaw Jankowsky ruled his workers with an iron hand, demanding that they bear themselves respectfully toward him and address him with the honorable title of a wealthy landowner, "Ponas."

Paulauskas, however, he honored and never made such a demand of him. They had known each other from childhood. Despite the difference in their ages, they had both served as volunteers in the Lithuanian army of liberation. Paulauskas had accompanied his friend at the outset of Jankowsky's journey to America and had been a rock of support for him when his wife died. Jankowsky would say of his companion, "He's got a sharp mind and a heart of gold, that Paulauskas."

When his friend asked that he receive Shula and her mother, Jankowsky did not hesitate overlong. He needed a housekeeper. His sister, Madam Helena, was an old spinster who found the work load excessive. She still walked around with the bundle of keys, but a lack of order was evident everywhere—in the kitchen, in the rooms, in the dairy, in the yard, and in the making of sausages before Christmas.

Jankowsky had a white head of hair, but he was still tall and strapping. His sister, though, was stooped and often fell asleep in the middle of a conversation.

In her youth, Madam Helena had been a servant in the count's house. She never stopped grouching about these bleak, gray times. She saved her special wrath for the brazen younger generation, so disrespectful of God and elders. When Mrs. Weiss and Shula arrived, she received them with a scowl. A Russian woman! All Russian women despised God. They never prayed and acknowledged no religious duties; besides, a woman from the city had to be vain and lazy.

Nonetheless, Mrs. Weiss soon won her over. Madam Helena suffered intensely from rheumatism of the legs. "Sofia Mikhailovna" would care for her, rubbing her down with various ointments and creams and giving her medicines to drink. Madam Helena swore that the newcomer could revive the dead; she never stopped praising her.

"She has a wonderful knack for healing," she would tell anyone who came to the house. "She just touches a sore spot or an ache and it's all better. She's worth more than all the doctors in the world."

Shula, too, won her affection. The old lady loved to listen to the girl's fluent Lithuanian and her smooth reading and observe her facility in embroidery and knitting. According to her identification papers, Shula was now Onyté, stepdaughter of the Russian Sofia Mikhailovna,

115

who had married a Lithuanian widower and had adopted his orphan daughter. Helena was quite pleased at the good relationship between the "stepmother" and her daughter. That Onyté was able to call the Russian woman "Mother" and love her surely indicated how good a woman Sofia Mikhailovna was.

The old lady found only one fault with the Russian—her Pravo-Slavic faith. Many times Helena tried to convince Sofia Mikhailovna of the superiority of the Catholic religion but after awhile admitted defeat. She learned that the Russian was not religiously oriented; she not only knew little about the rituals of the Pravo-Slavic Church, but also scorned them.

"Russia, Russia," she would sigh, "a godless land and people!"

But as for Shula—all religious obligations passed on to her. The daughter of a Lithuanian Catholic, she had to be scrupulously observant, not eating meat on Fridays, going to church every Sunday and on holidays, and the like. Madam Helena took upon herself the spiritual training of the girl. She saw it as her duty to train Onyté, who seemed woefully untutored, to become a faithful daughter of the Catholic Church and to diminish as much as possible the harmful influence of her stepmother.

At first Shula was repulsed by her religious duties.

"Mother," she would complain when they were alone evenings, "we have to lie every minute."

"We're not lying, child, we're only protecting ourselves."

Shula soon grasped the reality of the situation. She had to lead a double life. She knelt dutifully before the cross alongside Madam Helena, reciting the prayers after her.

116

At times, however, her conscience would bother her. She would look upon herself as a fraud and would be ashamed. After awhile, however, she went through all the necessary rites outwardly and mechanically.

The custom in the household was to say a short prayer before each meal. Jankowsky, who had become somewhat of a freethinker during his stay in America, would rush through the prayer by rote and would poke fun at his pious sister. The old woman would complain, while Jankowsky held his peace, winking across the table at Mrs. Weiss, whom he somehow considered an ally in his heretical thinking.

Every Sunday Helena would rise early, put on her black silk dress, drape a black kerchief over her white hair, and tuck her gilt-edged prayer book under her arm. In front of the porch the team of horses would be waiting, washed shiny and hitched to the wagon with reins brightly polished and decorated with shiny tassels and red ribbons. Wladislaw would give his arm to his sister and help her onto the buggy. Alongside the old woman would sit Shula, attired in her holiday best, which Madam Helena had bought for her. The driver's seat would be taken by Jankowsky himself.

Mrs. Weiss would stay at home to oversee the household. Jankowsky would whistle at the horses, Madam Helena would cross herself, and Mrs. Weiss would wave good-bye as the buggy pulled away.

After prayers Jankowsky would head into the city on business, and Madam Helena and Shula would go out for a stroll. In the summer they would walk through the

Tyshkiewicz Park by the seashore, and in the winter through the city streets, to look at the store windows.

Shula loved those walks very much, for they gave her a change in her boring routine. She especially liked the summer walks by the ocean. On the other hand, she was afraid to walk in the city for fear that someone might recognize her. More than once she had vacationed on the beach at Palanga in happier days, she and her mother having registered at one of the many lodges in that resort town.

Shula loved to walk through the ancient park which, after the establishment of an independent Lithuania, had become municipal property and served the summer throngs that swamped the town. In the past there had been a sign over the garden gate: NO JEWS OR DOGS ALLOWED.

Only a few years before, a few women of the family still inhabited the Tyshkiewicz Palace. Public report held that the Tyshkiewicz daughter was not completely sane and that consequently she stayed in the palace while the men in the family were abroad.

In the park it was always pleasantly dark. The trees cast large, deep shadows. Shula loved to sit on a bench in the shade of a spreading maple and dream.

June was at its peak. Light, whitish clouds hovered in the blue skies like flocks of sheep. The aroma of jasmine and linden blossoms filled the air.

Helena, fatigued from walking, slumped down on a bench in the shade of a golden flowered linden tree surrounded by the sweet lullaby hum of bees.

118

Shula, too, sat down on the edge of the beach and followed the flight of a bee, noting how it folded its silken wings, burrowed into a flower, then buzzed and hovered over a second cup to plunge again into the blooming gold. Then off the creature would wing to a destination known only to itself.

Shula envied the flying insect—to drink one's fill of nectar and then fly happily home! A bee did not have to disguise itself as a cricket. It went about its business with no one to bother it. She, on the other hand, could not even be called by her rightful name. When anyone tried to hurt a bee, he would be stung—but then the bee would die, she recalled from her science lessons. Well, that didn't matter. Let it die! If she were a bee, she would know what to do. She would not be concerned about her life.

So Shula reflected until the snoring of her aged companion broke her reverie.

Groups of strollers began to appear in the park. From time to time, as usual, someone would gaze with curiosity at the dozing old woman and the young girl sitting by her side. Shula felt herself invaded by fear and insecurity. She tugged gently at the old woman's sleeve. "Madam Helena, come, people are staring at us."

The old woman opened her eyes. "Eh, what's the matter with you, child? It's nice to sit here and watch people walk by."

"But you went to sleep. You've been sleeping for a long time."

"Nonsense, I haven't slept at all. Just closed my eyes for a minute."

Madam Helena did not like to be found out in her

119

weakness. Swiftly she rose and they headed toward the seashore.

"Let's go to the Cave of Biruté," Shula requested. She loved to visit there. The cave was located on a not-too-high hill that was covered with fragrant pine trees looking out onto the blue sea. Vaulted with stones and always dark inside, the cave had room for only five or six people. Outside it stood a statue of Mary, made of colored clay.

At the entrance the two women bent their knees.

"Pray to the Holy Mother to find you a bridegroom worthy of you, daughter, and that she grant you long life," instructed Helena as she stooped to kiss the hem of the statue's dress.

According to tradition, Prince Kestutis, ruler of Lithuania in the fourteenth century, had met the priestess Biruté in the cave and had wed her. The local people believed that all petitions young people made in the cave would be granted.

"Let's sit here a little while," Shula asked again. It felt good to be in the dark, concealed from human eyes.

"Do you know, Madam Helena," Shula asked, in an effort to detain the old woman further, "why this spot is called Biruté's cave?"

"I don't know, child, I wasn't taught that at school." The old woman had no pretensions to learning.

"Should I tell you?"

"Yes, you've learned a lot more than I have."

Madam Helena, like all old village women, loved to tell legends and listen to them. Shula knew that the tale would win her heart and that she would not be able to refuse a walk by the seashore. Generally the old woman shunned sea breezes, for their dampness pained her legs.

They sat down on a stone in the cave and Shula spoke of the mighty Prince Kestutis who defended the country against the invasions of the cruel Crusaders. One day he went astray in the forest by the sea and arrived at a cave where *vaidilutés*—vestal virgins—guarded the holy fire that burned in honor of the chief of the gods, Perkunas. Among them was the lovely Biruté. Kestutis was stunned by her beauty. Priestesses, however, were not allowed to marry, so he seized her and carried her off to his palace. Biruté the priestess became the greatest princess in the kingdom of Lithuania and bore her husband the hero Vytautas, who demolished the Crusaders so badly that they no longer dared cross the nation's borders.

Madam Helena nodded her head, straightened out her kerchief, and sighed. "Ay, ay, daughter, you can tell a story; it's a pleasure to listen, just like the priest in church. You would have become a real scholar if you'd gone on with your studies."

The old woman pondered for a moment, then added, "Now we don't have Kestutises and Vytautases . . . always the enemies come at us, unwelcome guests. Sometimes Russians, sometimes Germans, a curse on them all!"

"But Russians don't kill people," blurted Shula.

"Yes, they don't kill. But they come and force the people onto collective farms. Who asked them to come? Everyone should stay in the country that God gave him and we'd all be better off. But no. It's always the other fellow's loaf of bread they have to grab. Ah, a curse on all of them!"

121

It was August. A blazing sun hung in the sky, beating down on the heads and necks of the reapers clad in long-sleeved coarse linen shirts and white linen pants. In a long line they advanced, cutting down the grain. Through the air whistled the scythes, spilling the ripe ears. Men's shirts stuck to their backs, but the greater part of their labors lay before them. A sea of grain swayed in the wind. The ripe ears heavy with seed bowed toward the earth.

Whizzzz went the scythes, slicing through the air. The edge of the field was still far off, the sun still high.

Behind the reapers advanced the young girls, their backs bent, binding the sheaves.

"Shake a leg, Albina, or you won't find a bridegroom this year," jibed a pug-nosed reaper to the girl behind him.

"Hush your mouth, you devil," the girl laughed, grabbing a handful of straw and flinging it in his face. "You've been chasing the girls of this village three years now and you haven't married a one of them yet."

The ridiculed youth mopped his face to the sound of the women's laughter.

As the day wore on, talk died down and fatigue increased. A little more, two more hours . . . the end of the field was in sight.

Curved backs seemed on the verge of breaking and hands seemed heavy as lead.

One hour more, half an hour more. . . .

The younger women among the reapers had already turned aside to weave wreaths of grain and cornflowers to present to the lady of the manor.

One more sweep of the arm, one more.

One more sheaf, one more stack.

Soon the ache of backs and swelling of feet would be repaid. Half an hour more, then the owners of the farm would greet the reapers and binders with liquor, cheese, and other delicacies.

The sun was declining toward the tops of the trees. The last of the grain had been bound into sheaves and placed in a stack at the end of the field. That last bundle was larger than the others; all the leftover stalks had been crammed into it. It stood facing its brother stacks like a rich, pot-bellied landowner.

For three whole days the reapers had toiled in Jankowsky's fields. The harvest had been delayed somewhat, for it had been difficult to obtain workers—many had been drafted into the army, others had been transported to Germany to work, still others had gone to the city. There was no lack of employment during the war and livelihoods were easy to come by, especially after the ransacking of Jewish stores and apartments. Enterprising Lithuanians became businessmen, opening stores in the towns and turning their backs on their villages for good.

Jankowsky had traveled through the nearby villages, going from house to house, coaxing workers to save his crop. The humidity had grown unbearable. On the afternoon of the third day gray clouds had appeared on the

123

horizon. The swallows skimmed low over the earth, all but touching it with their wings.

"It's going to rain," the farmers had said. "Maybe even tonight."

"What do we get if we finish your harvest todày and haul it into the barn?"

Jankowsky had promised a royal feast.

The women of his house worked diligently to prepare for the reapers' banquet. Mrs. Weiss's hands were full. She baked, cooked, mixed the liquor, and salted the cheese. Helena supervised the housework and Shula helped her. Much had to be done before the harvest festival: milking the cows, straining the milk, skimming off the cream, feeding the poultry and the pigs, and bringing the chicks into the coop.

Until the feast day Mrs. Weiss had worked outside. Now she was busy in the house. She intended to lay out a festive board so appetizing that Jankowsky would rub his hands with glee.

"Don't spare the expense," he had warned them. "Be generous with the workers. Let them remember that Ponas Jankowsky made them a royal holiday celebration."

The tables, gleaming with their white tablecloths, groaned under the weight of giant bowls full of ham and sausages, huge yellow cheeses, braided loaves, and above all, bottles of liquor. At the end of the porch stood a barrel of golden, foaming beer.

Mrs. Weiss was somewhat nervous. Would her performance be adequate? This was, after all, the first time she had prepared a harvest festival in a village. Would anyone realize she was Jewish?

124

Jankowsky often said that he could tell a dish cooked by a Jewess from the way it smelled. Would he not recognize hers, then, this time? She did her utmost to prepare everything according to the village tradition, just as the old woman had taught her.

"I'm a nurse, really, I never learned to cook," she said apologetically.

"Heh, heh, heh!" the old woman cackled. "So you're a nurse—well, you sure know your way around a kitchen. You can't fool me. People can't learn that much overnight."

Mrs. Weiss's heart fluttered in fear. From a distance she could hear the song of the reapers.

First came the women, their arms linked. In the center of the line was round-cheeked Albina, the swiftest of the sheaf-binders. Her sweet voice rang loud and clear.

In the meantime three of the younger boys had managed to slip away and enter the courtyard on the sly. They filled buckets with water and stood behind the main entrance.

Jankowsky and his sister stood waiting in the gateway. Pink-cheeked Albina greeted the master of the farm and extended a cornflower wreath to Madam Helena. The owners of the estate then asked the rest to enter. The men pushed the women in before them. Albina opened the door and—ha! A bucket of icy water splashed over her head! The girl leaped back spluttering and laughing. From the sides the two other boys sprang, emptying their buckets over the other women.

A pitched battle ensued. The women did not stand idly by but darted to the well, drew up the chilled water, and

125

dashed it over the men. No one came out of the conflict dry. Even the owners of the farm got wet; Shula was soaked from head to toe. The room resounded with the laughter of men and the shrieks of women.

Madam Helena hung the wreath on the eastern wall near the dining room, beneath the portrait of Mary, and invited the "combatants" to dine. Singing erupted anew and mingled with the clinking of bottles and glasses and with the joking and laughter. The sun lit up the pine branches in the grove and long shadows stretched over the table.

Jankowsky rose from his seat. "Many thanks to you for your honest toil!"

"God bless the fruit of your soil. We thank you for the lovely feast," they chimed in response.

One by one the men filed up to kiss the hands of Madam Helena.

Mrs. Weiss, too, received her share. "Many thanks to you, too, Sofia Mikhailovna, you have served us well."

"Ho, ho! You got yourself a wonderful housekeeper, Ponas Jankowsky," the women teased. "Maybe you're looking to get married?"

"Well, I'd like to, but the girls all run away from me," he joshed in reply.

"Ha, ha! You'll find one yet. You're a man in your prime," a woman shouted encouragingly.

"Well, then, maybe you'll find me a match—young, pretty, and a hardworking housewife."

"Come on and choose! Is there any shortage of young girls in the neighborhood?"

"I would take Albina, but she doesn't want me. She says I'm old."

126

"Heh, heh. You're a sly one, Ponas Jankowsky," the girl countered. "You've looked out for yourself. You sent long distance for . . . no, you don't need me."

"What are you talking about? This is news to me."

"There she is, standing alongside you. Do you need a housewife better than Sofia Mikhailovna?"

Suddenly Mrs. Weiss found herself in the center of a circle, Jankowsky by her side and everyone ready to lift glasses and toast the couple. She could see that her peaceful stay at the farm was coming to an end. Again the ghetto rose before her eyes, the threat of death loomed over her daughter and herself. Her senses reeled. She found some excuse to hurry out to the courtyard.

Somewhere a bird took flight into the motionless sky. The flapping of its wings sent a chill through her body.

The sound of revelry burst from the house, the sharp cries of the girls mingling with the men's voices, the laughter, the song and music.

How foreign it all was to her! At that very moment bullets were thudding into her people's flesh. The brothers of Ponas Jankowsky were wallowing in Jewish blood. There was no justice.

Tears filled her eyes, her whole body shook. But this was not the time for crying. She hurried to the well, tilted the bucket and drank deep, washed her face, and tried to calm down. She had to control herself. She returned to the festive company.

The young people got up to dance. One after the other couples spun by in the gay folk dance, the *suktinis*.

Among them was her daughter, Shula. *Dance, poor dear, dance*, thought Mrs. Weiss.

127

> Dance and whirl,
> Dance and whirl,
> Learn to court a pretty girl.
> Give her boxes
> Full of candy,
> Give her apples fine and dandy.

Singing lustily, a young fellow swept his partner off her feet and whirled her about.

"Hoo-ha!"

"Ho, master of the house, dance with us!"

Plump Albina flew to Jankowsky and caught him by the hands. He tried to protest. "What are you doing, girl? You want to dance with me? Pick a younger partner."

But in another minute he was twirling about with her in the center of the circle, tall and upright, bobbing his head and swinging to the rhythm, left and right.

"Hoo-ha!" The men's feet stomped on the wooden floor.

"Hoo-ha! Hey, musicians, don't go to sleep! Faster, hey, some life!"

On the steps by the entrance stood the village fiddler, working his bow with all his might. The sweat poured off him as his feet tapped to the rhythm of the melody. Behind him the harmonica player puffed away, his cheeks blown out to the bursting point.

> Hoo-ha! Hoo-ha!
> Dance and whirl,
> Dance and whirl,
> Learn to court a pretty girl.

128

After the *suktinis* came the polka and a circle dance. The music stopped at last, and one by one the sweat-drenched dancers retired to the porch steps, sitting down and gulping air.

"To the sea! Come to the sea!" cried Albina, who was always first at work or play.

"You come, too, Ponas Jankowsky, Sofia Mikhailovna!"

"You young folks go. It's time for us oldsters to lie down on the stove."

"Pooh-pooh! Old! Look at him! You could teach ten young men how to live yet, Ponas Jankowsky. Come on, come along!"

Shula raised pleading eyes toward her mother. "Come, Mother, come to the sea, I so want to go."

The poor child, at last she's having a good time, thought Mrs. Weiss, regarding her daughter's glowing cheeks and sparkling eyes. *Let her forget her troubles for a while.*

The girls embraced each other and linked arms in a long line extending across the path. After them came the others, walking slowly, among them Jankowsky and Mrs. Weiss. Gradually they progressed, all eyes on the red ball of the sun sinking behind the woods. A few last rays gleamed on the horizon. By the time they reached the shore, those too had vanished, leaving only a pale strip of red separating sky and sea. The water was wondrously calm. Tiny waves curled forward in rows to lick the sandy shore.

"Come on, let's look for amber," called Albina.

"I'll make a wedding feast for the first girl who finds one," Jankowsky joked.

Tittering, the girls skipped away to dig in the wet sand, the others behind them.

129

"My mother found it," cried Shula.

"Hurray, Sofia Mikhailovna will get married first!"

"Ponas Jankowsky, ask us to the wedding right now!"

Why did I do as the child asked, why did I come? thought Mrs. Weiss fearfully. She looked at her daughter in ill-concealed anger.

The girl was confused. As soon as she heard the jubilant cries in honor of her mother and Jankowsky she began to come to her senses. She had blundered terribly, but did not know how to make amends.

"Come, let's go back home," said Mrs. Weiss. "It's wartime; it's not good to go far from the house at night."

"What's the war got to do with us?" Albina cried scornfully. "It's the Jews' war."

Mrs. Weiss and Shula caught their breaths involuntarily. Their skin turned to gooseflesh.

"I wouldn't kill 'em," said one young man, since the conversation had turned to Jews. "But it doesn't bother me if somebody else does."

"What have the Jews done to you?" another asked. "Even a whipped dog deserves pity!"

"The Yids are enemies of Lithuania, they sold the country to the Bolsheviks."

"Ridiculous!" scoffed another. " 'The Yids sold the country!' When did they own it that they could sell it?"

"I'm sorry for them," said one of the girls. "Even their wives and little children get killed. I was in the city when they took them through. I couldn't look."

"The Germans know what they're doing. If it wasn't for them, the Bolsheviks would have taken over here."

"And now the Germans have taken over," someone added hesitantly, then fell quiet.

130

"Ah, boys and girls, what are you talking about such things for? It's better to sing something!" urged Jankowsky, displeased with the trend of the conversation.

"You sing, Ponas Jankowsky, we all know you have a beautiful voice."

Jankowsky smiled, flattered. He took the stance of a professional singer, twirled his long mustache and sang.

> Where are you now, oh mossy hut
> That once I loved so well?
> And the leafy apple tree
> In the summer dell?

All were silent, even after he finished.

"Now you sing," said Jankowsky, breaking the stillness. "Something lively."

Albina rose, glanced at him with her greenish eyes, and began.

> I'll stroll down to the garden
> And there I'll pick three flowers
> For brother and for brother-in-law
> And one for my intended.
> Rue I shall give my brother
> And mint I'll give my brother-in-law,
> And to my fickle lover
> I'll give a prickly thorn.

"Just wait awhile, you'll have your fun when some fellow comes along and pounds your bones a little," laughed the pug-nosed reaper, giving Albina a shove.

"What are you doing, you devil!" the girl answered,

pushing him in turn. "I wasn't talking about you. As if you were my boyfriend!"

"Hoo-hoo, what a stuck-up, look at her! What do you think, you're going to be a *ponia*?* Ponas Jankowsky isn't going to marry you, he's already got himself a missus," jibed the pug-nose, winking toward Mrs. Weiss.

Jankowsky, seated near Mrs. Weiss, was all too clearly delighted with this exchange. His hand lighted on her shoulder. She shuddered, shrank away, and hurried over to Shula.

"Come, daughter, let's go home, it's late."

"Wait a minute, the harvest is over. What's the hurry?" Jankowsky would not let her off. "Who can tell us a story of the sea goddess, Juraté? You're a scholar, Onyté, you must remember. You tell us."

"Yes, tell us, daughter," whispered Mrs. Weiss, deathly afraid lest the conversation again turn to her or to the Jews. She did not dare get up and go home alone for fear Jankowsky would follow her. All she longed for was to see the party over so that they could return to the farm.

Shula began, her voice shaky. Such a large audience! Up till then she had told stories only to Madam Helena. Little by little, however, she calmed down and was herself caught up in the magic of the tale and the attentiveness of the group.

Many years ago the Baltic's waves had not yet tossed up drops of amber onto the shore. In the ocean depths, in all its glory, stood the amber palace of the goddess of the sea, Juraté.

* Wife of a wealthy landowner.

132

Beautiful was the palace but ten times more so Juraté; her voice was even enchanted.

Every evening she would arise from the depths, float upon the water, rock to the rhythm of the waves, and sing her song. The birds would stop their chirping, the very stars would halt in their tracks and give ear. From the heavens Pekunas, lord of thunder and chief of the gods, looked down. With all his being he hungered for the beautiful goddess, but she paid him no heed.

Every morning the handsome fisherman Kestutis would set sail on his lovely boat. One day he lingered overlong in the blue-green expanse and night leaped suddenly upon him. No sooner had the last rays of daylight expired than he heard a song wafting over the waters. He plunged forward with all speed, and there before him lay the most exquisite maiden he had ever seen, rocking on the waves and singing.

Shocked beyond belief, the fisherman let the oars slip from his hands.

Juraté no sooner saw Kestutis than her heart was his.

Nightly the fisherman would linger on the sea in his boat, and nightly Juraté would sing him her songs and entreat him to dive after her into the depths and live with her regally in the amber palace.

For a long time Kestutis resisted the temptation but finally, overcome by the magic of her song, he plunged after her into the depths of the sea.

Perkunas saw and was filled with rage. "Lo, because you have sullied your honor," he thundered, "the honor of a daughter of the gods, in bestowing your love on a mortal, you shall suffer grievously, for great is your sin."

133

Perkunas seized one of his largest and heaviest thunder-bolts and hurled it into the amber palace.

Kestutis fell down dead, his corpse floated to the surface of the turbulent sea, and the amber palace crumbled. Ever since that day the ocean waves cast up the remnants of the palace, and the unfortunate Juraté comes nightly to the shore to gather them up and bewail her lost love.

Shula had finished her tale, but the once boisterous group sat on in silence. Only the lapping of the waves ruffled the silence.

"Come, let's go home, before we meet Juraté," Mrs. Weiss urged in an effort to set them moving.

She rose and pulled Shula after her. Slowly the others got up too, gripped by the magic of the ancient Lithuanian legend that they heard, unknowingly, from the lips of a Jewish girl.

The party broke up, everyone went his separate way. Only Shula, her mother, and Jankowsky remained together.

Shula could tell how disturbed her mother was by her quick pace and the fact that she held her hand tightly and would not let go.

At the entrance to the house Mrs. Weiss was quick to wish Jankowsky good night and turn toward her room. He stopped her, however, and grasped her free hand.

"I want to talk to you."

Mrs. Weiss sucked in her breath. For weeks the land-owner had been trying to get close to her.

Despite all the grief she had undergone in the ghetto and during her travels, she was still an attractive woman. She was well educated, and her pleasant manner and charm were well known among the local farmers. Jankowsky,

134

who had seen the world in his youth, knew how to judge women.

Still pressing Shula's hand, Mrs. Weiss replied in a quavering voice, "Yes, good sir, I am at your service."

"I would like to speak to you alone."

Her knees shook.

"Can't we put the conversation off? It's late and I'm very tired."

"Very well," he said, disgruntled. "Good night."

For a long time she was unable to sleep. Her sixth sense told her that a dangerous storm was brewing. Shula, too, lay awake, her eyes open in the dark, her ears attentive to her mother's sighs. *Poor mother*, thought the girl, and a wave of pity swept over her.

Doctor Klimas

Weeks passed in peace and quiet.

The scent of ripened fruit floated on the breeze. Before the cherries were all picked, the apples and plums were ready to be gathered in. Shula feasted her eyes on the splendor of the garden and ate to her heart's content. She spent all her free time in the garden. Despite the general desolation, that year's crop was plentiful. The branches all but broke under the weight of the fruit.

Shula loved to sit by herself amid the greenery and listen to the song of the birds. She lay in wait for them among the bushes and followed them to their nests. She especially loved to watch the woodpecker at work. Leaning with his tail against a tree trunk, he would hammer away furiously at the bark, the echo of his attack bouncing from one end of the arbor to the other. At times even a cuckoo would visit.

One day Shula was surprised by the sound of human voices from among the trees. Out of habit she stopped and strained to listen. How great was her surprise to detect her mother in the company of Jankowsky, both of them deep in conversation and unaware of her presence. Unconsciously, the girl stepped to the side. Something compelled her to listen.

"Yes, Sofia Mikhailovna," she heard Jankowsky say. "You are running away from me, avoiding me every time I try to talk to you."

"That's not quite true, Ponas Jankowsky, it's just that I'm so busy and tired. I've so much work to do."

To Shula her mother's voice sounded unsteady.

"No, no, you are running away. Just now I called you and you didn't stop."

"I was looking for my daughter," Mrs. Weiss objected.

"Nonsense, your daughter's not going to get lost. We're not children, Sofia Mikhailovna. We know how matters stand."

Jankowsky seized Mrs. Weiss's wrist. "Sofia Mikhailovna, why do you act the stranger? We've both passed our eighteenth birthdays, you have white hairs on your head, too."

"Ponas Jankowsky, I respect you very much. In your home I have found food and rest, but. . . ."

"But?"

Mrs. Weiss looked all about as though seeking help. Shula, seeing her mother's eyes, the eyes of a trapped bird, emerged from hiding.

"Here's my daughter!" she cried jubilantly. "Where have you been all this time?"

Jankowsky scowled, muttered something, and left.

Mrs. Weiss continued in her work. She gathered tomatoes in the garden, picked fruit, fed the chickens, milked the cows, and engaged in every kind of household and farmyard task. She would spend long hours making butter, churning the cream in the wooden tub between her knees. The butterfat would become dense, the thick fat would separate from the liquid and congeal. Then Sofia would transfer the butter to the cellar in a huge, wooden ladle.

It seemed that Jankowsky had decided to let her alone, for he no longer tried to come near her. Once again he was master of the house and she merely a foreigner in his employ.

At times Mrs. Weiss began to think that the clouds darkening her skies were beginning to scatter.

Shula was healthy and happy. The physical work and life in the heart of nature exerted a wholesome influence on her. Her cough had vanished long since and her cheeks displayed a healthy glow. *It is good for my child here,* thought Mrs. Weiss. *I only pray it lasts.*

Summer passed and fall followed. Rain beat upon the windows, the wind wailed below the rickety roof, and the sea's roar grew stronger. Mrs. Weiss and Shula would come into the house from the courtyard wet and shivering. Their shoes ripped and their clothing began to wear out. Shula caught a cold and took to her bed.

Madam Helena peeked into Mrs. Weiss's room and found her seated on Shula's bed, her hand on the child's forehead.

"Oh, you city folks," she chided. "The rain just wets you a little and already you're in bed. A young girl like that, sick already."

Seeing the concern on the mother's face she smiled and added, "It's nothing, don't worry, Sofia. I'll brew some tea from dried linden leaves and she'll feel better. And you, you get on your knees to the Holy Mother and pray. Prayer comes before any medicine. Ah, but you Russian women, you don't have God in your hearts!"

The old woman gave the patient the yellowish brew to drink, put a hot-water bottle at her feet, covered her with a few blankets she brought in from her room, made the sign of the cross over her chest, and went out. But Shula felt no better. That night she fell speechless, seized with a raging fever. Mrs. Weiss was beside herself with fear.

"God in Heaven," she whispered. "Will You put me through this trial too, and take away my girl, my only hope?"

Shula tossed about in bed, mumbling uncontrollably. Her heart pounding, the mother listened to her words and shuddered.

"No, please," the sick girl moaned. "I'm Onyté, not Shula. Don't kill me! Don't shoot me, Jesus!" she cried attempting to leap from the bed.

138

Mrs. Weiss, who did not stir from the sick child's side that entire evening and night, swayed from exhaustion and despair. What would become of them were anyone to hear the girl talk? Their secret would be out and they would be destroyed.

What were they to do? God in Heaven! She wrung her hands. For a moment she wanted to pray, throw herself on God's mercies. The next moment she mocked herself; she could hardly qualify as a believer. She had never been religious, and was even less so now. How could God look upon the slaughter of entire communities, the butchering of women and children, without bringing heaven and earth down together? No, there was no God, nor was there any mercy or justice in the world. No God, none! She beat her fists upon her forehead in her anguish. There was nothing, nothing. . . .

So the night passed in mental and physical agony.

Before morning Shula fell silent and seemed to sink off to sleep. Mrs. Weiss, too, dozed off in the chair by the head of the bed. The creak of the door awakened her. Jankowsky entered the room. He approached the bed and looked at the sick girl's face.

"We'll have to call a doctor, Sofia, right away."

The woman lifted red, sleepless eyes to him. "Ponas Jankowsky, I haven't got a penny."

"I'll pay. We'll do everything we have to, to get the child on her feet again."

"How can I ever thank you for your kindheartedness?"

"It's nothing; we're Christians and we got to help anyone in trouble. I'd help any human being—except a Jew."

"Why not?" she whispered.

"I don't like Jews. Jews are Bolsheviks. They sold Lithuania. We don't need any *kolkhozes*.* I wouldn't turn them in, but I wouldn't lift a finger to save them."

Mrs. Weiss felt a chill grip her heart.

"Who will call the doctor?" she asked.

"I'll go to the city and fetch him."

When he left, Mrs. Weiss tried to calm down, but in vain. She had been thrown into too much of a turmoil.

What did we do to them? she asked herself. *Why do they hate us so? What power do we have that they should accuse us of being able to influence nations? And this Jankowsky—he's no boor, yet he repeats this nonsense like any ignorant peasant.*

Once again the patient began to mumble and groan. Mrs. Weiss did not take her eyes off Shula. Suddenly an unbearable thought flashed through her mind. What if the girl were to start ranting in her fever while the Lithuanian doctor was present and disclose their identity? This scheme would end in their ruin, not their rescue.

Had she best run after Jankowsky and tell him the girl was improving and there was no need for a doctor? But what if the child were to die, God forbid, without medical aid?

In a frenzy she snatched up her shawl and dashed into the courtyard in search of the landowner. In the gateway she encountered old Helena.

"Where is Ponas Jankowsky, Madam Helena?"

The old woman eyed her suspiciously and grumbled, "What impatience! Is the world coming to an end? What's the panic all about? As if someone were dying!"

* Russian collective farms.

140

"Madam Helena, is Ponas Jankowsky still here?"

"He left, he already left! A half-hour ago. Holy Mary, these city women are spoiled!"

Mrs. Weiss returned to the room. She tried to put it in order, to wash, comb her hair—no need for the doctor to spot her by her fear. But her fingers betrayed her. Only with the greatest difficulty did she manage to button her blouse.

A wagon stopped by the farm gate. Mrs. Weiss stared through the window openmouthed. Following Jankowsky was the aged Dr. Klimas. She knew him from the old days when she would spend hot August vacations in Palanga. More than once she and her husband had visited his home and he had been their guest, too, in the apartment on Mapu Street. What could she do? Dr. Klimas would surely recognize her. She could not be found in the room. Let him examine her daughter in her absence! She would slip out through the kitchen by the rear door.

"Sofia Mikhailovna, I've brought the doctor," she heard Jankowsky say behind her.

In consternation, Mrs. Weiss halted, her jaws locked in fright.

"This is the patient's mother, doctor," Jankowsky continued. "It's nothing, your daughter's going to get well, Sofia Mikhailovna, don't worry. If Dr. Klimas has been kind enough to agree to take care of her, everything will be all right." He patted her shoulder protectively.

The old doctor looked into her face briefly. "It seems to me that we have met, but I can't remember where."

Mrs. Weiss smiled weakly. "Oh, you must be mistaken, doctor. I've never been in this area. My name is Sofia Mikhailovna Dudainé."

141

The aged physician squeezed her hand, smiled, and replied, "Ah, then I must have been mistaken. Old eyes can play tricks on you. Let's have a look at the patient."

Dr. Klimas examined the girl thoroughly and diagnosed inflammation of the lungs. He prescribed medication and instructed the mother in caring for the child.

"Don't fear," he assured her. "The child will get better. I'd like to see her again in a few days. Good-bye, Mrs. Dudainé."

The doctor turned to go. Mrs. Weiss drew a long breath.

She accompanied him to the hall and helped him on with his coat as Jankowsky went outside to pull up the wagon, which had been parked in the shed.

She and the doctor were alone. Abruptly the old man turned and seized her hand. "Mrs. Weiss, if you ever need help, I am at your service."

Tears sprang to her eyes. "Thank you, Dr. Klimas, I did not dare to hope!"

"Courage, daughter, courage!"

The rattle of the carriage drew near.

"Good-bye, Mrs. Dudainé," said Dr. Klimas loudly.

Mrs. Weiss's eyes followed the wagon as it bore the upright figure of the elderly doctor away, and tears streamed down her face. How good, how easy it now was to cry.

Days of Confusion

Weeks passed. Shula, pale and weak, recuperated very gradually. During that period it became clear to Mrs. Weiss that she could not remain on the farm. Jankowsky's attitude had become that of a man who had saved her daughter's life and felt that the mother owed him a limitless debt of gratitude.

He became increasingly brazen. He would lie in wait for her evenings, as she returned to her room, or surprise her in the barn at milking time. Mrs. Weiss realized that there would be no escaping a frank talk that would leave her daughter and herself naked to the elements and the dangers of a hostile populace. She did all in her power to put off that decisive moment.

Madam Helena sensed that something was developing between her brother and the housekeeper. She was deathly afraid of Jankowsky's getting married, for his new wife would very likely deprive her of control of the house.

Mrs. Weiss was well aware of Helena's coldness.

The old woman began to throw barbs in her direction. One day she was looking for her ring of keys, which she often would misplace. Mrs. Weiss found them and returned them. The old woman grew sulky and said, scarcely under her breath, "So that's how it is. You take people in, you look around for a minute, and before you know it they're taking over while you're still alive."

143

Once on her way back from the barn, carrying a pail of milk, Mrs. Weiss heard shouts emerging from Jankowsky's room—the baritone voice of the landowner and the shrill tone of his sister.

"It's none of your business!" Jankowsky cried. "Am I master of this house or not? I can bring anyone I please into my family."

"You're of noble ancestry," his sister retorted, aiming at his weakness. "Do you know who she is or what she is? She's a Russian, an anti-Christ, she never prays."

An idea sprang to Mrs. Weiss's mind. Unwittingly, the old woman could serve her as an accomplice and protect her from Jankowsky's advances.

She would speak with Helena as soon as possible.

When Jankowsky next went into the city on business, Mrs. Weiss entered the old spinster's room. Helena was sitting in her armchair knitting.

"What is it?" she snapped, eyeing the intruder angrily.

"Something very serious. A matter of life and death. For my daughter and myself."

The old woman's face reddened. "Quiet, you hussy! Don't try to butter me up. I won't listen to you. As long as I live you won't be mistress of this household! Do you hear?"

She choked in her rage. A fit of coughing cut short her stream of abuse.

Mrs. Weiss patiently stood her ground, waiting for the old woman to calm down. Then she continued.

"You are mistaken, Madam Helena. I have no intention of marrying Ponas Jankowsky. Nor has he spoken to me of it."

144

"Not spoken to you yet? Not yet?" she asked incredulously. "That's because I'm opposed. And you come to wheedle me! No, no, my sweet. It shall never be, not as long as I live!"

"Madam Helena, it was I who prevented Ponas Jankowsky from bringing up the subject all this time. I intend to marry no man, not even your brother."

"Why not? The match doesn't suit you? It's beneath your dignity?"

"I want to return to my homeland and my family after the war."

"And what will you do there?"

"I'll work in a hospital."

"Nonsense! You'll prefer to marry and be the mistress of an estate."

"Madam Helena, I want to live in the city. Country life does not appeal to me. My husband was a doctor and I love that profession. Besides, after his death I vowed I would never remarry."

"Swear to me that you will not marry Wladislaw."

"I swear."

"By your daughter's life."

"By my daughter's life."

That seemed to placate the old woman. "Have you told this to my brother?"

"He hasn't proposed."

"No doubt he will—soon," she said uncertainly.

Another week went by. Jankowsky was away from the farm in Kovno on business.

Mrs. Weiss was able to relax a bit. Outside winter lay

145

in all its splendor, clothing the fields in sparkling white coverlets. There was less work to be done in the courtyard, and Shula had regained her full vigor. The child had begun to take walks outside. Even in the wintry weather she loved the garden, with its near-naked trees covered with snow.

Madam Helena was content. Her attitude toward the housekeeper underwent a marked change for the better.

Mrs. Weiss was cut off from the world. She had not been to the city for the longest time. Guests did not come to the estate; they had no radio nor did newspapers reach them. A short while before rumors had spread that fierce fighting was under way in southern Russia. The Germans, however, boasted of their victories, of the great number of Russian planes they had shot down and the masses of prisoners they had taken.

News of the Jews remaining in the ghettos was vague. Helena came back from church one day to report that the Jews of the ghetto in the town of Shauli had been transported to parts unknown.

Mrs. Weiss had no illusions. She knew where the Jews were being taken. Farmers told of trenches and deep pits dug a few miles out from the city and of troops blocking the approaches to the area.

Jankowsky came back from Kovno in a furor. All that night he did not speak a word. Only on the following day did he poke his head into the barn where Mrs. Weiss was milking the cows. "I've got news for you, Sofia Mikhailovna."

Her heart pounded fiercely.

"Not now, after dinner," he added.

146

That evening he looked intently at Mrs. Weiss and said, "Paulauskas is done for; they've arrested him."

Mrs. Weiss turned white.

"Someone informed on him. They searched his house and found a Jew in the cellar. Too bad, he was a good fellow. All for a rotten Jew. . . ."

Mrs. Weiss feared that her distress would be too evident. She mustered courage and asked, "What else has been happening in the world? And in the city?"

"They say the Bolsheviks have given the Germans another real shellacking. Kovno has become one big barracks. One army goes, another comes. Many have fled the city—it's almost impossible to live there."

Mrs. Weiss wanted to inquire about the ghetto but was afraid to show the slightest interest.

"Do you recall," Jankowsky asked, turning to his sister, "the janitor Antanas, the fellow whose wife used to take in washing for the Jews? They say he worked at Citadel Nine.* They brought home stacks of Jews' clothes. Now his wife wears a fox fur, looks just like a lady. You wouldn't recognize her."

Mrs. Weiss felt dizzy; in another moment she would faint. With all her remaining strength she rose from the table.

"I'm going to lie down, my head hurts."

Jankowsky, too, rose. "Wait, I want to talk to you."

She lifted her head and met the gaze of Madam Helena. "Is it all that urgent, Ponas Jankowsky? Can't it wait?"

"No, it cannot," he said impatiently. "I won't take up

* A site where thousands of Jews from Kovno were executed.

147

much of your time. Would you please come to my room?"

She entered his chamber in alarm. Jankowsky closed the door behind her.

"Sofia Mikhailovna," he began without delay. "I don't think what I have to say will come as any surprise to you. We are not youngsters anymore. We have both been married. Is there any need to mince words? I need a wife to look after my house. I'm a man in my prime and you seem right for me."

A huge lump rose in Mrs. Weiss's throat. "Ponas Jankowsky—you're a Catholic and I am Pravo-Slavic."

The landowner was shocked almost speechless. "Ridiculous! You already married a Catholic! We'll go to the priest and he'll arrange everything."

Suddenly he stared her full in the face and pressed his lips together. Mrs. Weiss saw his thoughts race swiftly ahead and fear seized her.

"And maybe you aren't Russian at all? Maybe you are Jewish. Paulauskas sent you to me, and they found a Jew hiding in his home. . . ."

Jankowsky did not take his eyes off her. By a mighty act of will Mrs. Weiss retained her composure. "Ha, ha, ha," she burst out laughing. "You are very egotistical, Ponas Jankowsky. One minute you tell me you are not young anymore, the next you think any Christian woman should consider herself blessed when you propose marriage."

Jankowsky was stunned. How was one to respond to such words, to such laughter?

"I don't want to stay in a village," she continued. "I don't like the life here, looking after pigs and cows. I'm not accustomed to that sort of thing. I'm a professional woman and want to work in a hospital."

148

"That's grotesque," he objected. "Any woman would choose marriage and the life of a mistress of an estate over slaving as a nurse! You're a Jew!"

"If I were a Jew, I would accept your proposal with joy, Ponas Jankowsky," she replied, lifting her chin. "Nothing is better for a Jewess nowadays than to marry a Christian, especially one of the nobility."

Jankowsky could not find an answer. Was she sincere or was she mocking his ancestry? His pricked vanity stirred his anger. He, a landowner, could have treated her like any common serving wench, but he had respected her honor and had proposed marriage. He had been confident that she would be overjoyed, that she would fly to his arms laughing—yet she had dared to refuse! He wanted to humiliate the woman, overcome her somehow, but he was completely at a loss. He stalked out of the room in exasperation.

Mrs. Weiss went back to her own room and collapsed on the bed.

What would come next? If Jankowsky began to investigate he would promptly learn that there never had been any Dr. Duda. She had to leave immediately. But where could she go?

She thought longingly of Paulauskas's cellar. Now her poor friend was languishing in prison, the captive of the hangmen. What would be his fate? And what would become of good Maré?

Shula was deep in youthful sleep, but Mrs. Weiss tossed about, unable to find rest. Finally she reached a decision. The next morning she would say that she was sick and had to visit the doctor. Dr. Klimas had offered to help.

Indeed, Dr. Klimas did not disappoint her.

149

Two days later Sofia Mikhailovna and Onyté parted
from the Jankowskys, pretending to return to Kovno. At
the first stop the train made, they got off and were met by
a farmer and wagon; Dr. Klimas had arranged for them to
stay in a village for the time being in the home of one of
his friends. Mrs. Weiss was to take care of the farmer's
sick wife and his two-week-old baby, and in the mean-
while Dr. Klimas would seek out a new refuge for them.

In the City Once More

At the beginning of February Mrs. Weiss and Shula
arrived by train in Vilna. "Sofia Mikhailovna" was dressed
in the uniform of a Red Cross nurse and Shula's face was
bandaged. Despite the congestion in the car, sympathetic
travelers made room for them.

On the trip Mrs. Weiss told the curious that the girl had
been struck by fragments of a grenade, one that had gone
off in the midst of a group of village children who had
thought it a plaything. Now she was taking the girl to the
hospital. Dr. Klimas had given her a letter of recom-
mendation to his friend, a physician in the municipal
hospital. Mrs. Weiss was hired as a nurse and would work
primarily at night.

150

She could scarcely contain her joy, but of course to have shown delight openly over night work would have easily roused suspicions. For payment she received a tiny room off the hospital courtyard, food for herself and for Shula, and some change for small expenditures.

Working conditions were hard. The hospital was jam-packed, bandages were in short supply, medicine and other vital supplies were lacking. There was a similar shortage of employees, especially professional people. Still, Mrs. Weiss was fortunate. At least she had the security of a job. More than once she asked herself why her luck had taken a turn for the better. Why was she more deserving than thousands of other Jews?

She was all too willing to work at nights for fear of investigations and night detentions. She was afraid to leave Shula alone in the room, so she found her daughter daytime work in the hospital kitchen washing dishes. At night the girl would sleep near her, in the room adjacent to that of the nurse on night duty.

When work was slow she would sometimes go out with Shula to the street, approach the ghetto walls, and look in. Weeping inwardly, she would hastily walk away. It was dangerous to be rambling about in the vicinity of the ghetto—someone might recognize her, call her by name. Still, she could not keep away.

The ghetto was in its death throes. Nurses and patients spoke a good deal of the atrocities at Paneriai, a lovely valley in the vicinity of Vilna that had become drenched with blood. They told of trains packed with Jews, headed no one knew where. The boxcars were sealed, and from inside burst cries of agony.

151

From time to time one of the women working at the hospital would breeze in wearing new clothes or sporting a new gold pin, bracelet, or watch. She would boast of having "inherited" the find from the Jews. Mrs. Weiss had to join in the conversation and ask how much the article was worth. She had to look amused, congratulate her "friend" on the new acquisition, blend in with the crowd. She dared not show anger.

Only at night when the long corridor of the hospital emptied, when the day shift went home and the lights in the patients' rooms were turned out, did Mrs. Weiss breathe freely. Then she could allow herself to rest and even cry. By that time Shula would already be asleep. Mrs. Weiss could unmask herself of indifference and alienation, be a Jew, and weep as much as she liked.

Every evening on her way to work she would pass the office of Dr. Kwiatkowski, the head of her ward for patients with communicable diseases. He would greet her with a quick hello and a nod of the head. Since she had begun work he had not conversed with her. Mrs. Weiss was not even sure if he knew her secret. Had Dr. Klimas told him? At their first meeting she had introduced herself as Sofia Mikhailovna and Dr. Kwiatkowski questioned her only on her professional qualifications.

Who was the man? she often wondered. Was he for the Jews or for their enemies?

She liked one woman in her ward, Sister Teresa, who took floor duty sometimes during the day, sometimes at night. Whenever she found Mrs. Weiss free at night the two would go to the sister's room and chat. The nun loved to talk. Slim and taller than average, she had narrow shoulders and delicate hands. Her face was pale and sensitive, her blue-gray eyes alert and merry. She was a lovely, captivating woman who poured her words out gaily and freely, which seemed so incongruous with her black and somber nun's habit.

Often Mrs. Weiss wondered what on earth had drawn such a lovely woman into a cloister. Sister Teresa never spoke of it and Mrs. Weiss, of course, did not dare bring it up.

Shula, too, was befriended by the sister, who at times would take her for a walk or to the movies or bring her a book.

Sister Teresa was Polish. Most of the foreign professional employees of the hospital had been replaced by Lithuanians, for the government had gone to pains to convert Vilna into a Lithuanian city after it was taken from the Russians in 1939. Government offices were transferred from Kovno and a large number of Lithuanian clerks, doctors, and nurses were brought in to replace the Poles, who had been fired. Only a few of the former employees remained—among them were the head of the department, Dr. Kwiatkowski, and Sister Teresa.

Mrs. Weiss had sensed instantly that the institution's employees were split into two warring camps. The head of the Lithuanian faction was Nurse Victoria, known as Vikte. She was a short, broad-beamed woman with stocky legs. Her flaxen-colored hair was always protruding from beneath her nurse's headdress. She would tramp through the hallway with much stir and bustle, somehow filling up all available space with her presence.

Vikte loved to deck herself out, put on something new

153

every day, wear glittering ornaments around her neck or wrist. She would always boast of her acquisitions, plundered from Jews, and Mrs. Weiss would go on smiling, holding her peace. Vikte never passed up an opportunity to vaunt her superiority over the newcomer. "The Russians thought they had the world under their thumb already, till Hitler came and put 'em in their place. The Russians will be *kaput*, just like the Jews!"

Mrs. Weiss tried to stay away from the woman as much as possible. She never responded to her insults and avoided getting into conversations with her.

Vikte, aware of the new nurse's attitude, sought her out constantly.

Anatoli

One day as Mrs. Weiss was on her way to work, she was called into the office of the ward director. She found Dr. Kwiatkowski seated at his desk, where he had been working overtime for quite a few days. Many deaths had occurred in the ward.

"Nurse Sofia," he said softly, "in room 14 we have a new patient. Please tend to him. During the day Sister Teresa will look after him, and at night, you will. See that

154

no one goes in who should not. The patient rambles at times in his fever. I think you understand me. In times like these we must be more than mere doctors and nurses."

He squeezed her hand and hurried out of the room before she had a chance to respond.

Mrs. Weiss was astonished. Room 14 was for dying patients. It was at the end of the corridor by the steps leading out of the hospital and had only two beds. Of late it had always been full. Mrs. Weiss knew that patients in room 14 were not given much attention.

She entered the room with anxiety. One bed was empty and in the second lay a man with closed eyes; patches of fever lit up his sunken cheeks. She looked at the patient's chart and read, "Anatoli Hakim—Karaite, twenty-one years old." It looked as if the sick man was sleeping, but Mrs. Weiss was startled when his face suddenly contorted in pain and a groan escaped his lips. A chill swept over her. Had he whispered in Yiddish?

She stood rooted to the spot, her eyes riveted on the patient. She waited for a fresh indication, another sound. But the man did not stir; he had sunk into sleep. As she was about to leave he moved again and once more came a soft groan. "Mama, Mama. . . ."

Her stomach turned over. The patient was—a Jew! How closely she would have to guard that secret! Like a flash came the next thought. If she tended him and he was found out, she would be lost. She pushed the thought away at once, and went back to work.

The next morning she tossed in bed, fear-ridden. What if Sister Teresa should reveal his identity? Could she be trusted? And what would happen if one of the Lithuanian

155

employees were to walk into the room and overhear him mumbling?

For long hours these thoughts tormented her. Finally exhaustion overtook her and she slept.

Most of the time the patient lay unconscious. His fever was very high. Sometimes he would leap from bed shouting and crying, as though ready to flee. Usually, though, he muttered disjointed syllables.

So passed six days and nights, during which time Sofia did her best to avoid the company of her co-workers. She feared their questions. At the end of her shift she would hurry to her room. Only to Shula did she speak of the patient in room 14. Shula was told of his condition by Sister Teresa, too, and became very concerned over the fate of the poor "Karaite."

On the seventh night when Mrs. Weiss entered the sister's room to receive instructions for the night, she did not find her. She headed for room 14.

The sick man lay in bed, his head raised slightly, drinking from Sister Teresa's hand. "The crisis is over," smiled the nun, coming to greet Mrs. Weiss. "He'll live. Let's hope that in a week he'll be able to get out of bed." Her eyes were radiant.

After a few moments she added, "I didn't let anyone into the room; I took care of him by myself."

Sister Teresa squeezed Mrs. Weiss's hand and went out into the hall, tall and slender, robed in black, and light of foot. Mrs. Weiss stood unmoving, her eyes fixed on the door behind which the nun had disappeared.

No doubts remained now—the sister knew her secret. It was as if a stone had rolled off her heart.

The walls of the hospital became familiar and beloved;

156

night work was no longer a burden for Mrs. Weiss, but somewhat pleasant once again. Lightfooted, she hurried from bed to bed, extending help and comfort. When she completed her rounds she would return to room 14.

The patient lay still, his eyes open. His cheeks were still pinched and his face was waxen. His black eyes were sunken deep in their sockets, but now they showed the spark of life.

She changed his bedding and rubbed his thin body down with alcohol. He would follow her every move with his eyes—it made her nervous.

"I hope you're feeling better," she would say. "Soon you'll be all well."

The patient would not answer. He would move his lips but no sound would come forth. Returning an hour or so later she would find him deep in slumber.

After a few days the sick man was able to sit up in bed. Mrs. Weiss sensed, however, that he was not sleeping nights. It seemed to her that he was shutting his eyes as soon as she came in. He feared her. She decided she had to explain to him that she was his friend.

She never discussed the man with Sister Teresa. As though by mutual consent their conversations never touched on him. One night she came into Hakim's room and found him sitting up. This time he did not pretend to sleep.

"Nurse," he asked as she came in. "Was I unconscious for a long time?"

"About a week."

"I see. . . . Who took care of me?"

"Sister Teresa and myself."

He fell silent for a moment, apparently struggling

157

toward a decision. Without warning he leaned forward and seized her hand. "Nurse, who is Sister Teresa? A good person?"

Mrs. Weiss saw the abyss of terror in the sick man's eyes and a wave of pity swept over her. Such a young man! She wanted to comfort him.

Gently she extricated her hand from his bony fingers and laid him back on the pillow. "Have no fear, Mr. Hakim, you can trust Sister Teresa."

The sick man, however, was not satisfied. Mrs. Weiss saw his fingers tremble on the bedcover. His breathing was shallow.

"Nurse, did I call out? Did I say anything in my fever?" he blurted out with an effort.

"No, nothing at all."

For an instant it seemed as though he sighed in relief. But again he seized her hand and locked glances with her. "Tell me the truth! Nurse, a man's life is in your hands!"

He's out of his mind, thought Mrs. Weiss. *Acting this way could be his ruination.*

"Look here, young man," she said firmly, "what are you bothering me for? You're healthy already, and soon you'll be leaving here for home. Do you have parents in the city? Relatives? Maybe you'd like me to have someone come for you?"

"I have no parents."

"Should I get in touch with one of your relatives?"

"Nurse," he said his voice trembling, "I'm a Karaite. My parents died long ago. I have no relatives. My uncle brought me up and he's been killed, too."

"Where will you go?"

"I don't know yet."

Why am I torturing the boy with all these questions?
Mrs. Weiss reproved herself. "Can I help you in any way?"

"Nurse, if you want to help me, ask the doctor to let me stay here in the hospital, until—until I can stand on my feet."

The next day Mrs. Weiss found a second patient in room 14. Her conversations with Anatoli came to a halt.

Days passed. Anatoli got up, although he could move his legs only with difficulty. He had to hold on to the edge of the bed for support. One morning, after work, Mrs. Weiss decided to go to the dining room and eat a light meal. There she found Sister Teresa, Vikte, and a number of employees.

"What I don't see is, why is Dr. Kwiatkowski playing games with the patient in room 14?" one of them remarked. "He's better already, so he can leave."

"Because he's not a Lithuanian. I don't get it; how come our government left a Polish doctor in charge of a hospital ward?" shrilled Vikte.

"And how does the Polish doctor annoy you?" Teresa asked calmly. "Isn't a Pole a Christian, too?"

"Sure, but only Lithuanians should serve in high posts in Vilna now. Vilna is the capital of Lithuania, for your information. Anyway, who is this Hakim? Hm-m-m . . . Hakim. . . . What kind of a family name is that? Is he Polish, too?" Vikte glared contemptuously at Sister Teresa.

"No, he's a Karaite," the nun answered softly.

"Karaite! What's a Karaite? I never heard of such a people. Maybe he's a Jew? That Russian woman isn't taking care of him for nothing." Vikte glowered in Mrs. Weiss's direction.

"The patient Hakim is no Jew," Teresa went on placidly. "The Karaites are descendants of the Tartars. Vytold the Great brought them to Vilna and settled them in the Trakai.* So I was told by a Karaite elder. They have their own religion, too. But here you are, proud of being a Christian and a Catholic and you want to throw a man out of the hospital when his legs can hardly support him."

"Stuff and nonsense," Vikte insisted. "It's no coincidence that you two are taking care of him."

Feeling herself turn pale, Mrs. Weiss hurriedly slipped out of the room.

"Nurse Sofia, Dr. Kwiatkowski wants to see you."

Mrs. Weiss entered the ward director's office. He rose and closed the door firmly behind her.

"Sit down, nurse," he said, motioning her toward a chair.

"Thank you, doctor. Has anything happened?"

"Nothing, but something might. Uh—yes, I wanted to discuss a delicate subject with you."

"Yes, doctor."

"Concerning the patient Anatoli Hakim. He cannot stay in the hospital any longer. But he has no place to go. I trust that you follow me."

"Yes, doctor."

"I would like to keep him in your room for a few days. I hope that will not disturb you too much."

Mrs. Weiss said nothing. The proposal came as a surprise and frightened her.

"I understand, Nurse Sofia, that this would be an impo-

* An old lakeside fortress in the region of Vilna and the ancient capital of the princes of Lithuania.

160

sition. But we must save a man's life. Your daughter will have to take care of him. We'll say that Onyté does not feel well and has received sick leave."

"Doctor——" said Mrs. Weiss but broke the sentence off. *What will Vikte say?* she thought.

That evening Anatoli was transferred from room 14. In the dining room Sister Teresa said that Sofia's room was being taken from her for the time being as it was needed for patients. A heart complication had been discovered in Anatoli Hakim following his recovery from typhus, and he had to remain under medical supervision. Vikte muttered something under her breath and there the matter ended.

Indeed, the new arrangement did prove a great imposition upon Mrs. Weiss. She no longer had a corner to rest in. After a hard night's work she would wander about the nurses' rooms in the morning to snatch some sleep and then return to her own quarters. At night Shula slept in the nurses' room and in the daytime looked after Anatoli.

Anatoli and Shula became friends. He told her stories and played checkers with her. Mrs. Weiss observed with joy how the color began to creep back into his pale cheeks. At times the three of them would eat together and spend the afternoon in each other's company. Mrs. Weiss never asked him about his family or what he did, nor did he ever discuss the matter with Shula. Officially, he was an auto mechanic by trade.

One night Mrs. Weiss decided to stay in her room and sleep. She was exhausted. The next day was her day off and that night she did not have to go on duty.

Swiftly she crossed the hospital courtyard. A snowstorm

161

was raging, not a star shone in the sky. In an instant her head and shoulders were covered with snow.

Upon entering her room she found Hakim dressed in a brown sheepskin coat, hat in hand. He looked exactly like a local peasant. "Mother," Shula leaped up as she came in. "Tell him——Anatoli wants to go! On a night like this. Don't let him, he's too weak."

"What's happened?" asked Mrs. Weiss.

He hesitated for a moment. Then he went over to her, grasped her hands, and said, "Nurse Sofia, you know who I am. So does Onyté. My name is Anatoli Rubinstein. Back home they used to call me Tulik. Nurse Sofia, thank you for everything from the bottom of my heart. But I've taken advantage of your good-heartedness and endangered you and your daughter long enough."

"But—if you leave, where will you go at night? And in such cold?"

"Where I came from—the forest."

"What brought you here?"

"My sister. I had a sister in the ghetto, seventeen years old. I came to save her." He paused. "I was too late," he continued in a choked voice. "She went with the transports."

"Dr. Kwiatkowski knows that you're Jewish?"

"Oh, yes, he knew me when I was a child. Anyway, then I caught typhus. When I felt I was on the verge of collapse I managed to stagger into his office. I don't know what happened to me there. When I woke up I was in the hospital."

"Why do you want to go back tonight? The snowstorm is raging outside."

"I know. Nights like these are a blessing for a man like

me," he replied with a sad smile. He embraced Shula, who blushed deeply, and kissed her on the cheek.

"If you find that you have no place here, try to get to the forest. A nurse would find a warm welcome among the partisans."

Again he squeezed their hands and grasped the door-knob.

But the door was flung open noisily. Into the room burst Vikte accompanied by a man dressed in the gray uniform of the Shauliai.

Shula emitted a cry of terror. Before them stood Jonas, son of the janitor from their old apartment in Mapu Street!

For a long time Vikte had suspected that Nurse Sofia was a Jew, and her suspicions only increased when Anatoli was moved into her room. Consequently she decided to keep a close watch over mother and daughter. Once she told her acquaintance Jonas, then on duty in Vilna, that the girl was well acquainted with Kovno even though her papers said she was from a town far from that city. Vikte had drawn Shula into conversation, had described to her the attractions of Kovno, Vikte's native city, and had invited her to come visit with her sometimes. The girl naïvely remarked that she knew the city.

"Oh, are you from Kovno?" Vikte had gone on to ask, and had noted Shula's confused response.

"I smell out Jews right off," laughed Jonas.

Vikte had smuggled him into the hospital kitchen. Shula was standing by the sink washing dishes. The guards-man, unseen by the girl, observed her. At first he did not recognize her, for she had grown taller and thinner, and her round face had lengthened. He peered at her again; something about her stirred dim recollections.

"I do know that girl! Where have I seen her?" he muttered.

Vikte's eyes lit up. "You've got to have a look at the mother."

They decided to take them by surprise that evening in their room.

The scene remained frozen only for an instant. With incredible agility Anatoli sprang forward and slammed his fist between the Lithuanian's eyes. Jonas staggered, his head crashed against the door, and he collapsed. Anatoli plunged outside and was swallowed up by the darkness.

"Jesus Maria, help!" shrieked Vikte.

"Get him! A Jew, get him!" shouted Jonas, quickly recovering from the blow and rushing out after Anatoli. Vikte ran out behind him.

Mrs. Weiss and Shula stood thunderstruck.

"Have to leave here, get away . . . quickly. . . ."

Mrs. Weiss tossed her coat over the child, flung her thick shawl around her own shoulders, and grabbed a small bundle she had prepared for any emergency. They left the hospital courtyard by a gate leading into a side alley.

The snow continued to come down heavily. The street was deserted. Shula and her mother sensed that they were being pursued. The shouts of Jonas and Vikte rang in their ears.

"Run to the convent, daughter, run," whispered Mrs. Weiss. "Ask for Sister Teresa. She'll surely help you."

164

"But you, Mother, where will you go?"

"I don't know, child, I don't know. Run!"

Shadows of men rounded the corner. "Ho there, halt!" Shots split the air.

Shula did not know how her legs carried her through the dark streets. Her coat, which she had not had time to button, had fallen off her shoulders. Her dress was covered with snow, but she did not stop running.

How long she raced through the city streets she did not know. Knifelike pains pierced her ribs and she stopped. She could scarcely breathe. Where was she?

She looked about and found herself at the end of a street leading to the top of a hill. Before her lay a dark grove sheltering tiny houses, their roofs asleep beneath the snow, their windows blind.

Tears fell from her eyes. Alone in a hostile street on a wintry night without warm clothing, not a penny in her pocket, with no friend or protector—where could she go? To whom could she turn? Where was her mother? Captured? Shula remembered her instructions: "Run to the convent, daughter, to Sister Teresa!" But where was the convent? She seemed to recall that it lay at the other end of the city.

Shula ran on and began to feel warm. The snow had stopped, the sky was clearing. Stars began to dot the sky.

Breathing became more and more difficult. The jabbing in her chest grew keener and more frequent. Time and again she had to stop to take in air and quiet the pain for a moment. She could hardly get her legs to move forward.

What's happened to me? Am I sick? she thought, terror-stricken. *I'm lost.*

165

Many-storied houses on each side of the street loomed like monsters in the pale dawn.

Everyone has a home. People are sleeping in their beds, only I'm in the street. "Mommy, Mommy," she whimpered.

On she pushed until she reached a high wall with a green iron gate. Trying to take a few steps further, she sank to her knees in a snowdrift.

Suddenly it seemed that the wall was moving, that the immense iron gate was wavering above her. In another instant she would be crushed. Shula struggled desperately to turn aside but could not budge.

"Mommy, Mommy," she whispered softly—and collapsed beside the bars.

At that moment Shula's mother lay motionless on the sidewalk of the alley behind the hospital, the snow about her red.

The Fateful Leap

After Shula and her mother had left the ghetto, Mrs. Cohen and Shmulik had remained alone in the apartment. Ghetto existence was even bleaker now. Evenings, after coming home from work, Shmulik would drag himself listlessly about from one corner of the room to the other. His mother would turn her weak eyes upon him, eyes red-rimmed from sleeplessness and weeping. Silently she would serve him his watery bowl of soup and withdraw again to her corner.

Stifled by depression, Shmulik would have liked to hug his mother and whisper soft words of comfort, but never found the voice. Once he screwed up his courage to ask, "Any news of Hanna?" Mrs. Cohen was so shaken by the question that he lowered his head and held his peace.

One day he was turned away from the gate and told not to go to work. Shmulik sensed at once that an "action" was in the offing. A deathly fear embraced the ghetto. The streets were deserted, but in his mind's eye Shmulik saw them crammed with screaming, elbowing mobs frantically seeking safety.

By the time he reached his quarters he saw the Lithuanian police fanning out through the streets and bursting into the courtyards.

He found his mother standing in the middle of the room distractedly stuffing a bundle with anything that came to hand, then emptying and repacking it.

He knew the residents of the neighborhood had been ordered to line up in the courtyard. Whoever was found in the apartment would be shot on sight.

Shmulik stood alongside his mother in the mass of Jews with bundles and packages. At first he looked in all directions for acquaintances, but quickly saw the uselessness of that. The summer sun blazed down on his head. His thirst was oppressive. From the ranks ahead of him rose cries for water. Someone fainted.

Shmulik regarded his mother seated on the ground, her head on her package. Was she asleep? Had she perhaps fainted? The sun set. Red and purple clouds floated across the sky, blue ones, then gray, then black.

After the heat of the day the night was doubly cold. Shmulik sat on the ground, back-to-back with his mother, and slept.

Mrs. Cohen awakened him. The boy leaped to his feet and flung the pack on his back. The front rows were already moving, the row behind them was pushing them forward.

Where to?

It was difficult for Shmulik to make out what was happening up front. He could only hear the curses of the police, the groans of the Jews, and sounds of weeping. They arrived in front of a railway freight car. In short order Shmulik was shoved inside and pressed against the wall. The door slammed shut. Hammers banged away. All was darkness.

Where was his mother? He had not seen her enter the car.

"Mom," he cried desperately. "Where are you?"

"Here, son, here."

He could not see his mother standing by him, he could only hear her voice and feel her warm hand.

Where are they taking us? he wondered. The weeping that rose from the darkness enraged rather than frightened him. A woman began pounding her fist on the locked door and banging her head against the wall.

"Citadel Nine," the terrifying name of the mass execution site, crept about the car.

Little by little Shmulik's eyes grew accustomed to the dark. By the dim light filtering in through cracks in the walls, he began to make out his neighbors. Haim, the shoemaker from his work brigade, and his wife, Hannah, stood by the wall where the light was coming in.

Shmulik saw that Haim was whispering to his two companions and decided to get close to the group. In the brigade Haim had a reputation for daring. More than once he had helped Shmulik slip out of the lines under the very noses of the all-seeing ghetto police. Shmulik reached Haim's back and listened. With the rumble of the train wheels it was difficult to hear a thing. Anyway it seemed they had stopped talking.

It was not long before the air in the boxcar was stifling. Shmulik's head swam and nausea overcame him.

The voices in the car quieted down and the crying ceased. The indifference that follows despair was all-encompassing.

The train stopped. Someone peered through the cracks. "A field."

No one knew how long the train stood there. No one seemed to care.

Half fainting from suffocation and thirst, people leaned on each other, sitting and standing.

Finally the car jerked forward, the wheels began to move, and they were rolling again.

169

The rays of light coming in through the cracks grew fainter, then disappeared. Shmulik's senses sharpened. Haim and his friends had begun talking again.

"Haim," Shmulik tugged at the shoemaker's sleeve. "Haim, where are they taking us?"

"Who's here? You, Shmulik? Alone?" The cobbler leaned over him.

"With my mother."

"Ah, so."

Haim turned back to his friends. After a few moments Shmulik heard the sound of quiet sawing.

"Haim," he attempted to engage his friend again. "They're sawing through the wall."

"Quiet, boy, we're trying to get a board out. Maybe we'll manage to escape."

"Let's tell everyone in the car to escape," suggested Shmulik.

"Shut up, you fool, they'll stop us in the middle yet!"

"What's that sawing sound?" someone asked from the side.

"There must be rats or weasels around," one of Haim's group replied.

The sawing was discontinued for a few moments, then started up again. Before long the creaking of boards being ripped from walls was heard and a stream of cold fresh air burst into the car.

"Ay, what's happening?" cried someone.

"Quiet, fellow Jews! We've made an opening in the wall. Anyone who wants to can jump."

A tumult arose. Shmulik felt himself shoved aside. Someone started to light a match.

170

"Douse it, you bastard," hissed a youth by the opening.

"Friends, don't jump. Have pity on us! The Germans will kill us all," someone pleaded from the dark. Shmulik felt Haim's strong fingers on his arm.

"Let's jump, Shmulik, no sense waiting."

"Jump, boy!" someone urged him.

"I can't."

"Jump, I say! You scared?"

"I can't leave my mother."

Haim's hand lifted.

Shmulik watched as the cobbler's figure pressed through the dark to the opening. A rush of wind—and in a wink he had disappeared into the thickness of the night. Haim's wife, then two men plunged out after Haim.

"Shmulik, my son." He felt his mother's warm hand.

"Woman, don't stop him. Let the boy try to save himself."

Shmulik saw an older man who had been standing to the side all the while, as though set apart from the general consternation.

"Jump, boy," the stranger continued. "You'll be of no help to your mother, but you might save your young life."

Shmulik said nothing. His heart thumped wildly.

"Woman," the stranger continued, "speed him on. A little longer and it will be too late."

Hot tears fell upon his hand. His mother embraced him and pressed his head against her breast.

"Jump, my son, jump. . . . Perhaps the man is right."

"Mother," he whispered, "Mother. . . ."

Suddenly he felt someone pushing him from behind. He stood by the hole in the wall. Another instant and a

171

vigorous shove yanked the ground from beneath his feet. Icy wind swirled about him. A deafening roar rendered him senseless.

When Shmulik opened his eyes the first thing he was aware of was a searing pain in his left knee and in his arm. He gingerly touched the hurt areas and felt a sticky moistness between his fingers. Blood! *But I'm alive*, he thought.

It was night. A full moon shone. By its light he could see that he lay at the foot of the incline of the railroad tracks. A small distance away loomed pine and fir trees. Somewhere a rooster crowed and a dog barked.

A forest, Shmulik thought. *There must be a village or a lone farm nearby. What will happen if someone finds me? Where are the Jews who jumped off before me? Where is Haim the shoemaker?*

Carefully he rose to his feet and tried to walk in no particular direction, only trying to move at first. It was agony. Again he touched his wounded leg; it was on fire. He dared not fall sick. He had to stay strong and healthy.

To continue along the railroad tracks would be folly. He would have to penetrate deep into the forest.

Shmulik limped through the stumps bordering the tracks and plunged into the woods.

Thicker and thicker the forest grew, ever sparser the stumps. The darkness turned inky. Night birds sounded eerie cries, and the croaking of the frog choirs was deafening.

Watch out for swamps, Shmulik warned himself fearfully, advancing with great caution.

Tall forest grasses stroked his legs. Firs and pines were replaced by leafy trees with tangled branches that let only

172

scattered drops of moonlight through. The dry piny forest was falling behind him; he was nearing swampland.

He remembered stories he had heard as a child, of bogs that sucked in travelers and left no trace.

Lost and tired, he could hardly drag himself on. His head sagged. He collapsed beneath a broad-branched tree, leaned his head against a trunk, and slept.

With an odd feeling that someone was close by, he awoke and opened his eyes. At first he wanted to run on, but he could not even move. During the night his wounded leg had become swollen. Pulling the throbbing limb after him, he crawled into a clump of undergrowth.

The sun was high in the blue, unclouded sky. Shmulik felt his insides burning from hunger and thirst. For thirty-six hours no food had crossed his lips.

The tantalizing odor of ripe strawberries rose in his nostrils. He looked around and his eyes lit up—he was sitting right at the edge of a wild berry patch. Shmulik forcibly propelled himself to the bright red berries, snatching them off the plants and cramming them into his mouth.

He was startled by the sound of approaching footsteps. In a flash his hunger and thirst were forgotten. He slithered to concealment.

Had he been spotted? If so, hiding was useless.

The voices grew louder. Obviously the speakers were drawing near his bush. Suddenly his ears perked up. Had he heard Yiddish?

A tremor passed over him. Yes, now he was certain; Jews were indeed in the vicinity. Could they have been the ones who jumped off the train, now in search of hiding?

Shmulik began to crawl in the direction of the voices.

173

Between the trees he spotted a gray wool coat and the figure of Haim took shape.

As though thrust forward, Shmulik staggered to his feet flinging caution to the winds. "Haim, Haim!" he cried jubilantly.

Indeed it was the cobbler, with a member of his band. The boy stretched his hands out to embrace him but was repulsed by Haim's glowering eyes.

"What are you yelling for! You're not at home!" he rasped.

"Oh, Haim, I'm so happy I met you. I've been so lonely," Shmulik went on weakly, letting his arms drop.

"Fine, fine. We're all lonely here, all of us. . . . If a thousand Jews joined us we'd still be lonely."

Taking in the black look of the cobbler, Shmulik asked uncertainly, "Haim, where's your wife?"

The man's face twisted in grief and rage. "Gone. Beneath the train wheels. . . ."

"Ah," cried Shmulik, grief-stricken.

"Don't be sorry, boy . . . we'll all meet soon in the next world."

They fell silent. One instinct fired Shmulik: not to remain alone in the forest, to be with people, with fellow Jews. They walked on together.

Haim stopped, looked at the boy, who was dragging his swollen leg with difficulty, and barked, "Look here, Shmulik, we're in the forest among strangers and enemies. It looks like we've crossed the Lithuanian border into Byelorussia. There are no bosom buddies in the forest. Everyone's out for himself and goes where the breeze takes him."

Shmulik looked at him in horror. "Haim, you wouldn't

174

leave me here. I won't drag you down. I won't ask anything of you. I just don't want to be alone."

"No, boy, your being with us endangers our lives. You
go your way in peace. We can't take you with us. We have
a long, hard road ahead of us; you couldn't take it."

Shmulik wanted to say more, plead with them, but the
two turned their backs on him and strode off into the trees.

Overwhelmed with his utter aloneness and helplessness,
he collapsed, laid his face to the earth, and wept.

Vaska the Shepherd

A harsh chill woke Shmulik. He opened his eyes and
could make out nothing. All was utter darkness. The
silence was unbroken but for the hooting of an owl and
the hollow croaking of frogs, the rustle of dry leaves, the
plop of acorns.

Shmulik rose to his feet. His clothes were wet from
dew and the dank forest floor. He was hungry and thirsty.
Except for the few berries he had plucked, he had eaten
nothing for two days and nights. An awful weakness came
over him; he could not move. He groped about with trembling hands and found a pile of dry leaves. He sank into
them, covered himself over, and closed his eyes, but sleep
escaped him. Unconsciously he plucked a few green leaves

from the tree and began chewing on them. They tasted bitter, but their faint moisture somewhat refreshed his dry lips.

Gradually the sky grew brighter. Stars glimmered among the treetops.

Shmulik got to his feet and tried to go forward. His leg did not ache as much as it had before. He began to walk. After half an hour he reached the fringe of the forest.

I'll have to take to the road, he thought.

Looking about, he made out, by the moonlight, a broad meadow not far off and in it a large pile of hay. He burrowed into the fragrant stack until he was completely covered.

A sudden thrust shook him awake. Opening his eyes he saw a horse standing over him, hungrily chomping away at the pungent fodder near his head. The animal was hitched to a wagon alongside which stood an old farmer fixing a wheel.

In a panic, Shmulik struggled to his feet. The farmer cast his eyes upon him.

"Ah, the times, such times are upon us," he shook his head in vexation. "Chasing people from their homes! Don't be scared, boy," he reassured Shmulik. "I don't kill Jews. Where are you from?"

"From far away," blurted Shmulik, weak, cold, and agitated.

Again the old man muttered something angrily and crossed himself. "You must be hungry." He pulled a loaf of bread from his pack, broke it, and gave half to Shmulik.

"Grandfather, where are you going?" asked Shmulik, gathering courage.

176

"A long way, past Svienzianni. . . . They dragged me off with my wagon to haul lumber for them . . . three days and three nights they've been running me ragged, damn them," he cursed softly.

Shmulik yearned passionately to be with Jews again. Svienzianni was not far from Vilna where the Wilenskys were.

"Grandfather, can you take me to Vilna?"

The old man turned his head aside. "Vilna's still far off. We'd only get to the main road by tomorrow night. . . . And how could I lug you around in broad daylight? I don't know, we're not allowed to transport Jews."

Shmulik recalled the gold chain his mother had hidden away in the lapel of his upper garment for any emergency. He ripped open the lining and extended the slim chain to the old man. "Grandfather, I'll pay you; I'm not asking you to do it for nothing."

The old man scrutinized him carefully. Satisfied with Shmulik's appearance, he took the chain and said, "Oh well, get onto the wagon. Lie on top of the straw and not a peep out of you."

Dawn broke. The old man traveled on through the morning hours, stopping only for half an hour in a field to feed and water his horse. Then he drove on in the heat of the day. They wound through snakelike country roads, rarely crossing a main thoroughfare. The aged driver skirted any towns that lay in their path, choosing to go through the villages. Twice more he halted to draw water from wells. Shmulik also quenched his thirst and washed his face. The chill, refreshing water inspired new hope within him. At times they would pass other wagons on the road. The farmers would exchange a few words and con-

177

tinue on their way. No one paid any attention to him. His blond hair and ragged clothes led them into believing that he was a farm boy. At times they passed German soldiers on the road. The soldiers would look at the cart and the boy stretched out on the straw—seemingly sick with God knew what—and hurry off.

The weary nag plodded on at her own good speed. The rocking of the wagon and the creak of its wheels made Shmulik drowsy.

A frantic shove in his ribs awakened him. "Jump off, quick . . . police," muttered the old man.

Shmulik bolted awake. The wagon was advancing on a dirt trail flanked by a thick forest. Two men on bicycles were coming at them swiftly. The rifles slung over their shoulders glistened in the rays of the setting sun.

Shmulik turned to leap from the cart, but it was too late.

"Halt! Where are you headed?"

"Home, to the village of Shidlovtsy," the old man replied in a shaky voice.

"What have you got in the wagon?"

"Nothing, nothing at all. . . . I'm coming back from work."

"Where are your papers? And who's this?" The second man pointed at the boy. "Off that wagon!"

When Shmulik saw that the two men had forgotten about him for a moment as they poked about the straw in the wagon, he leaped across the ditch into the underbrush.

"Halt, halt!" echoed the cries of the policemen after him. A bullet whistled passed his ear and thudded into a tree in front of him. Another whistle followed, and another.

Shmulik ran. Pine needles lashed his face. At times he fell, hitting his forehead, but on he ran. Finally his strength gave out and he stopped. All around was silence. He stood in the midst of a forest with no road and no human beings in sight. The sun had long since set, all was cloaked in darkness.

His mother came to mind, as he had seen her last, seated on her bundle in the corner of the boxcar, pressed against the wall. *Mother, Mother, how could I have left you like that?* he accused himself. Then for an instant he took comfort; his mother herself had urged him to jump. Maybe he would live to help her, too. But the very next moment he was stricken with remorse.

Again he closed his eyes and it seemed as if his mother were standing before him serving him a cup of hot cocoa and a fresh buttered roll. Shmulik reached out for the cup and inhaled the delicious aroma. But his hand fell helplessly to his side, hitting a broken branch. He licked the drop of blood from the scratch. Finally he got up, wobbly on his feet, not knowing where to turn. He had to find something to eat and some water to drink or he was done for.

Shmulik plunged through the thick woods, over a carpet of moss and rotted leaves, without even looking for a path.

How long had he been wandering? he wondered. Moments? Hours? A whole day? He had lost his sense of time.

His ears began to realize how overflowing the forest was with life. Above him floated the song of birds, and a woodpecker attacked a hollow trunk, sending echoes

179

reverberating through the forest. Black and red ants scurried over the moss. From time to time tiny forest animals, rabbits or whatever, would scurry from their nests in fright, almost between his legs.

Suddenly he felt the earth sink beneath him. As he advanced, water gurgled up beneath his feet. The trees grew sparse, and thick bushes predominated. The tall reeds that covered the area began to pierce his rags, gashing his legs.

He had reached the swamps. He stopped.

Then he heard footsteps. He stood motionless.

Silence. Again, footsteps, stopping and starting. Clearly he could hear branches snapping. Breathlessly he hid in a thicket.

"Mooo-o-o," bellowed a cow, once, then twice, followed by a man's hot rebuke. "Where are you heading, you devil? Get back here or I'll crack your head open!"

First the brown, horned head of the animal appeared among the reeds, then that of a long-haired old man huffing and puffing. He was struggling in vain to head off the cow and bring her back.

His joy at seeing a human being overcame Shmulik's fear. He emerged from the branched thicket in the cow's path. The animal halted in fright, then turned and retreated.

The farmer saw Shmulik for the first time. He looked him over from head to toe, then asked between pursed lips in Byelorussian, "Who are you? A Jewboy?"

Shmulik did not speak at once. Then an answer flashed through his brain. Speaking in Russian—the second language of many families in Kovno—Shmulik replied, "No,

I'm Russian. My father was a soldier. The Germans captured my family and I ran away." Then he added immediately, "I'm hungry."

The shepherd sized him up again suspiciously. "Jew or Russian, it's all the same to me. Lots of people running around the country nowadays without a roof over 'em. Eh, eh, eh, what times. . . . God help us!"

He motioned to Shmulik to follow him.

The farmer tied a rope to the stubborn cow and tugged her after him, bawling at her the while. "Ah, you rotten beast, getting smart, huh? Men act like animals nowadays, and animals learn from 'em. A nice habit your first pregnancy gives you—running away. Dumb carcass!"

For a moment Shmulik hesitated, but continued after the farmer and his cow. Not knowing what to make of the man's anger, though, he felt very uneasy.

After a few moments they were standing in wild grass and shrubbery that reached almost to Shmulik's waist. This was a forest clearing where a few sheep, a cow, and a calf were munching on the flourishing vegetation to their hearts' content. The old man walked over to a tree stump, lifted a decrepit-looking linen knapsack, took out half a loaf of bread and a slab of ham, ripped off large-sized chunks, and handed them to Shmulik. "Eat, boy!"

Shmulik grabbed what was offered him and began chomping away with a will.

The shepherd observed closely as Shmulik devoured the ham. He certainly seemed to be enjoying it. *No hesitation at all*, the old man thought, putting his suspicions to rest.

Suddenly the oily meat stuck in Shmulik's dry throat. Still following the boy's every expression, the farmer observed, "You're a hungry little Jew, but you still can't take pig meat, can you?"

"I'm thirsty. Where is some water?"

Again the shepherd peered into the pale face before him, hesitated, then motioned him to follow. He approached the grazing cow and said to Shmulik, "Bend down."

Then the farmer knelt, approached the cow's belly, and began pulling on the full nipples. A thin stream of warm milk shot into the grass. Waiting for no further invitation Shmulik stuck his head under the cow's teats and gulped down the life-giving liquid. After he quenched his thirst, he continued to devour the bread and meat.

"Where are you headed?"

"Dunno. I don't have a home."

"Where have you been till now?"

"Wandering around the villages."

"Why didn't you stay where you were?"

"Germans came to the village looking for Russians. I ran away when they took Mother."

"Where did you sleep last night?"

"In the forest under a tree."

"Why are you limping?"

"I hurt myself in the dark on a tree stump."

The shepherd fell silent, as though weighing something. Then he rose, assembled his small flock, turned his head toward Shmulik, and pointed off to the distance. "I live over there at the end of the village. The last house is mine. Come around tonight to sleep."

Then he flicked his whip in the air and strolled off with his flock, disappearing among the foliage.

Shmulik stood still, his eyes following the gray figure of the shepherd. Then he decided to trail him from a distance. For about half an hour they advanced through the trees and thick brush, the shepherd hurrying on and Shmulik scarcely managing to keep up with him.

Gradually the forest began to lighten as more and more sunlight slipped in. They were approaching the woods' end. A broad meadow unfolded before Shmulik's eyes. On the other side a field of rye rippled in the wind and behind it lay the isolated farmhouses scattered over the broad, green plain, far apart from one another. The peasant led his flock through the field and around the grain, then vanished.

Shmulik returned to the forest, made his way into a thicket, stretched out on a mattress of dry leaves beneath a thick ash tree, and sank into melancholy reflection.

A stinging sensation made him start. He rolled up his shirt sleeve and found a number of red ants on his arm. He crushed them and flicked them off. Looking about, he discovered a nest of ants nearby. Shmulik sat on a stone and followed the colony's activity with keen interest. A tiny ant was hauling a piece of straw—or was it grain?—many times larger than itself. A few of the insects were pooling their efforts to move a sheep turd, no doubt a treasure to them. Seeing their fruitless efforts, Shmulik took a stick and rolled the find toward the nest. Instantly ants were swarming over it from all sides.

It's better to be an ant than a Jew, thought Shmulik. *Ants have a home. They know what they have to do. But me—what will I be doing two days from now?*

Still, the day was so enticing, the forest scent so intoxicating, and the feeling of being full so pleasant that Shmulik soon exchanged his gloominess for a surge of good spirits.

The sun dropped low in the sky. Dusk enveloped the forest, one shadow swallowed another, all sank into darkness.

Carefully Shmulik made his way through the field and the standing grain to a dirt road; he turned into the yard where the shepherd and his flock had disappeared. Shmulik saw a fence woven of branches with a gate in it, and nearby he made out two large buildings and one very small one, almost a shed. He entered one of the large buildings, which was made of boards and beams turned black in the rain and snow. Two wide doors, set at one end, were flung open. A sharp odor of hay and manure struck his nostrils.

Shmulik opened the gate and entered the yard. He stopped at the sound of a barking dog, gripped his stick, and walked in.

He was greeted by the neighing of a horse. "Who's there?" a familiar voice inquired.

In the dim light of the barn he made out a team of horses, a human shape alongside them. "It's me—Vaska!"

"What Vaska?" The shape stirred and grew near. "Ha, you, is it? Come for the night, eh? Fine. Get up there on the haystack." The farmer pointed to the other side of the barn. "You must be hungry. One meal's not enough, 'specially for young fellows like you with bellies that work better than their brains. Go to that hut and you'll get something to eat." He indicated a building, at the far end of the courtyard, whose windows gave off a dull light.

184

Shmulik did not move.

"Go on, what are you waiting for? There's no Germans there, only my old woman. I have to feed the horses."

"That's all right, I'll wait for you."

"So young, and already a mule," muttered the farmer. "Any way you like."

The man finished his work and left the barn. Shmulik followed him to the lit-up building.

Again a bark resounded and a black creature leaped toward them, sniffing the air and baring his teeth at Shmulik.

"Quiet, Tzigan, quiet, he's one of us," explained the farmer, stroking the animal's back. Then he turned to his guest with a chuckle. "Don't be afraid, Tzigan won't do anything to you. He hates Germans, too."

They entered a dark corridor. Shmulik bumped into the high threshold and almost lost his footing. The old man opened a heavy wooden door and walked inside with the boy behind him. By the weak light of a burning torch stuck into a crack in the wall, Shmulik at first saw only a long wooden table flanked by two benches. Then alongside a big stove appeared a woman with her back to them.

"Klava, more potatoes," the old man ordered, "I've brought a guest."

The woman was small and gaunt. As she swiveled her head about Shmulik saw many creases on her face and white hairs peeping out from beneath her kerchief.

The old woman scrutinized the boy. Two large yellow teeth protruded from her lips, stretching her mouth into a grin.

Not uttering a word, she took a pair of tongs from the

185

corner, reached into the red-hot oven, gripped a black pot, and dexterously slipped it out. Holding the lid of the boiling vessel with a rag, she tipped the pot over on top of a wooden bucket and drained the water. After a few moments she set the large crock of steaming potatoes on the table.

The old woman next brought forth a bowl of sour milk and placed alongside it a few wooden spoons, a knife with a wooden handle, and half a loaf of black bread.

"Come to the table, boy," the farmer invited Shmulik. "Grab a spoon and dig in. We're not city folk, we eat from one bowl like our fathers did and our fathers' fathers."

"Hmph, you and your manners, Afanas," scolded his wife. "Even in the villages people eat from porcelain plates and with shiny spoons."

"Sure, they eat from plates. They come from no good, those porcelain plates and shiny spoons. From no good," the old man repeated. "Someone eats from a plate, someone else gulps tears. Help yourself, boy, don't be shy," the old man urged. "Eat of what God has blessed us with."

"God's blessed you, all right," muttered the old woman, her bitter tone clashing strangely with the smile spread across her face.

"Don't sin with your lips, woman, there's a war on in the world."

"One man starves, another man feasts," his wife persisted.

"My *baba** is right, she's right by God," Afanas added,

---

* Woman in Byelorussian—a somewhat insulting term.

186

loudly sucking in a spoonful of milk. "People live on their land peacefully, plowing and reaping, and out of the blue, like wolves they come—stealing, killing, driving people away. War they want! Damn 'em!"

"It's the Germans who are to blame for it all, they attacked us," Shmulik ventured.

"The Germans . . . but the Reds started it! Why did they come here? Who invited them?" the old woman cried out in anger.

"My old woman can't stand the Russians," Afanas explained, smiling weakly. "We had a son, they took him into the army. He went off with them and we haven't heard a word from him since. Who knows if he's still alive?"

"He was my only boy, my Nadya, and they took him," sobbed the old woman.

"Ach, the Poles took boys, too, foolish woman," the old peasant tried to placate her. "And not only to the army. And they took every piece of good land, those *osadniki,** what did they leave us? The sand dunes and the swamps."

"And the Russians didn't take grain?" argued the old woman as though she had not even heard her husband's last remarks.

"Ech. All governments take. They take from everybody and it's few get anything back from 'em. But these—just stupid dogs."

"Sh!" his wife warned, eyeing Shmulik suspiciously.

_____
* Polish colonists in Byelorussia and the Ukraine granted special privileges by the Polish government and despised by local inhabitants.

"What's the 'sh'ing about? Every government takes. That's the way the world runs. What can you do? The peasant's got to take orders and do his job. It's not our business to get mixed up in politics. But these Germans—men aren't enough for them; give 'em women, too. . . ."

The old wife burst into tears, rocking back and forth in place, wailing, "My Nadya, my dove. . . . Where did they take you to? Where have your young bones wandered to?"

"Such times have come, damn 'em all to doomsday. They took our daughter to Germany, too," the old man explained. "As if they were really taking her to work. . . . Ach," he waved his hand, "what's the use talking? You can't ever satisfy that kind, they swoop down on you, sniff around, peck in all your corners, out for anything else they can grab. Lots of times I had to take off to the forest with what's left of my sheep and cattle. Then they'd go to work on my old woman. Give 'em eggs, butter . . . they stuff themselves to the gills, rot 'em all!" The old man spat angrily toward the door.

"What's the use talking? Enough yapping for nothing. Time for bed! I can't leave you in the house, boy. Someone could come in at night. Don't be scared," he added, seeing Shmulik looking askance at the dog, who sat quietly under the table, his head resting on his master's lap. "Just clear out of here in time, so no stranger spots you."

Shmulik thanked his host and left. Inside the barn, he sank into the pile of hay and quickly fell asleep.

"Hey, up, you slept enough." Someone was shaking Shmulik by the shoulder. "Get up, dawn will be here any minute. You have to get out of here."

188

In a flash Shmulik snapped out of his sleep. He slid down the haystack and landed in front of the farmer, who held a bottle of milk and half a loaf of bread in his arms.

"Take these," he said.

Shmulik took the gifts, thanked the farmer, and returned to the forest the same way he had come.

Two days passed. The bread the old man had given Shmulik had gone, and hunger gnawed at the boy's empty belly. As bad luck would have it, a stinging rain slashed down for a day and a night. Shmulik sought shelter beneath a tree but the rain sliced through the branches, soaking him to the bone. True, he could not complain of thirst, but his hunger was monstrous. He gathered wood sorrel to chew on. He also found some shriveled-up seeds among the leaves. All these, however, merely served to intensify his tortures. Trembling from cold and aching all over he stood beneath a fir tree, the strength draining out of him. *What will become of me?* he thought sadly. *I have to get food, no matter what.* He turned back to the village.

It was twilight. The farmers were occupied with making arrangements for the night and the women were busy preparing dinner.

Shmulik crept through the meadow, which became a swamp, and slogged on through the muck and brackish water until he reached the village. Lacking the courage to go to Afanas again for bread, he decided to sneak into the second courtyard.

As he drew near the fence, cries reached his ears—a woman's howl and raucous male laughter. Shmulik jerked back and darted behind the barn. From his hiding place

189

he saw two German soldiers lunge out of the pigpen, laughing uproariously, dragging a pig by the ears. The animal filled the yard with its squeals as the woman ran behind, waving her hands frantically and weeping aloud. A man dressed in clothing not quite village or city style tried to comfort her.

Shmulik was so frightened by the sight of the Germans that he forgot his hunger. Calling on all his reserves of strength, he slithered over to the field of grain behind the fence and hid among the tall grasses. The Germans hauled the pig to the road, skewered it, and flung it atop a wagon hitched to a team of horses. The man accompanying them cracked his whip and the cart pulled up the hill, scattering mud and water.

Shmulik waited until the cries from the farm died away and darkness cloaked all. With his last strength he plodded into Afanas's courtyard and entered the barn—but it was empty. Without thinking too long he walked toward the house. Silently he approached the dwelling, but he heard no sound. The door was locked. He remembered that at the end of the corridor there was another door. He pulled on the handle. The odor of manure hit him in the face as he entered. Obviously it was a cowshed or sheepfold, but there was nothing inside except manure and a pile of hay. *Afanas must have vacated with his herd in fear of the Germans*, thought Shmulik.

Shmulik began rummaging about in the yard and the corridor. Then in a corner by the barn door he found a black iron pail containing potatoes cooked in their skins. He began to cram them into his mouth, swallowing them with all speed and stuffing his pockets as well. As he turned to leave, he heard steps approaching. His heart sank. What would happen if the farm owners should walk in? They would think him a thief!

Swiftly he leaped outside and tried to slip around the back of the house. But it was too late. The figure drawing near let out a cry and stopped in its tracks.

Shmulik recognized the farmer's wife and walked toward her, whispering, "Don't be afraid, ma'am, it's me—Vaska."

The woman drew in her breath sharply and burst out in anger, "What are you doing here? Why did you come at night?"

"I came to ask for food. I'm starving."

"Starving, starving—as if we have to feed all the tramps in the world. You give to people once, twice, and they hang around afterwards, there's no getting rid of 'em. Get out of here, or. . . ." She retreated into the hallway and banged the door closed after her.

Shmulik stood motionless, overcome. He turned to go. Suddenly the window opened and he heard a muffled cry. "Vaska, Vaska, come here."

He approached and she pushed a loaf of bread into his hands.

"Here, take this and get out. Into the forest with you, the Germans are all over the place. And don't come back again." She swiftly shut the window.

A day and a night passed, the rain stopped, the sun shone. Shmulik dried out his wet clothes and enjoyed the heat.

His bread gave out. The night before he had tried to enter a few houses in the village and ask for food. At one home he got no answer at all; at a second, a window opened and a dry crust of bread and some potatoes were flung out. Then the window slammed shut, leaving Shmulik to grope about in the mud for his handout. *Things can't go on like this,* he thought. *I've got to find work and a permanent shelter.*

He decided to seek out Afanas and try to talk to him. Weary and hungry and thirsty, Shmulik roamed about the forest for an entire day. Finally, in the distance, he heard lowing. Tracing the sound, he discovered in the thick undergrowth the black cow whose milk he had tasted more than once. Afanas was seated on a tree stump, puffing on his pipe.

Shmulik opened his mouth to greet the man but lost his voice. For a moment they looked at each other.

"Still roaming around here?" Afanas asked.

"I've got no place to go."

"Why don't you go to one of the villages?"

Shmulik made his move. "Maybe you'd take me in," he asked. "I don't want charity, mind you. I'm big and I know how to work already."

"What do you know how to do?"

"I could shepherd your animals."

"Hm-m-m. Yes . . . actually, I do need a shepherd. I'm late in harvesting the hay and getting it into the barn. And corn harvest isn't far off."

"*Khozyain,** I'll watch your flock faithfully, and you'll be free to do all the work you want to do on the farm. I don't ask much, only food and a place to sleep. I don't eat a lot. A slice of bread and some potatoes will do me fine. I

* Master of the house.

could help out your wife, too—draw water for her and cut wood. I could even peel potatoes."

The old man looked at him with a smile, exhaled smoke, and replied, "We'll see. You come to the yard tonight."

Shmulik stayed on the Afanas farm, sleeping in the stable. Every morning before dawn the old woman would waken him, give him a cloth knapsack with bread and cheese, occasionally a chunk of meat or fat, and shoo him off to the pasture.

Whenever news would get through that the Germans were confiscating farm animals, Shmulik would pass the night in the forest. With Afanas's help he constructed a lean-to out of branches and lived there. While the cows and sheep grazed leisurely or knelt in the pasture, Shmulik would lie at his ease in his shelter and let his thoughts wander.

The old woman, Klava, had accepted him with some grumbling at first, but he won her over soon enough. He would snatch a full, heavy basket out of her hand, or a bucket—anything she happened to be lugging about. He would draw up water for her, even sweep the house and the yard. On his return from the forest he would bring back dry twigs to light the oven. In the end his quiet way and good work won the old lady's heart. She even began to worry about him. She would patch his pants, wash his shirt, and every Saturday night give him a clean shirt to put on.

Saturdays the old man would light the bathhouse behind the stable. It was an old wooden shed alongside a narrow brook. Almost every courtyard in a Byelorussian village had a family bathhouse of that sort. In villages, where buildings lay close together and where farmers had not yet set up separate dwellings in their individual fields, the fire would be kindled in a different house every week and the owner would invite all his neighbors over to wash. There were fixed hours for men and fixed hours for the women. A bathhouse had a special type of clay oven—low, something like a baking oven. Kindling was put in through an opening underneath. Stones would be heaped high on top of the stove, alongside which stood a large kettle with water to be heated. In the middle of the bathhouse stood a wooden barrel full of cold water. Along the walls ran long tiers of wooden shelves. The bather would take a vessel full of water from time to time and pour it out over the hot stones on the stove, filling the whole bathhouse with steam. Stretched out on the ledges, the bathers would beat themselves or each other with brooms of slender green shoots. In the thick vapors of the bathhouse the naked figures loomed like ghouls and devils. The atmosphere was suffocating, the room reeked of human sweat. From time to time someone would burst outside and plunge his fiery naked body into the cold brook.

Bath day was a holiday not only for children but for adults, too. Ten or twelve at a time would enter the bathhouse, one man scrubbing his neighbor's back, or thwacking away with the broom till flesh glowed red and groans of delight resounded: "Ah . . . ah . . . yes . . . yes . . . um-m. Lay it on, no mercy! Beat every sickness out of my body."

One Saturday Afanas set up his bathhouse and invited Shmulik in to wash. "Come on, Vaska, get clean for Sunday."

The youth drew back, blushing. "Uh, l-later," he stammered, "I'm not used to getting undressed in front of strangers."

Afanas regarded him for a moment, smiled into his mustache, grabbed a towel, and pulled him by the sleeve. "Come on, don't talk nonsense! You're not an old maid to be ashamed of your body."

In the bathhouse the old man stripped with the agility of a youth, dashed a pitcher full of water over the white-hot stones, and began washing and scouring.

Shmulik slowly began to unlace his shoes, his heart full of apprehension. What would happen when his host saw that he was a Jew?

Suddenly Afanas was beside him looking straight into his eyes. "Don't be afraid, boy. Hurry up and strip. I know you're a Jew. It's not easy to fool old Afanas. I've seen a lot in my day and for years I dealt with Jews. Don't be afraid, I won't tell your secret to anyone, not even my old woman. You see, I didn't invite anyone else over to the bathhouse. It doesn't matter to me. Jew, Russian, Pole—we're all human, we all want to live."

Speechless, Shmulik stood with tears in his eyes.

"Grab a broom," the farmer said to the youth after he had undressed, "and go to work on my back." He lay down on the shelf. "That's it, that's it. . . . Harder, you're a man, not a *baba*. . . . Now you lay down and I'll give you a going over."

Shmulik felt that momentarily the skin on his back would rip, so tight and burning was it from the heat. Unable to endure the steaming vapors any longer, he flung open the door and sprang outside.

The farmer bellowed uproariously. "Ach, ach, ach! Oh

195

my God, what a Russian. . . . You can see you're a Jewboy right off. Call this steam? Till you've sweated it out seven times straight, a bath is no bath."

When Shmulik came back in, he found the old man reclining on the uppermost ledge where the steam was so thick he was all but invisible.

Many days passed, weeks became months. Shmulik grew accustomed to his new home and his work. He felt good on the lonely farm; the oldsters treated him as one of their own. When his clothes ripped, Klava made a new outfit for him from her son's pants. Barefoot, in his white flaxen shirt, Shmulik looked for all the world like a true-born peasant lad. Even his speech changed, as he adopted the mannerisms and dialect of the local people.

After awhile he got to know the neighbors, particularly their children. Like himself, the young boys were shepherds in the forest. He grew close to one of them—Vanka, who had crossed eyes and hair as yellow as flax.

Their friendship began one day as Shmulik was leading his animals back home. He heard cries for help. Rushing to their source, he saw Vanka flat on his stomach and Sashka, older and stronger than he, slamming his fist into the boy's head and shoulders. Blood flowed from Vanka's nose, but that did not stop Sashka. Writhing and yelling under the attack of his foe, Vanka was unable to struggle free.

Shmulik's blood boiled. He threw himself upon the attacker and with one blow of his fist felled him. Sashka was ready to counter, but Shmulik stood over him, fists clenched tightly, eyes flashing with rage. "Just try and get near, you bastard. . . . Pick on a weak little kid, huh? I'll ram your teeth down your throat! Look what you did to him!"

Sashka lowered his head and turned aside, cursing, but Vanka continued to howl.

"Stop yowling like a *baba!*" Shmulik snapped. Vanka fell silent.

"You're tough, you beat Sashka up," Vanka murmured. "Me, my name's Vanka, I live there"—he pointed to a farm near Afanas's place surrounded by cherry trees and spreading lindens. "I know where you live," he added quickly. "But where are your parents?"

"I have none," blurted Shmulik, as his mother's face rose before his eyes. Suddenly, the conversation had become oppressive; Shmulik wanted to be alone. He spun about and strode off toward the forest.

Vanka was taken aback. What was the matter with the fellow?

He must have pained his newfound protector, he decided, and was deeply sorry. Vanka ran after Shmulik and put his arm around his shoulders, and said gently, "Ah, don't get mad. I didn't say nothing. Want to be friends? You know, I don't have a big brother anymore. My oldest brother was killed in the war. You can be like a brother to me. Want to?"

Shmulik stopped and looked at the boy, who at that moment cast his eyes aside.

"O.K.? Want to be like brothers? Here, take this."

Before Shmulik could reply, Vanka removed from his neck a bronze chain with a small round medallion displaying a portrait of Mary and draped it around his friend's neck.

197

"No, no, I don't want it," Shmulik protested.

"Take it, take it, don't be embarrassed. It's a sign of friendship. It's got to be that way. A holy medallion helps you out when you're in danger. Listen, when the Russians retreated through our village, there was a terrible battle, right here alongside the road. Golly, what happened then! You saw the burnt-up trees behind the barn? The Germans attacked so hard all the windows in the village were blown to smithereens. We all ran out of the houses and jumped into the canals and the rye, almost dead. I was lying next to my brother. When the shooting was over with, I raised my head and there he was, dead beside me. That's how it happened. And you know how I was saved? All that time I held tight to this medallion in my fist and I prayed! You don't believe me? I swear it!"

"So why are you giving it to me?"

"Because you don't have a father or mother. Or anybody to protect you. And I want us to be like brothers."

Shmulik gave no answer but concealed the gift beneath his shirt.

So it was that Shmulik and Vanka became fast friends. Together they would shepherd their flocks in the forest and together they would come home. At nights they would kindle campfires. Shmulik would gather dry twigs and Vanka would bring potatoes to bake. The potatoes, half burnt, pleased his palate more than the sweetcakes old Klava baked in honor of All Saints' Day.

At times the two friends would be joined by other children from the village. Shmulik adjusted to this life and wandered freely about the village, even visiting in the homes of his shepherd companions.

198

On Christian holidays the farmers would invite him in and offer him a hunk of meat or a fat pancake.

"Poor child," the farmer women would nod their heads, "an orphan. It's good the Afanases took him in."

Still, on Christian holidays and on Sundays, Shmulik would be plunged into gloom. Amid the courtyard hubbub of the family's preparations for churchgoing, a feeling of aloneness and alienation engulfed him. He recalled the Sabbaths and festivals in his parents' home, the candles shining in silver candlesticks, the pure white cloth on the table, and the two twisted loaves. While Shmulik's parents had not been rigorously observant, they had been traditional. His mother had even been scrupulous when it came to the dietary laws, and on festivals his father had taken him to synagogue.

Now, however, Shmulik had lost track of time. He no longer knew when the Jewish holidays fell.

His benefactors did not force him to go to church with them. On the contrary, they were glad that he was content to forgo the pleasure of a trip to the city and stay home to keep an eye on the property. Eventually, though, the old woman began to protest, holding it a sin to leave Vaska behind; after all, he was a Russian boy and had to be brought close to God.

Afanas would burst out laughing. "Ach, you foolish old woman! Don't you know that the younger generation has its eyes lifted to Satan and not to God? It's not us who will change the world!"

But Klava held doggedly to her opinion. Finally Afanas stayed home and Vaska took his place on the wagon seat.

Afanas kept his promise and seemingly forgot that he ever knew Vaska's secret.

199

Swiftly the summer days whirled by, like leaves shed from chestnut and linden trees. The grain harvest over, the fields emptied of people, Vaska and his friends led the sheep through the golden autumn fields while the cattle grazed at the edge of the forest. Mornings, flocks of migratory birds streamed overhead through leaden skies. Cold autumn winds carried the dead leaves over the fields. Between rains the skies would clear and Shmulik would wander off among the trees of the forest, gathering fallen leaves to weave into multicolored chains of yellow, purple, and red.

At times he would be joined on these walks by Vanka. The younger boy was an expert on forest birds, caterpillars, and insects. He could recognize every bird by its cry and was quick to discover birds' nests and foxes' lairs. Vanka had acquired this skill from his grandfather Karl, who was still alive. Although incredibly old, Karl hadn't lost a tooth in his mouth and could hear the slightest movement in the forest. Only his vision had dimmed slightly and Karl argued that it was the war, not old age, that accounted for that.

He had served as a soldier in the army of Nikolai and loved to brag about his exploits. "Like oak trees the men were then, and now?—women, not soldiers!" He would spit to the side in contempt.

It was said that in his youth old Karl had gone into the forest on the Night of Saint John to find the fern in flower. In the villages of Poland, the Ukraine, and Byelorussia it was the custom for young people to pass that night, June 24, in the forest, dancing and sporting by the campfire. According to tradition, the fern bloomed only on Saint John's Night and instantly withered. Whoever found the flower would have his every wish fulfilled. To do so, however, he would have to get by the evil spirits guarding it zealously.

What happened to Karl that night no one knew. Karl himself never disclosed his secret and turned furious whenever asked. All that was known was that farmers found him unconscious at dawn in the forest.

The shepherds still had to lead livestock into the forest overnight whenever news arrived that Germans were about, confiscating sheep and cattle. At times the village boys would also lead the horses out to rest after a hard day's work.

Karl loved to accompany the youths to night grazing. He would always be wearing—even on hot summer days —a short sheepskin coat, a warm hat, and a large shepherd's pack on his shoulder. Staff in hand, he would stride forward so briskly that the two boys could scarcely keep up with him. In the forest, he would kindle the fire. Karl knew just how to light a fire and keep the flame going even on rainy days. He would sit down on branches piled atop the moss and tell the boys of days gone by.

"Ah, what do you know?" he would turn to Shmulik. "There's no men or soldiers either nowadays. One raindrop on the nose and already they're moaning and groaning and rushing off to the doctors." He wrinkled up his nose in contempt. "In my day, whoever had a head on fire and a shooting fever would pour a pint of liquor down his throat, lie down on the stove, stay there till he'd sweat seven times, get up the next morning, and load eighty pounds on his back.

"Once," the old man recounted, drying his soaked leggings at the campfire, "we were in the Caucasus Mountains when our regiment was hit with a weird sickness. Men suddenly turned pale, foamed at the mouth like mad dogs, yelled and thrashed about with their fists. One man fell sick, then two, three, ten. . . . A panic seized everyone, doctors were rushed for. No one knew what was happening. Was it rabies? But there were no dogs in the vicinity, not even puppies. We let the doctors go whistle and went out to the villages to get hold of a charmer; maybe he would iron things out quickly. Then, what do you think? The local people brought us an old man. We asked his advice, drilled him, grilled him, but he wouldn't open his mouth. When we threatened him with clubs he loosened up and told us that on a nearby mountain there was a certain kind of plant with roots shaped like a human body. The root had to be found and boiled, and if the liquid was served to the patients, the plague would be wiped out. Straight off the commanding officer sent five men out to discover the root. For days they searched and came back empty-handed.

"Then I got up and said, 'Send me, sir.' Three days and three nights I roamed around the rocks and crannies until I found it. It was no cinch uprooting it, either. Moving a house would be easier. But I yanked it up sure enough, shook off the dirt and . . . Holy Mother! A man's body, plain and simple, with a head, arms and legs. I brought it to the camp and the old man boiled it in water, gave the drink to the sick troops, and cured them. The general shook my hand in person.

"And there's no comparing generals then with generals now. Today you've got generals? I know what's what! In

202

my time, when a general walked by, you'd go blind from the glitter. Gold epaulets, stars, straps, decorations—a regular rainbow. But today. . . . Ah, why waste the spit!" The old man flung some dry twigs into the fire contemptuously.

Shmulik loved to sit near the fire and listen to Karl's stories. And the old man, for his part, seemed to like the boy.

Autumn grew more bitter day by day. The sun peeped from behind the clouds only rarely. Shmulik, barefoot and inadequately clothed, shivered from the cold. He would look enviously at Vanka, dressed in a Polish army uniform and big boots. While Klava had given Shmulik a sack sewed together on one side to keep out the rain, it was not substantial enough to warm him. Old Karl's campfires were his salvation.

Generally Shmulik would find himself standing forlornly alone under a tree, dripping water from head to toe. More now than in the summer his thoughts went to his mother, his neighbors from the courtyard, and his acquaintances. Frequently he heard from the shepherds what was happening in the nearby village. Boxcars packed with prisoners would go by, the passengers shouting. He heard of a Jew that a farmer came upon in the road, robbed of his boots, and then turned over to the Germans.

After a while Shmulik almost began to believe his own story—that he was a Russian who had arrived in the vicinity with his family during the Soviet occupation. He was locked in an internal struggle. For a while he had struggled to live only day by day, not thinking of either past or future. But then Shmulik felt the "Vaska" within him recede and his true identity pained him more and more. And the question of "What will happen?" oppressed him and robbed him of sleep.

Shmulik Meets the Partisans

One morning, Shmulik opened his eyes to discover a gleaming world mantled in pure snow. He ran to the window and looked outside. The whiteness of the yard was unbroken by the imprint of a human foot, and the snow continued to fall.

Shmulik bound his legs with the clothes that had dried out by the stove, pulled over them the wooden shoes Afanas had made, and went outside. Only at that point did he notice that the farmer's bed was empty. Had the old man really gotten up ahead of him? During the preceding days Afanas had been getting up late. Because his back hurt him, he would stretch out in the early hours of the morning and pamper his weary limbs.

Shmulik felt the cold wet nose of Tzigan on his hand. The dog, long grown used to him, accompanied the boy wherever he went.

"Tzigan, where's your master, huh?" asked Shmulik, stroking the animal's black fur.

The dog growled intermittently, then wagged his tail

and looked at Shmulik with knowing and devoted eyes.

"You don't know, Tzigan, you're worried, eh?" Shmulik went on conversing with the dog.

Suddenly the animal let out a happy bark and sprang forward in the direction of the forest. Shmulik shaded his eyes and made out a figure of a man on the road leading from the woods to the farm. He quickly saw it was Afanas in his sheepskin coat. The snow sparkled on the hairs sticking out of his sheepskin hood and on his mustache and beard. The farmer entered the courtyard, saw Shmulik and stopped; he was not pleased at their having met.

"What are you doing here? What devil pushed you outside?" he snapped, shaking the snow off his hood and sleeves as he entered the house. Indicating to Shmulik that he should keep quiet, the farmer hurriedly undressed and went to bed.

Shmulik's eyes stretched wide in amazement but he did not dare ask anything.

"Vaska, hey, Vaska!" he heard Vanka call him. "Come on out behind the barn!"

"Right away, just wait a minute."

Shmulik quickly finished his tasks, shoveled some dung aside, scattered fresh straw by the cows, and went outside. Vanka was waiting for him alongside the fence.

"Come on, come on, I got news to tell you. I saw partisans last night."

"Partisans?" Shmulik looked at his friend in amazement. "Partisans?" he said eagerly. "Really?"

"Honest, honest, I swear on my life—with rifles and red stars on their hats."

205

"Where did you see them?"

"They visited our yard last night. They got grandpa out of bed; he only got home at dawn, cursing like mad. They say the partisans were at Theophile's farm last night and took a pig and a lamb."

"You mean the partisans are robbers?"

"Grandpa Karl thinks they're just like the Germans. The Germans grab, and they grab, too, he says. But I think it's different."

"Why?" asked Shmulik.

"Because the Germans are strangers, enemies, and the partisans are on our side; they speak Russian."

"Ah, that's it. Partisans live in the forest, and if they don't take things, who would give them anything to eat?"

All that day Shmulik walked around in a daze. It was really true, they were walking about near a partisan hideout. He had heard much of them during the summer. More than once the farmers had talked among themselves of sabotage carried out by partisans in the vicinity—of a train heading in the direction of Minsk and the front blown to kingdom come with everyone on board; of the revenge taken on a certain farmer whose son worked for the police force.

All such stories were circulated by word of mouth in fearful or admiring tones. What mattered to Shmulik was that the partisans were enemies of the Germans and were fighting them in that part of Byelorussia. That meant there were people who were not afraid of the Germans, who went their way as free men with weapons in hand, who lived in the forest, that same forest in which he had felt so desolate and abandoned. How he yearned to see with his own eyes those wondrous partisans.

206

At times it seemed to him that all such reports were fairy tales spun out by the farmers for their amusement in the long winter nights or summer nights at pasture, to stave off boredom. But Vanka had actually seen them. Then they really, truly existed!

"Vanka," Shmulik whispered into his friend's ear, his face aglow. "Where can you see them?"

Vanka shrugged his shoulders. "That's real secret," he said solemnly. It felt nice to be asked advice by Vaska, whose fists had protected him from tougher boys and who even knew how to read and write.

"So? How do you find them?" Shmulik persisted. "Come on, tell me. You swore we were buddies . . . like brothers!"

"Sh-h-h, we can't talk about it. The fence has ears. Grandpa Karl gets awfully angry when you just mention them. Anyway, it's better not to gossip," he added, sliding across the snow on their way home.

Shmulik now was driven by one urge—to see the partisans with his own eyes and speak with them. He had pictured them in his dreams and daydreams. Often, standing by the fence behind the barn, or peering across the broad, snow-covered meadows and the road leading to the forest, it seemed to him that amid the blackness of the trees their rifles glistened in the sunlight. At times he would wake up in the night, dress hurriedly, and go outside hoping that luck would be with him and the partisans would pass by.

At times he was deeply depressed. He was only a boy; the partisans would surely pay him no mind.

His outdoor duties had long since ended, including the pasturing of the animals.

207

Shmulik would go out to the forest with Afanas to chop wood, which they would then saw into logs, load onto the sleigh, and take to the city to be sold. Shmulik did not accompany Afanas to the city very often. On the way back from the forest he would remain in the courtyard and the farmer would continue the journey alone. On entering the woods very deeply—woodcutting was forbidden to farmers by law—hope would well up within him. Maybe this time, maybe. . . . But the forest was always empty of people, and only echoes from afar answered the ring of their axes.

"Get up, Vaska, get up!"

Someone was shaking him by the shoulder. He opened his eyes to find Afanas standing before him, wearing his sheepskin over his underwear. Obviously he had just gotten out of bed.

"Your head clear yet, or are you still sleeping?" Afanas asked mockingly. "Can I talk to you?"

Perplexed, Shmulik looked at the farmer in silence.

"Vaska, know how to keep your mouth shut?" Afanas asked suddenly. "You're a Jew, you have to keep secrets."

Shmulik nodded affirmatively, his eyes alive with excitement and curiosity.

"Here's a note." He stuffed a piece of folded paper into the youth's hand. "Go into the forest to the place we first met. In the stump of the willow we sat next to you'll find a crack; stuff the note in there. You remember the spot?"

"Sure," Shmulik replied.

"You hate the Germans, don't you?" the old man continued to sound him out.

Shmulik's expression was answer enough.

"And you want to hurt them?"

He nodded his head vigorously, his eyes sparkling in the dark.

"Then you won't be afraid of running to the forest alone at night. Get to it now and come right back. No delays, got me?"

From that night on Shmulik lived in a new world. He felt himself part of a great effort. He was especially happy that the farmer had put such faith in him. On the surface nothing changed in their relationship. Afanas continued to be the master of the house, giving him orders, and he the orphaned shepherd boy who had found refuge in his home. At times, however, he would catch Afanas winking slyly at him and he knew that they were in league together in a secret and adventurous undertaking.

After that first trial mission Afanas sent him on many errands—at times to the city to deliver a few words orally to a certain person unknown to him and at times to the neighboring village.

One night Shmulik was snapped out of sleep; Tzigan was barking and someone was knocking on the window. Afanas, already awake, was standing by the door.

"Who's there?"

"Open up! Comrades!"

Afanas pulled out a dry sliver of wood from behind the stove and kindled it. He went to the window and looked out. Apparently he was satisfied, for he quickly opened the door.

Into the room pressed three men wearing sheepskin coats and boots. One was armed with a submachine gun,

209

the others with rifles. All three wore military leather belts and rifles. The man with the submachine gun took the stick from Afanas and held it out in front of him.

"Master of the house! Aren't there strangers here? And who's this?" He lifted his torch toward Shmulik.

Afanas thrust the burning torch into the crack in the wall and pressed the hand of the arrival. "Part of the family, don't be afraid," he said. "How are you, Kolka? Good news?"

"Good, very good, *khozyain*," Kolka laughed, his face exuberant. "You'll hear about us in the morning."

He shook the snow off his cap and shoulders, unslung his weapon, took it in hand, and sat down on the bench, his back to the wall. His two friends sat alongside him, their rifles between their knees.

"We've come a long way, *khozyain*, we're worn out. But the Germans . . . ha, ha, ha," he laughed loud and clear. "They won't forget us so quickly. . . . Not until our next visit, ha, ha, ha!"

Immediately upon awakening, Shmulik had sprung out of bed, dressed, and thrust his feet into his shoes. So these were the partisans. He longed to draw near them, seize their hands, but lacking the courage, he drank in their faces avidly from afar.

"Where is the missus?" added Kolka, apparently in command of the group. "We're famished."

"I'll get my old woman up right away."

Klava got out of bed with a scowl, looked over the uninvited guests, and began grumbling. "This way a body gets no rest day or night. One minute the Germans, the next the partisans. You sweat out a living and everybody comes along and eats it up."

210

"Hey, lady of the house, stop that grumbling," laughed the commander. "Get the fire going and make us some pancakes. But good and oily, so the oil runs down our chins. *Khozyain*, your old woman isn't too happy to see us," joked the partisan, turning to Afanas. "Well, what's there to do? We'd like to stretch out on a hot stove ourselves instead of roaming around all night in the wind and storm."

"What to do, what to do," Afanas, echoed. . . . "And you, my good friend, don't take it to heart, that's the way my old lady is, she likes to complain—but she's not really a bad sort. Just wait, Kolka, until you see the kind of pancakes she'll make you."

Shortly the smell of fried fatty oil filled the room. The partisans took their boots off and began drying their leggings by the fire.

From outside came the sound of human voices and Tzigan's urgent barking. Shmulik opened the door and plunged outdoors. On the road leading into the village he could make out in the distance figures wrapped in white cloaks. A black machine gun stood out against the snow-covered earth. *Lookouts at the entrances to the village*, he thought.

As he stood leaning against the barn wall staring at the moving figures, from the opposite direction came the sound of loud laughter and singing.

A sleigh drawn by two horses emerged from Karl's farm carrying a few armed men. The carriage stopped alongside Afanas's house and the jovial group burst inside, laughing and singing.

They sing so loud—they are not afraid of the Germans,

211

thought Shmulik joyfully. He returned to the room, which was full of smoke and the aroma of fried pancakes, sat at the edge of the stove, and followed the doings of the noisy guests.

Bottles of liquor were brought to the table, poured into large glasses, and immediately emptied into the mouths of the guests. Shmulik followed their conversation closely, and though he did not understand much of it, he learned that the drinking was in celebration of the successful completion of a mission.

The gray light of predawn began to cover the village. The band of partisans left Afanas's house, climbed into the two sleighs, and disappeared into the forest. For a long time Shmulik stood leaning against the fence accompanying the men with longing, awe-filled eyes.

The next day farmers in the region told how a train headed toward Minsk on the main track had been derailed in the night. Two days later it was said that hundreds of Germans headed for the front, as well as cars packed with supplies and arms, were blown sky high.

From that night the partisans' visits to the village farms became increasingly frequent. They would even appear in the daytime, openly walking through the village streets. Their weapons slung on their shoulders, they would chat with the village farmers and flirt with the girls. The partisan called Kolka became a member of Afanas's household. He would materialize suddenly, accompanied by only one comrade, and would ask that the bathhouse be readied and fresh underwear laid out. They would go in to bathe and come out red and glowing. At times Afanas would send in Shmulik to serve them. Kolka would go up to the highest ledge and his friend would lay into him with the broom. Suddenly he would leap down, burst outside, roll his burning flesh in the snow, and reenter the steam-filled bathhouse. Shmulik all this while would be serving them—pouring water on the white-hot stones, feeding fresh twigs into the stove, and bringing water to the bathers.

Shmulik lost his shyness and learned to speak with the partisans. Upon their arrival he would sit down at the table with them and would even be privileged to receive whiskey. The first time he tasted the cloudy potion it felt as though fire had been poured down his throat, setting his insides aflame, but then he got used to the drink. He strove to be just like the partisans. At times he was allowed to carry a rifle. He learned to take apart and reassemble the bolt. Enthusiastically he would remove the magazine and fill it with clean, well-polished bullets. He would polish the rifles zealously and return them to their owners, beaming with joy.

Kolka would slap him on the back in a comradely fashion and say, "You're a fine partisan. Now you can say you've learned to polish a rifle and drink *samogon*."*

Once when he was alone with Kolka, Afanas having left the room, he gathered his courage and asked, "Kolka, take me with you into the forest . . . I want to be a real partisan."

Kolka looked him over and burst out laughing. "And what would a pip-squeak like you do in the forest?"

"Kill Germans."

* Primitive home-brewed whiskey made from corn or potatoes.

213

"All we need," laughed Kolka, "is to open a kindergarten in the forest. Little one, you stay tied to Mama's apron strings for a while. Three years from now, when you're grown up, we'll come get you."

Then he added gravely, "A partisan's life in the forest is no game; it's not for children. Today, you're alive and tomorrow you're a trampled corpse."

Shmulik left, restraining his tears with difficulty.

The Hand of the Enemy

The news from the front became more and more encouraging. The partisans arriving at the village would tell of the Red Army's victories, of the defeats inflicted upon the Germans, and of Stalingrad.

The Germans stopped visiting the village out of fear of the partisans. Neighboring farmers felt safer. Villagers would lend the partisans horses or would take them about themselves, and the village women would wash the fighters' underwear.

It seemed that the German oppressors could not set foot in the now peaceful area. The partisans would come to take part in village celebrations, playing on harmonicas and accordions and dancing with the girls.

Karl alone would walk about scowling at this revelry.

"Ach, it's not brains that leads to such goings-on, no brains at all," he would warn them. "The Germans will get back at you yet, they'll get back at you yet."

He was particularly infuriated upon hearing how the partisans, drunk with victory after a successful sabotage mission in the area, strolled about the village singing so loudly that their voices rang in the distance. As their ranks and their arms supply swelled, they began to feel cocksure of themselves. The Germans, they were sure, would not dare break through to the area, now under partisan rule, without a vast force.

"With their own hands they're digging their graves, with their own hands," the old man would mutter and go back to his hut, close the door and lock it.

The day old Karl predicted was not long in coming.

One morning at daybreak, the rumble of vehicles awakened Shmulik. He leaped out of bed and rushed to the window. Down the road leading to the village from the main highway rumbled a tank, its cannon barrel protruding. Right behind it came more vehicles.

"Germans in the village!" The cry leaped from his lips of itself. "*Khozyain*, Germans!"

In an instant they were all on their feet.

"Vaska, run to the barn, get the animals into the forest," Afanas cried to him, as he burst into the courtyard with Klava behind him.

But Shmulik was no longer listening. Germans! All his senses were sharp, tuned to one goal. To flee! To flee as quickly as possible.

With all his strength he began racing down the path

215

leading to the woods. His wooden shoes slipped off his feet. Once again he was a tiny animal, pursued by hunting dogs. He quickened his pace as shots rang after him.

Only when he had gotten past the first tree of the forest did he pause for an instant to gulp down air, but then he plunged immediately into the thick undergrowth as deeply as possible so that the murderers might not find him; no doubt they would be coming there, too, to search out survivors from the village.

Feeling that he had gone far enough, he chose a thicket of young pine trees, plunged into them and curled up, praying that his heart would stop pounding so wildly and straining to take in what was happening in the village.

Shmulik did not know how long he lay on the forest's frozen floor. It seemed to him that he was neither Shmulik nor Vaska but someone else entirely—an old man trembling from cold and fatigue. His head spun, his eyelids were heavy, forcing his eyes shut. With all his might he struggled to prevent exhaustion from overpowering him. He could not afford to sleep! The pine branches swayed lazily, strewing his head and shoulders with snow.

Shmulik arose, and tried to exercise his aching limbs. It had grown less cold. No longer did the snow crunch beneath his feet; rather, it was soft and wet. His leggings, which that morning had been covered with a thin layer of ice, were now wet. The shots grew ever fainter.

What's going on there? he wondered. Why had no one from the village come after him? Could they have fled and hidden elsewhere? The forest was huge after all, affording many hiding places.

The shots had ceased. Dusk was falling. It was growing

colder again; thousands of needles began to pierce his flesh.

He had to move, he could not stand in one place. But where to? He decided to see what was going on in the village. Perhaps the butchers had left.

Shmulik emerged from the thicket into tall pines. The trees hid the sky completely. A little further and he would reach the forest clearing where he had regularly brought the animals to graze. From there he would have a good view of the fields and the road leading to the village.

The sharp caw of a crow split the silence. Shmulik shuddered, stood still, and held his breath.

"Nonsense, it's only a crow," he whispered, trying to calm himself.

Suddenly his knees shook. From the village columns of smoke rose heavenward. He emerged from the forest, looked in the direction of Afanas's farm, and saw a black patch flung across the whiteness of the snow, sending up a thin column of smoke. Soon, it too would vanish. Thick clouds were still spiraling up from the neighboring farms.

As though rooted to the spot Shmulik stood staring at the burnt village. What had happened? Where were all the people? Wasn't there a soul left alive? And Afanas and Klava—had they been able to escape?

Long shadows stretched across the snow. The smoke clouds over the village began to blow away. Over the black heaps stretched a blue sky, now growing dark, strewn with thousands of blinking eyes. It seemed that the life had been wrenched out of the scorched earth and had ascended into the heavens.

The shrill cawing of a crow chilled Shmulik once again.

217

He ripped himself from the spot and began running toward the village.

On the way he ran into a large dark object and almost tripped over it. He looked. It was the carcass of Afanas's black cow, whom Shmulik had loved to milk and look after.

With faltering steps he approached two gutted pillars, the remnants of linden beams, sticking out of the earth like two sooty skeletons over a heap of glowing coals and cold embers. Only the day before, Afanas's house had stood on that spot. Now only a few charcoal poles remained and the two stone steps.

Helplessly Shmulik sank to those steps and lowered his head into his frozen hands.

Suddenly he felt a hot soft body rubbing between his legs. He opened his aching eyes and a cry of joy burst from his lips.

"Tzigan, Tzigan—you're still alive!"

The dog leaped up to lick Shmulik's face and hands.

"Poor Tzigan," Shmulik stroked the dog's head with both hands and pressed the animal to his chest.

The dog freed his head from Shmulik's hands, lifted his sharp chin, and wailed long and pitifully.

"You're the only one who stayed alive in this graveyard. The two of us are without a roof over our head, Tzigan. We're in the same boat."

Shmulik decided to pass by all the other farms in hopes of meeting one of the villagers. Slowly he walked down the path leading to Karl's farm, with Tzigan running after him.

Suddenly the dog stopped. Again he emitted a prolonged and plaintive wail, ran forward, came back, and

218

then stopped again. Shmulik moved closer. By the moon's light he made out a human form in the snow. He bent over and shook in every limb—it was Vanka! Trembling, he touched his friend's face and his fingers leaped back; the face was frozen hard as ice.

Shmulik could not wrench his gaze from the dead boy. Vanka's eyes gaped open wide.

His fingers shaking, Shmulik tried to close the dead boy's eyes but could not. He jumped back from the corpse and began to run. Drenched in cold sweat he arrived at old Karl's courtyard. The dog, who had been running before him, began to bark. Shmulik made out a figure huddled on a pile of rubble alongside the wall of a half-gutted house. At the sound of the dog's barking the man lifted his head. It was Karl. Shmulik leaped toward him, his heart thudding.

"Uncle Karl, Uncle Karl!"

The old man looked at Shmulik in a daze, as though he did not know him. Then his eyes flashed anger. "All of them killed, and only you left alive, you damn worm. . . . Bolshevik spawn! Get out of here before. . . ." His voice dropped off.

Shmulik halted and started back in astonishment and pain. His eyes clouded with tears. He stood before the old man trembling and utterly confounded. The latter raised his head, and the two regarded each other wordlessly. Karl's face softened and grief filled his eyes. He waved his hand as though flicking aside a bothersome mosquito.

"Merciful God," he groaned. "What are you to blame for, poor child, if people older and smarter than you didn't have brains in their heads?"

Not looking at Shmulik, he motioned the boy to him

219

and continued, as though talking to himself, "How many times did I warn them: 'It's no good, no good, this mad roaring around. The Germans will come and finish us all off.' They didn't want to listen, an old man's voice is the same as a dog's. . . . Partisans they loved. Damn 'em all. . . ."

The old man fell silent. His shoulders drooped and his head swayed from side to side.

"All of them?" Shmulik finally dared to whisper.

"All of them . . . all of them. . . . They came at dawn, like wolves on the hunt. They surrounded the farms on all sides. One house after another. . . . Didn't even let them get dressed. . . . They led them there. . . ." With a bony and shaking hand he pointed the way. "And afterwards . . . you see for yourself."

"They didn't run away? No one was saved?"

The old man shrugged his shoulders.

"Maybe someone else will show up. God knows. . . . I went down into the cellar in the yard, into the potato pile. I saw our Vanka running toward the forest."

Shmulik shuddered.

The old man caught the motion and cast searching eyes upon him, at once frightened and full of hope.

"Vanka's body is there," Shmulik murmured, "on the road."

The old man said nothing, only closed his eyes. Shmulik thought he had fallen asleep from grief and fatigue. After a few minutes he shook himself, got up, and began striding in the direction Shmulik had pointed out, with Shmulik behind him. They came upon the body. The old man knelt in the snow. His lips moved, but no sound came

220

forth. He made the sign of the cross over the dead boy's forehead and chest, lifted the body, and slung it over his shoulder.

Silently they returned to the scorched yard. The old man set the body down among the burnt cherry trees. He poked about the piles of embers, turned the rubble over, and took out two spades. Momentarily he straightened up, then bent over and began shoveling the snow aside. Shmulik, too, took hold of a spade and the two of them began digging a grave. Silently they lowered Vanka's body into the earth.

The old man set up a cross with two boards and planted it in the newly dug earth, and rolled up a pile of stones alongside.

They sat on the stony mound for a moment, each one deep in thought.

"What will you do now, boy?" The old man touched his arm. Shmulik lifted the eyes of a beaten pup.

"Listen, now," the old man said, "go to the village of Druzdai. I have a relative there, name of Andrei Palka. Tell him what happened to us. Tell him I sent you so he'll take you in. He's a farmer and well off, too; there'll be bread enough in the house for you. Don't go to forest villages anymore. Go to Druzdai, it's near a town and a German garrison. Partisans won't get there. You'll be safer from a disaster like this."

"And you, Uncle Karl, what will you do?"

"I . . . I . . . ."

He hesitated a moment, then went on. "I'll wander around here a little while yet. Then the hut will have to be rebuilt and the farm too."

221

"I'll go with you, Uncle Karl." Shmulik's eyes were full of pleading.

"What is it with you, boy? You would die of hunger. Go to Andrei Palka. Tell him I sent you. Go right down this road." He pointed out the way to Shmulik. "You'll arrive at the village, then just ask for him. Be well," he pushed him affectionately from behind. "I'll come visit you sometime."

"Good-bye, Uncle Karl!"

"God keep you, boy!"

Karl turned and disappeared down the road leading to the other end of the village, the same road taken by its residents on their last journey.

Shmulik in Druzdai

Before nightfall Shmulik arrived in the village of Druzdai. On the way he met a farmer half sitting, half lying on the seat of his wagon. The man gave him a short lift into the village and pointed out the yard of Andrei Palka.

"Is he a relative of yours, the *Starosta** Andrei?" the farmer asked, giving Shmulik the once-over from tip to toe.

"No. I'm bringing him regards, though," answered

* Head of the village.

Shmulik reluctantly. To avoid a thorough investigation, he jumped off the cart and began dragging his shoeless and injured feet up the hilly road leading to the village.

"Hey, where are you going, Jewboy?" called one of the village children seated on a fence, a band of ragamuffins around him. "Where you heading? There are Germans in the village." Shmulik heard laughter behind him as a snowball, hard as a rock, thwacked into his head.

He quickened his pace. It was not long before he found the yard of Andrei, apparently the richest of all the local farmers. Unlike the other houses, whose roofs were of straw, his house had a shingled roof and the fence in front was made of yellow pickets. He found the master of the house beside the gate, smoking a pipe and chatting with a neighbor.

"Hello, *khozyain*," Shmulik greeted him, his voice quavering with fear and hope.

Andrei removed his pipe from between his teeth and looked askance at the strange lad. "What's your business here?" he demanded.

"Aren't you the *Starosta* Andrei Palka?"

"And if I am?" the man answered irritatedly, looking at Shmulik's rag-encased feet.

"I'm from the village of Sosnovka. Karl sent me to you."

The two farmers were suddenly alert. "From Sosnovka, you say? You escaped from Sosnovka?"

"Then you know already?"

"We know, ah, we know," sighed the second farmer, a white-haired man. "A little bird brought the news."

"Is my godfather, Karl, still alive?"

"Alive, thank God. He sent me to you."

223

The *Starosta* saw that an inquisitive circle was beginning to gather. He tugged at Shmulik's sleeve.

"Come, let's go into the hut, we needn't talk of this outside."

"Times, such times," groaned the neighbor, as he entered after Andrei.

Shmulik looked about desperately for a place to sit down, but dared not do so without being invited to. He remained standing by the doorway.

Andrei took note and indicated a spot alongside him on the bench. "Sit down, boy, you must be exhausted from the road."

Only when he had sat down was Shmulik aware of the searing pain in his feet. Inadvertently he let a groan escape from his lips.

"Tell us how it happened," Andrei said in an ill-humoured voice, puffing smoke.

Shmulik began to speak. He tried to paint the massacre as he had heard it from Karl's lips, adding to the tale from his own bitterness and hurt.

Despite the *Starosta's* precautions, a few more neighbors entered the room, particularly women. Fearfully they followed the story, nodding their heads and wiping away the tears. "Oh, Jesus, oh, Holy Mother! The women, too, and the children. . . ."

Dour-faced, Andrei let Shmulik go on to the end without interrupting him. Shmulik was afraid to look into those angry, half-closed eyes peering from beneath bushy black eyebrows.

"And who are you, boy?" asked one of the women. "Are you one of the villagers?"

224

For an instant Shmulik was tempted to say that he was a village orphan who had survived by chance, but he decided at once that lying was too risky. Were it ever learned that he had been a foundling shepherd in the Afanas household he would not be able to ward off disaster.

"No," he said firmly. "I'm a war orphan. Good people in Sosnovka took me in. I'm Russian and my name is Vaska." He paused a second, then added with emphasis, "Old Karl took care of me. He was a good man." There was no need to mention Afanas, Shmulik decided.

Andrei eyed him suspiciously.

Shmulik repeated the tale he had told upon his arrival in Sosnovka.

"A Russian, you say?"

"A Russian, a *Vostochnik**—a Bolshevik, in other words," pronounced one of the farmers, wrinkling his lips.

"Bolshevik! Stop that! He's still a child . . . and an orphan," one of the neighbor women said. "Aren't you hungry?" she asked compassionately.

"Antonina, bring the boy something to eat," called Andrei. Turning to Shmulik again, he asked, scowling, "And who have you come here looking for?"

"I thought maybe . . . maybe you'd take me in. . . . Uncle Karl sent me," stammered Shmulik, hopelessly.

Andrei looked him over again.

"No," he declared icily. "I can't take strangers into my home. And besides, besides"—he stumbled momentarily

* A person coming from the Eastern regions that belonged to the U.S.S.R. before the war.

225

—"I'm the *Starosta*; guests come here. No, you can't stay with me."

Shmulik rose. He looked at the faces around him in despair. A dark night peered in from outside. Where would he sleep? He turned to the door.

"Hold on, boy," Andrei stopped him. "Maybe one of the farmers will take you in. I won't stand in the way of your staying in the village," he said with generosity. "Just don't show yourself to the Germans and the police. Spend the night and ask around tomorrow. Maybe Vasil will take you in, or Anton."

"*Starosta*, sir," answered Shmulik in a weak voice. "I'm big already. I can work. I don't want handouts."

"Big," smiled Andrei. "You're as skinny and small as a cat. What could you do on a farm?"

One of the farmers' wives tugged at Shmulik's sleeve. "You go to Fedka tomorrow, friend. He needs a worker. Come to me. I'll look after you."

No sooner had Shmulik set foot on the threshold of Fedka's house than terror gripped him. The table was covered with a green satin cloth with a flower design on it, and beneath a portrait of Mary stood a large silver menorah just like the one he recalled from his grandfather's home at the holiday season. A candle was burning in the menorah. A thickset woman with a colorful kerchief on her head was vainly attempting to put together two pieces of glass over the picture of a young man dressed in the uniform of a Polish soldier. Shmulik stopped in the doorway, not taking his eyes off the burning candle.

The peasant woman turned her head, looked at him

impatiently and said, "Are you the Vaska who's come here to work for us?"

"That's me," gulped Shmulik.

"You're too little. We won't get much out of you. . . ."

Shmulik said nothing.

Noticing how fixedly he eyed the menorah, the peasant woman remarked, "I vowed I'd light a candle every day before the portrait of the Holy Mother if my son would come back whole from the war"—she pointed to the picture of the soldier in her hands—"and now my Fedya has come home."

Before two weeks had passed Shmulik came to learn that the tablecloth and candelabrum were not the only things that had once belonged to Jews.

"Vaska, hey, Vaska, where have the devils run off with you?" That one cry of Fekla, the lady of the house, was always ringing in his ears. Her voice rasped through the yard from morning till night: Vaska, bring me water; Vaska, bring wood; Vaska, light the stove; Vaska, bring the sheep into the fold. . . .

Shmulik ran from one end of the yard to the other. She never left him alone for a minute. His food consisted of leftovers from their meals, his bed was a pile of hay in the stable loft. One morning when he came down half frozen, his big toe oozing, her pity was sufficiently stirred to give him a worn sheepskin coat.

It was not Shmulik alone who shuddered at her fuming. None other than the master of the house, Fedka, stood in fear of this Amazon. More than once Shmulik saw her hit him with a heavy fist. Fedka, lean and short, would shrink together, draw his head down between his shoulders, and

227

speed outdoors. From the yard Shmulik could hear him cursing her.

Fedka and Fekla had a daughter named Theophilia, a moronic girl who usually lay stretched out on the stove sucking her thumb. Deathly afraid of her loud-voiced mother, the daughter would hide in her corner whenever Fekla would sound off and would not emerge until the odor of food reached her nostrils. Theophilia was a glutton. Frequently she would leap up to snatch Shmulik's meager portion right from beneath his nose.

"Hey, you cow!" Fekla would guffaw at the sight of her daughter's gluttony, disregarding, in the process, hungry Shmulik's empty plate.

One day Shmulik was summoned hastily by the lady of the house and ordered to chop wood quickly and light the stove, as important guests were expected.

Fekla covered the table with a white cloth and set it with fine china plates and cups, and red and green crystal goblets. Then she opened the large wooden chest standing in the corner by the wall and always covered with a colorful blanket, and took from it a big bundle wrapped in a towel. For a moment she held it in her hand, indecisively. Then she began to unroll it; silver spoons and forks rang on the table. At the bottom of the trunk lay a gleaming silk tallis. Fekla seized it and said, "From this I'll sew a going-to-church blouse for the holidays. I'll set out the silverware myself," she added, pushing aside Shmulik who had been helping her.

Shmulik, however, stood rooted to the spot, his eyes roving from the tallis to the spoons. The Jewish initials were inscribed on every fork and spoon.

228

"What are you gaping at?" yelled Fekla. "Have a mind to steal anything? If I find one piece missing, I'll skin you alive!"

Suddenly she became suspicious. Shmulik's eyes were glued to the Jewish letters. For a moment she said nothing, then demanded accusingly, "Say, what are you so scared of those Jewish letters for, huh?"

Shaking off his temporary paralysis, Shmulik found himself on the brink of an abyss. He smiled and answered, "I never saw silk or silverware like that in all my life. We don't have anything like that in Russia. Are they really made of silver?"

A broad grin spread over Fekla's lips and she answered disdainfully, "Ah, what do you have there in Russia? *Kolkhozes*, that's all."

"And all this is yours? I never saw such nice things in one house."

Fekla beamed at her young helper's admiration. Her suspicions melted away.

"Anyone with brains in his head gets everything. From the Germans you can get all kinds of valuables only Yids had before. You've just got to know how to get along with the Germans."

"Your *khozyain* sure must be important to get hold of something grand as this." Shmulik pointed to the set table.

"My *khozyain*! All his life he never even managed to get a decent kerchief for his wife. That's from my son, Fedya. He's got the head of a *voyevoda** on him. Ah, he does all right for himself, my Fedya . . . and strong as the devil himself."

* Polish district chief.

229

"And what does your Fedya do?" Shmulik continued to ask, noting that the conversation was drawing her attention away from him.

"Don't you know yet? He's a policeman, my Fedya, a policeman in the county capital. He hobnobs with greats. The Germans respect my Fedya. He hasn't been home for two weeks now. You'll see him today. He's invited a few of his friends over for lunch. But what are you standing there for with your mouth hanging open?" she suddenly shouted. "Go on and get the wood ready to light the oven."

At dusk Shmulik heard the rumble of an automobile. He shook all over. The car stopped at the gate and from it emerged a man dressed in an officer's uniform. Three Germans wearing bright greenish outfits marched after him gravely. Shmulik darted behind the house and hid in the stable.

All that night Shmulik stayed in a corner of the stable, peering through a crack in the wall, his very bones dissolving. From the house, lit up more than usual, floated the sound of drunken voices. From time to time the door would open, a staggering figure would take a few uncertain steps, vomit, and then go back inside.

Shmulik stayed in his hiding place and did not come out even at the cries of the lady of the house. Before his eyes floated the silken tallis and Fekla's hands, holding large scissors and cutting away, cutting away. . . .

Days passed. Shmulik would carry buckets of water in his frozen hands as he ran over the ice and snow, his feet wrapped in filthy rags. He did all the work that was to be done, but never satisfied Fekla. She was always complain-

230

ing, and at the table she would administer a sound tongue-lashing to him and her "good-for-nothing" husband, too.

"The worker's just like the boss," she would jibe. "They both know how to eat all day. They could gobble down a whole ox, but when it comes to work—they're lumps of wood. You're just supposed to dance around and give them food and drink."

Fedka, long used to his shrewish wife's nagging, would go on eating his meal as calmly as if nothing but a persistent fly were buzzing about. But as for Shmulik, the food would stick in his throat, his eyes would fill with tears, and he would push away from the table before he finished the meal. Theophilia would polish off his food.

The house was all astir in preparation for visitors: Fekla's son was to receive a promotion. This time Fekla would not let her husband rest. She ran him from pillar to post, from the cellar to the coop, and from the coop to the attic, where fat sausages and ham hocks had been hanging since Christmas.

From the stove she removed a cake that filled the whole house with its rich aroma. Shmulik's mouth literally watered as he riveted his eyes on the wondrous concoction of fine flour, eggs, and raisins.

"What are you squinting at like a cat over cream?" he heard Fekla cry out in anger. "It's not for you, Jewboy!"

"Jewboy"—that was what she habitually called him. Was that merely her way of showing contempt for a Russian, a *Vostochnik,* or was she aware of his Jewish origins? *Still,* he often thought to himself, *they are keeping me here even though their son is a policeman and*

Germans come to the house. And maybe that's just why they're not afraid of working me like a slave. He tried to puzzle out the matter to his own satisfaction.

All during the long hours of baking, cooking, floor-scrubbing, and polishing, the cowlike Theophilia lounged about behind the stove taking in the goings-on with her bleary eyes. At the sight of each item her mother took out of the stove she would emit a purring sound, accompanied by sharp cries. Especially excited at the sight of the raisin cake, Theophilia leaped down from the stove, approached the table, and tried to sink her fingers into the soft, steaming mass. Her mother's rebuke chased her back to her lair.

The aroma of the delicacies prepared for the evening aroused Shmulik's appetite, as he had not eaten enough that day. He had been running about the farmyard from one job to the next, hungry and bitter. Upon returning to the room after chopping wood he found a few pots on the stove, in them leftovers of the morning meal and a few crumbs that the mistress of the house had put in the corner. Shmulik took what was there, sat in the hallway on the threshold, and ate. Fekla came in. She glared at her scullery boy, who shriveled beneath her gaze and went back inside, grumbling. Suddenly she began to scream.

"Ay, Jesus Maria, Jesus Maria! Murderers, thieves!"

Shmulik swiftly plunged in after her.

Fekla stood by the table, her kerchief pushed down onto her shoulders, wringing her hands and groaning. Before her on the plate lay the cake, mashed and broken, a third of it gnawed away as if by rats.

Fekla's face turned beet red and her eyes flashed fire.

"I'll kill you, I'll strangle you like a dog!"

232

"Theophilia did it!" gasped Shmulik.

Fekla turned toward him, her face twisted in rage. Suddenly she seized him by the hair and began pounding her fist into his face and shoulders.

"I'll give you 'Theophilia,' I'll give you 'Theophilia,' you damn little Jew bastard!" she gurgled, beating him unceasingly.

"It wasn't me. . . . I didn't even touch it. . . . I was chopping wood outside!" Shmulik struggled to break free from her grip.

"Not you, eh. . . . And who was it sitting in the hallway stuffing his guts? Theophilia, huh?"

Shmulik felt the darkness closing in on him; the walls of the house began to reel. With his last remaining strength he pushed Fekla away. Her head hit the wall and Shmulik burst outside, raced past the fence and on into the field. . . .

He stopped. The cold sliced through his ragged clothing. He looked about him: a barn, a few bare trees, but not a living soul. With faltering steps he drew near the building. The door was not locked. The granary was all but empty; in the corner there was only a pile of hay.

It turned dark. Shmulik still remained in the empty granary. Dull yellow patches illumined the village windows. Hunger began to oppress him. The cold grew more severe, pricking viciously. Shmulik climbed atop the haystack, burrowed deep into the hay, and curled up. He felt somewhat better. He tried to go to sleep, but fear for his future would not permit him.

What lay ahead? He could no longer return to Fedka's. Where to, then? What farmer would take him in?

233

Weary from these bleak thoughts and hunger, he sank off to sleep. At daybreak he wound his way back to the village.

Shmulik came upon hard times. He could not find a second farmer to take him in. He had to wander from farmyard to farmyard, chopping wood, tending animals, or doing any odd job for a crust of bread or a cup of milk. He would spend his nights in granaries and barns. More than once he was hooted or booted out of a stable or silo into which he had crept on the sly. For the longest time he had not changed clothing and his flesh was covered with lice.

He came to know many houses in the village and found in almost every one of them Jewish booty: expensive and delicate underwear, a Jewish matron's fur coat, silver Sabbath candlesticks, and even trunks full of merchandise plundered from Jewish stores.

Wandering among the courtyards, Shmulik became aware of an atmosphere of nervousness and disquiet widespread throughout the village. People would gather in small groups and whisper among themselves, casting glances in his direction. If he mustered enough courage to approach such a group, they would glare at him angrily and chase him away. "Off with you, Bolshevik spawn!"

Still he managed to pick up bits of information here and there. All the fragmentary reports contained the same word—partisans. The partisans—forest bandits as far as the local people were concerned—were roaming about the area. Of late they had become so bold that they even came near to the city, penetrating into the suburbs of the district capital. Once Shmulik heard how the night before they had burned down a mill under the very noses of the German army garrison. Fear glittered in the eyes of those relating the incident. The partisans were very cruel; they killed farmers and set fire to their farms.

Policemen began to appear in the village and the residents formed a civil guard. At night squads armed with rifles and submachine guns would walk about the village streets and alleys. The weapons were supplied by the Germans. Rifle shots and the rattle of machine-gun fire echoed not far from the village.

Shmulik's position grew ever more uncertain. Only infrequently would a farmer allow him to enter his yard, and give him some work to do for a mere crust of bread. Usually Shmulik would be chased away as soon as he turned up by the fence. Moreover, finding shelter for the night became more and more difficult. Roaming about at night was forbidden, and he was not always lucky enough to find himself a place to sleep, in some stable or barn. before curfew fell.

It was twilight. Night was swiftly falling and the cowsheds were giving off the odor of manure. The village women were carrying pails of steaming milk and the farmers were chatting leisurely as they puffed away on their pipes. At the end of the village, passing by one of the farmyards, Shmulik came upon a group of armed guardsmen grouped around a stranger, apparently an officer. Around them stood some of the village farmers and their children. The stranger was reading aloud from a leaflet that he held in his hand.

235

When Shmulik appeared at the end of the street, one
of the young boys picked up a stone, heaved it at him,
and yelled, "Jewboy! Get the hell out of here before we call
the Germans!"

The stranger raised his eyes and fixed them on Shmulik,
who had begun to turn away.

"Who is that rag?"

"He runs around between people's legs. . . ."

"He's from the village of Sosnovka, says he's a Russian,
from the eastern regions."

"From Sosnovka?" the officer sneered.

"Must be related to the bandits. . . . Maybe he's feeding
them information."

"A spy, no doubt," added another voice.

The officer eased the submachine gun from his shoulder.

The villagers pressed to the sides of the street, their
eyes greedily waiting to take in the drama.

But Shmulik was not waiting. Suddenly new strength
surged through his weary legs. His body uncoiled like a
spring and with one leap he was over the fence separating
him from the side alley. He was running full speed as the
submachine-gun bullets began raining in pursuit. When
he stopped for breath, the village lay far behind him.

Shmulik found himself in a desolate field mantled in
snow. Before him lay a broad dirt road, also covered in
white. The snow, which had been falling since noon, had
wiped out all traces of man or beast. Not far off loomed
the blackness of the forest.

I'll go back to Sosnovka, he thought in a flash, *maybe
I'll find Uncle Karl there.*

No, he reconsidered. *Old Karl hates the partisans; he*

236

sent me here to this village of murderers. I'll sit down a minute and rest, he decided. He recalled that it was dangerous to go to sleep when exhausted; it might lead to death by freezing. *I must reach the partisans. I'll surely find them in the forest,* he thought, and began trudging forward along the road leading into the woods.

When he reached the edge of the forest, the last lights of the village were swallowed behind him. Shmulik felt his limbs chained with an overwhelming weakness that he could not resist. He leaned against a lone pine tree standing by the crossroads and collapsed as his lids fell shut.

He was awakened by the cawing of a crow and the tread of an animal drawing near. Shmulik opened his eyes. From among the trees he could hear the rustling of dead leaves and the soft sound of footsteps being swallowed in the darkness. Shmulik shook snow off his arms and shoulders. His head was spinning and his every limb ached.

He tried to warm his frozen hands with the mist from his mouth. His toes pained him severely. He sat down on a stone and tried to remove his rags, but they were stuck to his toes which, he could see by the moonlight, were infected and oozing.

Shmulik recalled a Jew who had returned to the ghetto from a work camp with frozen toes, which after awhile became gangrenous and had to be amputated.

A feeling of despair attacked him.

"Mother, Mother, why didn't I go with you?" he wept softly.

Suddenly it seemed to him that he heard men's voices and neighing of horses. He strained his eyes in the dark and made out a sled hitched to a team of horses gliding lightly over the snow. Partisans! His heart stood still. But what if they were policemen, coming back from a patrol? Protruding from the sleigh before him he saw the rifle barrels of three armed men.

I'll run up to them, no matter what. . . . Better they should kill me, he resolved, and began racing toward the trampling horses.

By the light of the moon he could make out the fur hats atop the travelers' heads. No, they were not Germans!

"Partisans, stop, stop!" he shouted in the faces of the horses that were almost upon him. The sleigh halted.

A tall man armed with a submachine gun jumped down and approached Shmulik.

"Partisans, take me with you. . . . I have no one here."

"Who are you, boy?" the tall man asked him.

"I want to be a partisan. I'm thirteen already, I'll learn how to fight."

"Go home, boy, we don't have time to take care of babies."

"I have no home. They want to kill me. I'm a Jew," Shmulik blurted out in desperation.

The tall partisan who had turned to climb aboard the sleigh, stopped, grabbed Shmulik, and gazed into his tear-streaked face.

"A Jew? You're a Jew? I'm a Jew, too. . . . How did you get here?"

"I jumped off a train. I've been wandering around the villages here for half a year. Just today they shot at me. . . ."

The tall partisan laid an affectionate hand on Shmulik's shoulder.

238

"Boys," he cried, "we've found a son. You're in luck, youngster; you've met up with Jewish partisans."

Shmulik felt encompassed by relatives. He heard the others address the tall soldier as Anatoli. Swiftly he was swung aboard the sled, bundled into a fur coat, and someone's canteen was pressed to his lips.

"Taste this, my boy, a little liquor. You're freezing."

The sleigh pulled forward. Shmulik felt a pleasant warmth race through his limbs. He dropped his weary head onto the shoulder of one of the partisans and sank off to sleep.

In the Convent

When Shula opened her eyes it seemed that she was dreaming. The room in which she lay was small and white. Through the single window sunbeams streamed into the soft grayness, gilding the small square table standing by the wall and spilling onto the floor and the bed. Shula stretched out her hands; the sunbeams rippled through her fingers onto the clean white sheets.

Again she closed her eyes. She tried to bring back the events of the preceding few hours. *Maybe I'm still lying in the snow*, she thought, *by the iron fence, freezing, and just*

239

dreaming about a clean warm bed. Soon I'll be frozen stiff and the dream will end.

Suddenly she remembered her mother, left behind in their mad dash for life as the shots rang out behind them.

"Mommy, Mommy," her lips moved. "Where are you? Are you still alive?"

"What are you crying for, child?"

Only at those words did Shula realize there was someone else in the room. It was a woman with bright eyes and pale cheeks; robed in black, she sat alongside the bed. Why—she was a nun! Dressed the same way Sister Teresa had been! The woman bent over the bed and pressed a cup of milk to her lips.

"Drink, child, you'll feel better . . . you almost died. But Jesus' mercies are many."

The nun lifted her eyes to the portrait of the crucified Jesus hanging on the wall over the bed and made the sign of the cross, first upon her own chest and then over Shula's forehead and heart.

Shula tried to lift herself to a sitting position but immediately felt sharp shooting pains in her chest. She fell back on the pillow.

"Sister, tell me, where am I?"

"You are in a safe place, my child, in a convent of humble maidservants of God. Sister Teresa brought you here."

Sister Teresa, Sister Teresa. . . . Thoughts raced through Shula's weary brain. She could not piece together how she had gotten to Sister Teresa or what had happened to her. Her recollections were clouded. Her consciousness was filled with a vast, limitless whiteness streaked with black

240

and red. With a great effort she pulled up the blanket and closed her eyes.

Upon awakening she was aware of someone bending over her and stroking her hair.

"Mommy." Hope sprang up in her breast. She was afraid to open her eyes. Through her heavy eyelids she saw a black veil. A sigh escaped her lips.

"What is it, my child, does something hurt?"

Shula recognized the deep, caressing voice of Sister Teresa and opened her eyes.

"Sister Teresa," she whispered joyfully, catching the nun's hand. "How good that you are near me. . . . What will happen to me here? Won't they hand me over to the Germans?"

A sad smile flitted across the nun's lips.

"Nuns are not informers. Jesus commanded us to love even our enemies."

Shula understood that the question had raised dangerous suspicions about her origins and fell silent in confusion. Mrs. Weiss and Sister Teresa had met principally during working hours. They had spent many nights together on duty, speaking of the patients, doctors, and hospital employees and of what was going on in the world and on the front. But Mrs. Weiss and Shula had never talked with Sister Teresa about their private lives, their past, as though there were a silent agreement between them not to touch upon dangerous subjects. Mrs. Weiss had felt very strongly, however, that the nun was really not mistaken about their origins. She had been deeply indebted to the sister for her kindly ways and for the generosity she had shown herself and her daughter.

On this occasion, too, Sister Teresa understood the girl's

241

concern. For a moment she looked at her in silence and then said, "You are in a convent, my child. The authorities still respect these walls. But it would be best if you stayed here under the name of Onyté Dudaité. Only you will have to confess everything to Mother Anna Beatta. This is a holy place and heaven forbid that you should taint it with falsehood."

Shula tried once more to muster her courage to recall how she had reached the convent. A chill shook her body beneath the blanket as she experienced anew her fall in the snow by the iron gate.

"Sister Teresa, how did I get here?"

"On my way back from night duty at the hospital I found you unconscious in the snow by the convent gate."

"And my mother?" Shula's pale lips trembled. "Do you know anything, sister? I lost her . . . they shot at us."

The nun held her peace. Silently she stroked Shula's blond hair. She did not want to tell the sick child the bitter truth. Mrs. Weiss's dead body had been brought into the hospital that very night. She had been found in an alley not far from the hospital gate. Sister Teresa did not tell Shula that the kindly doctor who headed the department had been fired. For the time being they had left her alone —the Lithuanians still respected her nun's habit.

"When you are up and around I'll introduce you to the mother superior. But now don't torture yourself with sad thoughts. You were lucky that I found you. Sister Felicia will look after you. Try to get well quickly. I'm sure that in two days you'll be on your feet."

During her illness Shula was fed by Sister Felicia, the watery-eyed nun who had been at her bedside when she had first opened her eyes. She did not see Sister Teresa often, for the nun was busy with her work in the hospital. On the way back from night duty she would look in on her to see how she was getting along and offer words of encouragement.

Sister Felicia was tall and lean with hands as hard and bony as a man's. Shula was fascinated by her prominent blue veins. Those hands frightened her, but they knew how to flip over the mattress agilely, rub down Shula's body with alcohol, and break any resistance within Shula. They kneaded her inner being, as it were, making her like putty in the sister's hands.

Sister Felicia went about her work silently, giving out orders in a clipped monotonous tone as though she were dealing with someone far off or with a matter unconnected with the present time and place. After every meal she would have Shula say a blessing, facing the figure of Jesus on the cross hanging over her bed.

Her period of bed rest stretched on unbearably. All day she was enmeshed in absolute silence, broken only by the chiming of the church bells in the morning and evening and the occasional sound of human conversation rising from the yard. The sister would look at Shula without saying anything.

When Shula began to feel her strength returning, she mustered her courage and asked the nun to bring her something to read. One night she brought her two books. Shula took them gladly. On opening them, however, she saw they were *Lives of the Saints* and the New Testament. She began to leaf through the latter.

At the same time came the disciples unto Jesus, saying, "Who is the greatest in the kingdom of heaven?"

243

And Jesus called a little child unto him, and set him in the midst of them and said, "Verily I say unto you, except ye be converted and become as little children, ye shall not enter into the kingdom of heaven.

"Whosoever therefore shall humble himself as this little child, the same is greatest in the kingdom of heaven.

"And whoso shall receive one such little child in my name receiveth me.

"But whoso shall offend one of these little ones which believe in me, it were better for him that a millstone were hanged about his neck and that he were drowned in the depth of the sea.

*   *   *   *   *   *   *

"Take heed that ye despise not one of these little ones; for I say unto you, that in heaven their angels do always behold the face of my Father which is in heaven.

". . . It is not the will of your Father which is in heaven that one of these little ones should perish."

Shula stopped reading. She remembered the murder of Yisraelik.

But those two Lithuanian killers were Christians and spoke in the name of Jesus, she thought. *And Ursula, our maid, how she used to run to church every Sunday. She used to lecture Mother for not praying. But my mother never murdered anyone. None of the Jews I know ever did.*

Shula dropped the book. After a moment she picked it up again. What fault was it of Jesus if people corrupted his teachings? Why was this so, she wondered as she continued reading.

244

And behold, one came and said unto him, "Good Master, what good thing shall I do, that I may have eternal life?"

And he said unto him, "Why callest thou me good? There is none good but one, that is, God; but if thou wilt enter into life, keep the commandments."

He saith unto him, "Which?" Jesus said, "Thou shalt do no murder, thou shalt not commit adultery, thou shalt not steal, thou shalt not bear false witness.

"Honor thy father and thy mother; and thou shalt love thy neighbor as thyself."

The young man saith unto him, "All these things have I kept from my youth up; what lack I yet?"

Jesus said unto him, "If thou wilt be perfect, go and sell what thou hast and give to the poor and thou shalt have treasure in heaven; and come and follow me."

But when the young man heard that saying, he went away sorrowful, for he had great possessions.

Then said Jesus unto his disciples, "Verily, I say unto you, that a rich man shall hardly enter into the kingdom of heaven.

"And again I say unto you, it is easier for a camel to go through the eye of a needle, than for a rich man to enter into the kingdom of God."

But those who killed Jews included many poor workers, thought Shula, *and people without a penny to their name.* How did it all make sense then?

Unenthusiastically, Shula opened the second book, but soon found it engaging. The sufferings of the saints reminded her of the persecution of the Jews.

One morning Sister Felicia brought Shula a long gray dress that reached to her ankles, a white apron, a dark headdress, and a pair of sandals.

245

After Shula dressed, the nun looked her over from head to toe and wrinkled her lip. From beneath Shula's headdress a few golden curls protruded, hanging down over her forehead.

"You're not heading to a ball, but to Mother Beatta," she whispered sternly between compressed lips. "Remember, you are in a convent; primping is an abomination."

Shula was confused. The nun tugged at the headdress until it came halfway down her forehead, covering the wayward hair, and then motioned to Shula to follow her.

The door to the tiny room opened and Shula emerged into a long, gray hallway. On both sides were closed doors that shone bright in contrast to the dull vaulted ceiling. The floor of the hallway was carpeted with dark matting that swallowed up the sound of their footsteps. At the end of the corridor was a circular room enclosed by walls containing ceiling-high windows. That room also contained no furniture, except for unpainted wooden benches that stood beneath the windows. From the two walls opposite, portraits of the Holy Family looked down. To the right, beneath a large oil painting, were a few steps leading to a doorway concealed by heavy curtains.

Sister Felicia went up the steps and cautiously knocked on the door. It opened and Shula saw before her a room slightly larger than the cell she occupied. Two large windows flooded the white walls with sunbeams. It seemed to be an office or someone's living quarters. By the window stood a writing desk covered with dark green material under glass; on it were writing implements and office materials. Alongside the desk stood a bookcase crammed with folders and thick leather-bound books with gold let-

246

ters imprinted on them. On the other side was a narrow couch upholstered in dark green leather, and on the wall between the windows was a large wooden cross with the figure of Jesus. Two steps led to the figure. A small pillow, also encased in green leather, lay on the top step.

Upon entering, Shula raised her eyes. She saw an old woman, about seventy, whose face was deeply lined but whose eyes were full of life; they flashed as she looked at Shula.

"I have brought the girl, Mother Beatta," said Sister Felicia, respectfully kissing the old woman's shriveled hand.

"Thank you very much, Sister Felicia."

The nun left and quietly closed the door, leaving Shula very much confused, standing in the doorway.

Mother Beatta looked at Shula and a half-mocking smile passed across her lips. She motioned Shula nearer.

Shula approached the table.

"What is your name?"

"Onyté Dudaité," she answered softly, her lips trembling.

The nun's face grew stern, her smile vanished, and her eyes grew piercing.

"Don't forget whom you are standing before," she uttered gravely. "You're not in a Jewish shop. Here you have to speak the truth."

Shula turned white.

Seeing that Shula was shaking with fear, the nun tried to soften her approach. "This is not the Gestapo, daughter, you needn't fear."

Shula remembered what Sister Teresa had said: "You will have to tell the truth to Mother Beatta."

247

"My name is Shula Weiss," she whispered in a strangled tone.

For an instant that mischievous, mocking light flashed in the old woman's eyes, but then they were quiet and somber.

"I realized immediately that you were a Jewess. This is a very grave matter. You know that anyone harboring a Jew is liable to the death penalty. We cannot give refuge here to the despised of God. The Jews themselves are to blame for their calamity. The curse of God lies upon them. So our Lord Jesus said to them:

O Jerusalem, Jerusalem, thou that killest the prophets, and stonest them which are sent unto thee, how often would I have gathered thy children together, even as a hen gathereth her chickens under her wings, and ye would not.

Behold, your house is left unto you desolate.

For I say unto you, ye shall not see me henceforth till ye shall say, "Blessed is he that cometh in the name of the Lord."

"Thus the Jews will never know salvation until they repent for their rebelliousness and acknowledge the Messiah of God, Jesus."

Shula said nothing. She realized that under the circumstances she dare not. Her silence pleased the nun.

"How old are you, daughter?"

Shula was about to say "twelve," but she remembered that since the outbreak of the war two and a half years had passed; but then, could those years be considered life? At times it seemed to her that her childhood had fled, never to return, and that she was rapidly growing old.

248

"Fifteen," she said, after a moment's hesitation.

"Fifteen," the nun repeated. "You are still young, and I hope that the Holy Mother will have mercy upon you and illumine your spirit with the Holy Ghost. Sister Teresa has asked me to help you as much as possible, so I am ready to take the risk of giving you shelter. Perhaps in the course of time, you will be privileged to join the large body of those who sanctify Jesus' name, and will find within these walls rest for your wandering soul."

The old woman rang. Silently the door opened and Sister Felicia entered.

"Transfer her to the wing of new pupils," said Mother Beatta. "Sister Felicia will be your sponsor and will look after you," she added, again facing Shula. "You can turn to her for anything you need. If the Holy Mother be merciful I will receive no complaints about you," she concluded. Shula turned to leave.

"Bend your knee and kiss the mother's hand," whispered Sister Felicia, stopping Shula at the door.

It was not long before Shula adjusted to the routine of her new life. Her peace of mind seemed to return. On the surface, she was content.

She did her assigned tasks faithfully, even painstakingly. She stood out because of her keen grasp of things and her fine memory. Her teachers were pleased with Shula. They felt that she was destined to become an exemplary nun. Never did they see her go idle or engage in activities unfit for a trainee, such as prettying herself before a mirror or chatting with a man who chanced to be near. No one ever heard her laugh or talk loudly with the other girls. Gener-

249

ally she would be off by herself in a corner bent over some task or a book.

Three major activities occupied the pupils' day: prayer, work, and study. About thirty girls from the ages of nine through seventeen lived in a special wing at the end of the convent courtyard. Eight to ten girls lived in one long room, their narrow iron beds standing by the walls. Between the beds stood small night tables, one for both adjoining beds. It was cold and uncomfortable in the sleeping quarters. Covered with white sheets, the beds looked like soldiers lined up in formation.

Before sunup, the nun on duty would awaken the girls for morning prayers. Shula was glad to jump out of bed at the sound of the bell, quickly put on her gray uniform, straighten the sheet on her bed, and hurry out of the room. The girls would go out into the courtyard in pairs and from there to the convent's small chapel.

The grayness of the wintry dawn was illumined by a large chandelier hanging from the ceiling and by a second, smaller chandelier in front of the pulpit. The girls would come in two at a time and kneel to one side of the pulpit. Then the other residents of the convent—the novices and nuns—would enter and kneel on the other side. Finally, when all were in their places, the mother superior would appear, accompanied by a priest who would conduct the mass.

After the mass came two hours of work. Some girls cleaned rooms, others worked in the kitchen or the yard. Breakfast was accompanied by brief prayers, again followed by work until noon. Some older students also had various jobs in the city. The convent owned a kindergarten for abandoned children and orphans, together

250

with a laundromat and a sewing workshop. There the girls learned how to look after little children and to sew and embroider.

Following afternoon prayers they would gather according to age groups in classrooms. There were eight girls in Shula's group. Brother Boniface, a young monk, taught them. Mostly they studied religious topics: prayers, principles of the Catholic faith, the history of the Church, hymns, and saints' lives. The studies depressed Shula. She yearned to study nature and literature. Once she even fell asleep during a lesson, but a roommate saved her by poking her in the ribs. She was aided greatly by her excellent memory. Very quickly she learned by heart the numerous quotations from the hymns and the saints' lives. The teacher would comment on Onyté's industriousness in class and would praise her to her supervisors.

One thing Brother Boniface found difficult to understand—why such a talented girl never took part in class discussions. The monk had studied education and looked upon himself as a modern teacher. He strove to develop "independent thinking" in the girls through discussing and debating the tenets of the Church. All the arguments and all questions had one answer though: "It is God's will; we mortals with our feeble minds cannot grasp His wondrous ways."

Shula's classmates were not friendly with her; they considered her stuck-up. She did not take part in their chitchat, or the laughter and tricks with which they would purposely tease the sisters. Many of them had no intention of becoming nuns. They had wound up in the convent for lack of a home due to the circumstances of war. Most of them wanted to learn a profession and leave the convent after the war. Some of them even mocked the religiousness of the nuns, sticking their tongues out at them behind their backs. Others would get in good with the nun in charge of their education, taking upon themselves fasts and mortifications to show how pious they were; secretly, though, they would break such fasts.

Shula found all these devious schemes disgusting. At first the girls tried to mock her, calling her Davatka—a holier-than-thou spinster—but deep down they respected her. In the end they left her alone.

Still, after the many months of torment Shula had endured since the war began, she found that the convent afforded her peace and safety. It seemed to her that only the mother superior, and Sister Teresa, and the nun responsible for her education, Sister Felicia, knew her secret. From time to time Sister Felicia would invite Shula to her room, talk with her of many things, and sound her out for her future plans.

Shula did not conceal from the nun her desire to become a nurse. She still hoped to meet her mother someday and work with her. Sister Felicia encouraged her and said that the convent would help her learn that profession. Many nuns worked in hospitals. But to do so she would have to bind her future up with the convent. Shula would say nothing, infuriating the nun. Sister Felicia was used to hearing all kinds of vows and promises from the girls as they sank to their knees and raised pious eyes heavenward. Still, Sister Felicia was experienced. More than once she had caught the girls lying to her. Shula, on the other hand, called forth her respect. *It is not easy to penetrate into this girl's closed-off soul,* she thought.

252

When feelings of loneliness overwhelmed her, Shula would slip out of her room at night to wander alone through the halls and corridors of the convent. The building would be meshed in dark shadows, giving the hallways and vaulted ceiling the character of an ancient cave, a hiding place for the first Christians fleeing tyrannic persecution.

Happy were the hours when Shula was in the company of Sister Teresa, but only rarely was she allowed to accompany her friend to the city. Sister Teresa, an art lover, would lead Shula through churches and monasteries, explaining to her the various architectural styles and art objects. Shula loved to visit the lovely church of Saint Anne or even feast her eyes from afar on its many towers and ornamentations.

Two or three times a week the girls would emerge from the convent walls to take a walk together. Paired up in a long line, they would stroll through the city streets, sloshing through the melting snow, peering into houses and half-empty display windows to break the boredom.

Shula, however, found these walks somewhat refreshing. She would fix her eyes on the passersby in hopes of meeting a certain someone. At times the girls would come upon a group of Jews cleaning the streets. The Star of David showed yellow on their bent backs, and their ashen faces blended with the trampled snow, which these shadows of human beings were shoveling with their last strength into the gutters.

Heart pounding, Shula would glance at the tortured faces. Perhaps? . . . But she looked in vain.

The bitter winter was almost past. The residue of fierce snowstorms had covered the ground for months. Despite the blood that had been absorbed by the earth, the snow showed no red. It remained sparkling white in the pale rays of the winter sun until it turned gray beneath pedestrians' feet.

By April murky, melted water filled the gutters. At times a foul wave of the stuff would slosh over the sides of the gutter and flood the adjacent sidewalk. Pedestrians would wrinkle their noses, lift their feet, and mutter, "Seems there aren't any more Jews around, but Jewish ways of fixing things haven't changed. . . ."

Sister Teresa had promised to take Shula with her one evening for a walk. After studies, therefore, Shula entered the round waiting room in front of the mother superior's office. She wanted to go on to the long hallway with two sets of doors leading to the nuns' cubicles. Suddenly she froze. A group of girls was bunched together in the hallway by the window, all wearing black headgear and dark, long habits similar to the attire of pupils in her own convent. The girls seemed frightened and utterly perplexed. On the bench, which was loaded down with bundles and baggage, sat two strange nuns. From beyond the door to Mother Beatta's room burst voices. Shula wanted to turn about, but her curiosity got the better of her. She crossed the hallway, stopped before Sister Teresa's door, and knocked. No one answered. What had happened to Sister Teresa? she wondered. Had she forgotten about their appointment?

This was the first time Shula had not found her in the room at the set time. She had made up her mind to go back when the tall, slender figure of the nun appeared at the end of the corridor, tripping forward swiftly, which was most unlike her.

Without saying a word, she opened the door and motioned Shula in.

"Sit down, Onyté," she said, pointing to the footstool as she herself took a place by the window. A few minutes passed in silence. Shula looked at the nun's slightly bent back hiding the window and waited. Finally Sister Teresa turned. Her face was redder than usual and her eyelids were fluttering nervously. Apparently the nun too had been seized by the prevailing general disquiet.

"Child, have you seen the group of girls?" the nun suddenly asked, striding to and fro in the tiny room. "This morning they were ejected from the Convent of the Ursuline Sisters. They don't even respect holy places anymore, these anti-Christs," she fumed, "and still they consider themselves Catholics. The pagans!"

Shula kept silent, uncomprehending. Who were the pagans? The Germans?

"Ah, God in heaven—'Don't give the pig horns, for he will gore the whole world,'" sighed the nun as she fell into her chair. "Only a few years ago they got Vilna* and

* In 1921 Vilna was captured by the Polish general Zeligowski. Through the years the Lithuanians demanded from international

255

already they think they own our souls," she continued to mutter between her tightly pressed lips.

It seemed to Shula that the nun was not aware of her at all but was simply talking to herself.

Finally she realized that Sister Teresa, a Pole, was talking about the Lithuanians. From her friendly contact with the nun Shula had concluded long since that Sister Teresa had no great love for Lithuanians. Even "Christian charity" did not soften the irritation which crept through her remarks from time to time. She was unable to accept the subjugation of Poland and never forgave the Lithuanians for taking over Vilna.

After she calmed down a bit, the nun told Shula that the Lithuanian authorities had closed down the convent for fear it had been maintaining links with the Polish underground. A few of the nuns had been arrested and the remainder had been exiled. The pupils had been transferred to their convent.

"Such anti-Christs!" Sister Teresa would not remain calm. She knelt beneath a cross and sank into prayer.

That night, upon entering her sleeping quarters, Shula saw how congested they had become. Two beds had been added. In the one adjacent to hers chestnut-colored hair peeped out from beneath the blanket. Shula's new neighbor was sleeping, her head buried in the small pillow.

Shula woke up with the nagging feeling that someone was staring at her. She opened her lids and met two dark

---

agencies the return of the city, the capital of their nation. Their pleas went unheeded. Only in 1939 did they get it from the U.S.S.R., and they in turn began to oppress the Polish population.

brown eyes fixed on her. Shula was shaken. *I know this girl*, she thought, vaguely recollecting the face.

The new girl trembled, turned over, and pulled the blanket over her head.

Who is that girl? Where have I seen her? The question tormented Shula. Suddenly the answer floated up from the back of her mind: *I know her. It's Rivka! Rivka Wilensky from Mapu Street!*

A wave of happiness swept over her. Rivka Wilensky was alive and at her side!

Shula looked about her. Everyone was sleeping. Pale moonbeams illumined the hall faintly, together with the dull light of a small candle flickering beneath the portrait of the Virgin Mary. Without a moment's hesitation Shula got out of bed and approached her friend. Carefully she drew the blanket aside, revealing the girl's head. How changed her face was, how long and how deep-sunken the cheeks that were once so round. There were blue rings about her eyes as well.

"Rivka," she whispered. "Rivka, is it you?"

The girl's limbs snapped together as though she had been bitten by a snake. The fear of death was in her eyes.

"Rivka, don't be afraid, it's me, Shula." She tried to seize her friend's hand and embrace her.

The other's body began to quake all over, her face contorted, her lips trembling.

"I'm no Rivka. . . . I don't know any Rivka, I'm Birutė Magdalena," she cried in Lithuanian. "What do you want with me, Jewgirl?"

She pushed Shula away and curled up at the end of the bed. "I'm a good Catholic and soon I'll be a nun. You

257

see?" She cried in a choked voice as she brought from beneath her shirt a large, thick cross hanging on her chest. She began to kiss it passionately.

"But, but . . . I recognize you. We lived together on Mapu Street," Shula protested, her voice weak and tearful.

"No, no. You don't know me. I never lived on Mapu Street. . . . I never had anything to do with Yids!" she almost shouted. Shula feared that she would awaken the other girls.

"If you don't leave me alone, I'll yell and tell everybody you're a Jewgirl who snuck into the convent," she hissed, snakelike, into Shula's face. "I hate Yids; Jesus cursed them!"

Shula pulled back in shock. *Could I have made a mistake?* she wondered. *Why did I tell her who I was?*

For hours she tossed in bed, sleepless. When she woke up in the morning she no longer saw her friend in the hall. She did see her in the chapel after prayers, where a brief introduction ceremony took place. The mother superior announced every girl by name and each one kneeled before her and kissed her hand.

"Biruté Maria Magdalena," she called out. "The sisters have informed me that already you have decided to join the brides of Jesus. Be blessed in our midst."

The mother superior bent down and kissed the girl on the forehead.

Leaving the chapel, Shula noticed that the girl was not in sight. She paused a moment in the doorway and looked inside. Biruté was lying face down on the empty chapel floor before the crucifix.

258

At lunch, too, her new neighbor was missing. When she inquired of Sister Felicia, the latter informed her that the new girl excelled in her fervid piety and that in observance of her move to new surroundings had taken upon herself a special fast. She was praying that the Holy Mother would brighten her path in her new home.

Only at supper did the girl enter the hall accompanied by the nun on duty. Her pale cheeks contrasted sharply with the chestnut brown curls hanging down from beneath her veil, and her dark brown eyes.

"This is Biruté Maria Magdalena," said Sister Felicia. "She is still young but is already outstanding. She is as serious in her love of God as a mature nun. Learn from her."

No, I didn't make a mistake, that's Rivka and no Biruté Magdalena, said Shula to herself, no longer hesitant now that she had seen the girl a second time. *That's Rivka Wilensky from Mapu Street, only she's grown a lot during the war years.*

Shula decided to stay close to the new arrival and find an opportunity for an additional conversation. "Biruté Magdalena" sat alongside Shula at the table and greeted her with a nod of the head as though they had first met that very moment.

One week followed upon another, months went by, and nothing out of the ordinary broke the monotony of convent life. The new girls joined the classes. Every morning they too would go out to work and in the afternoon attend the lessons of Brother Boniface. Rivka did not do as well in her studies as Shula. Frequently she would make a mistake

259

in quoting from the writings of the saints. But in "theoretical discussions" she had the upper hand. The teacher always praised her answers.

She prolonged her prayers more than the sisters. Often she could be seen kneeling or lying full length before the crucifix, and she would frequently take on fasts and additional mortifications. As far as Shula was concerned it was as though Rivka did not even see her. Never did Rivka turn to her, and whenever they approached each other she would walk around Shula.

Shula, too, stopped seeking an opportunity to converse with the new girl. Rivka's comments and answers in class discussions of religion revolted her. She was particularly hurt to see the girl emphasize her hatred of Jews and justify the Germans.

Once Shula could not restrain herself. "You're so religious," she challenged, "and yet Jesus says, 'Forgive . . . until seventy times seven.' Why do you justify the murder of the Jews?"

Biruté turned her back on her. "The Jews didn't sin seventy times seven, but many times more. Two thousand years have passed since the time they crucified our Lord Jesus and still they have not repented. There is no atonement for them."

The Meeting

The spring days of 1944 stretched out in the city of Vilna, which seemed calm and peaceful, going about its daily life. Yet a discerning eye could see ferment beneath the peaceful outer shell of stability and security.

Lines outside the food stores grew longer. Here and there people would gather to whisper among themselves, but at the sight of an army man they would scatter, disappearing inside the gates. The men wearing uniforms with the sign of the skull on the lapel had disappeared; the number of young people in general shrank. From time to time the roar of airplanes would cause panic, as citizens' eyes fearfully scanned the skies.

The calm arrogance that had characterized Lithuanian faces had changed to a drab fear. The more Lithuanian uniforms—gray with a thin yellow stripe—that disappeared from the street, the more brown and light green German uniforms seemed to appear. Only the soldiers' pace seemed more hurried now, as though they were afraid of missing a train. Frequently automobiles would rush by, rumbling and honking deafeningly, and disappear around a corner.

The news from the eastern front was ominous for the Germans. Most of the civilian patients had been evacuated from the hospitals to make room for military casualties. Convoy after convoy of trucks and railroad cars arrived bearing wounded soldiers. Sometimes they would un-

261

load in the city, but usually they would carry the troops westward. Rumor had it that the forests were full of army deserters. Travel along the roads bordering the forests was impossible—they were under the control of armed gangs of bandits.

Bit by bit this information trickled into the convent. At times Sister Teresa herself would let something drop. The nun had grown even more silent and only very rarely did she turn to Shula. One day she did not come back from work. Shula wondered what had happened to her. Nothing was said in the convent, and Shula's question was greeted with grim silence on the part of Sister Felicia.

At times when the girls walked through the city, a barrage of shots would slice through the air and people would scatter to hide in gates and courtyards. Only Shula did not panic. Pandemonium of that sort bolstered her secret hopes. At times she would recall the winter's evening when Anatoli had fled their room and she had lost her mother.

One day Sister Felicia told her that the convent, aware of her desire to be a nurse, would send her to work in a nearby hospital the next day. Biruté Magdalena was sent along with her. One of the older sisters accompanied the girls.

From that day on they made their way back to the convent at dusk. Bone-tired after twelve consecutive hours of work, they would eat, pray quickly, collapse onto their beds, and sink into sleep.

Group strolls through the city became rare but Shula did not mind missing them. She was too tired.

One Sunday, when Vilna's throngs were streaming out

of the churches and flooding the streets, Shula, walking with her convent companions, noted a boy dressed in a brown peasant's sheepskin coat, standing to the side on the pavement, his hands thrust into his pockets. She was in the process of going around him when the boy turned his face and their eyes met.

Shmulik! Her senses reeled in fear and joy. She was scarcely able to suppress a cry. Shmulik paled and took half a step forward. All this happened in the blink of an eye. Then Shmulik's face assumed a mask of indifference; he turned and looked about like a village boy thrust for the first time into the hubbub of a major city thoroughfare.

The girls behind Shula bumped into her. Turning her head, she saw that the boy was following the procession.

A car moved out of an open gate, blocking their path. The lines came to a halt. Shula observed that the boy too had stopped.

There was no doubt about it—it was Shmulik and he was trailing her.

Looking again, she saw Shmulik take a piece of paper from his pocket, fill it with tobacco, and roll a cigarette between his fingers like a ragamuffin imitating his elders. Shula followed his movements intently. He lit the cigarette, drew near the line of girls, and flicking his eyes at Shula casually dropped the pack of matches on the sidewalk. Then he swiftly passed by her and disappeared into a side street.

Shula slipped out of her shoe, which was slightly too large for her, and stopped to put it on again. In bending down she picked up the matches and hid it in a pocket of her dress. Before long she was standing in front of the convent gate. Her sixth sense told her to look about once more. Standing by another gate was Shmulik, watching the girls as they filed into the convent courtyard.

Her heart pounding, Shula rushed to the bathroom and opened the pack of matches. Written on the inside cover in pencil was the message: "I'll wait for you at 10 P.M. Come."

Ten o'clock . . . ten . . . Shula knew that she could not get out of the convent courtyard at that hour. The gates closed at nine. And even if she managed to slip out, how would she get back? she wondered. But she had to meet Shmulik; and she had to speak with him.

Her brain worked feverishly. With difficulty she forced herself to eat that night, so that she would not attract the attention of her companions.

She decided that at eight o'clock she would leave the convent, go to the hospital where she worked—she could find some excuse later—and at ten be at the meeting place.

But then, where was she to meet Shmulik? She would walk down the street slowly, she decided. No doubt he would be waiting for her somewhere. . . .

At nine-thirty Shula was advancing along the city's main street, which was steeped in darkness. It was the first time since her arrival in the convent that she had been alone at that hour in the empty street. Strolling toward her slowly she saw a policeman. He cast a quick glance at her and passed by. Soon the convent rose before her.

Fear gripped her. What had gone wrong? Had her imagination misled her? Would Shmulik not come? Had he been caught?

"Shula!" she suddenly heard a voice behind her. "Don't

turn around, don't look at me. Walk toward the ruins."

It was Shmulik's voice. She would have recognized it among a hundred others. Shaking with emotion she turned into the alley containing a row of houses damaged during the bombing, but still half standing amid the rubble.

Drawing near the second house, she saw a figure disappear inside it. She shuddered. Was someone trailing her?

"Over here, Shula, over here," she heard Shmulik's voice.

For an instant they stood before each other, speechless. Then Shula burst into tears and fell into her dear friend's arms.

Shmulik hugged her and stroked her hair. He too had no words. In the joy of their first reunion Shula did not notice the presence of a second man in the ruins, who regarded them in silence.

"Why, that's my warm-hearted nurse, Onyté!" she suddenly heard a joyous voice from the darkness. Before she could turn her head she was in the strong embrace of Anatoli Hakim.

In the Partisans' Forest

After Shmulik had swallowed some of the liquor given him by one of the young partisans, he fell into a deep sleep. When he woke up he found himself lying in an earthen hut propped up with tree beams. In the center of the hut stood a tin barrel dispersing heat. Through the small opening in the barrel the fire showed red—a partisan stove. Shmulik smiled in contentment at the sight of the red glow carpeting the floor.

A pleasant warmth spread through his body. After the months of hard living he had experienced in the village, at last rest and peace were his.

At first he was afraid to stir his hand or foot lest the wondrous dream dissolve and once again he find himself frozen beneath the icy winter skies. But the more he took in his surroundings, the more he grew certain that this was no dream. Gingerly he withdrew his hand from beneath the sheepskin coat and felt the wall. It was a pine beam; he could even scratch into the wood with his fingernails. And the window, though very small, did let the light in. His eyes sought out the hut's doorway.

Alongside the tiny window Shmulik made out a few dirt steps leading up, but he did not see the opening. Then fatigue overcame him and he slept.

"Hey, boy, how long do you expect to sleep? A partisan's life isn't for snoozing!" he suddenly heard someone chuckle nearby. Shmulik opened his eyes and jerked up to a sitting position.

"What are you so scared of? You a field mouse or something?"

Standing before Shmulik was the tanned, mustachioed Anatoli, whom his friends called Tulik.

"How are you doing, lad?" he asked quietly. "*Nu*, manage to get some rest? Here, I've brought you lunch."

266

He handed Shmulik a tin mess kit filled with thick soup containing chunks of meat. Smiling, he watched the youngster gobble down the food.

"Come along, young fellow, I'll introduce you to the commander," he said.

Shmulik was confused. "What do I have to say to the commander? Won't he kick me out?"

"Let's hope not," smiled Anatoli, as before. Shmulik was about to get out of bed but no sooner did the soles of his feet touch the floor than he doubled up in pain. His frozen toes had warmed up under the sheepskin and now felt as though they were on fire.

"What is it, boy?" asked Anatoli, peering into Shmulik's face.

"My feet—I can't walk."

Anatoli looked closely and said nothing. Quickly he left the hut and very shortly returned with another partisan.

Shmulik opened his eyes wide. From beneath the other partisan's brown hat fell chestnut-colored curls reaching down to a man's coat collar. Then Shmulik realized it was a girl dressed in man's clothing.

"Lisa, look at the boy's feet," Anatoli turned to her, bending down to remove the rags that clung to Shmulik's wounds.

The partisan named Lisa unslung her bag and took out a few bottles, scissors, and bandages.

"I need some hot water," she said softly, seeing that the rags were stuck so firmly to Shmulik that every tug was agony. Shmulik did his best to hide his anguish.

"It's nothing, I'll take it off," he said, yanking at the rag clinging to his right foot. The cloth ripped off, together with flesh from his toe, revealing a deep, putrid, pus-filled wound.

Lisa scowled. "That doesn't look very pretty," she said. She bathed the wounds, bandaged them, and ordered Shmulik to stay in bed.

"When will I be able to get up?" he asked worriedly, "It's no fun lying here; I want to fight the Germans."

Anatoli and Lisa looked at each other, then burst out laughing. Shmulik flushed deeply.

Why are they laughing at me? he thought. *Did I say something foolish?*

"Never mind, young fellow, you'll get some fighting in yet," Lisa patted him on the shoulder. "In two days I'll be back to change your bandages. For the time being you just lie quietly and see that they don't get wet, hear?"

Shmulik looked into the girl's face. She seemed very young. *She can't be any older than me,* he thought, *and already she's a real partisan. And me . . . ?*

He did not remove his eyes from Lisa. Were it not for her long hair, he would have taken her for a boy. She was tall, and her men's clothing and boots fit well.

"So long, kid, get well quick." She turned to him once more, and Shmulik saw that her face was steeped in sadness.

Who is this Jewish girl? he thought, once he was left alone. *How did she reach the partisans?*

For about two weeks Shmulik lay a prisoner in his bed. His toenails dropped off and his wounds slowly began to form scabs. Whenever Anatoli was not in the hut, Lisa and Anatoli's friends looked after him.

268

Shmulik had managed to become acquainted with most of the Jewish partisans and with the non-Jews, Russian and Byelorussian, as well. Three young men besides Anatoli lived in his hut—two Russians and a Jew. But only rarely would they all be together. Someone was always missing, out on a mission or on guard.

There were fourteen Jewish partisans in the regiment. Anatoli was in command of a platoon. Shmulik liked two of the Jewish partisans especially: Gedalia and Asher. They were staunch comrades who never parted. They went out on missions together, came back together to the hut to rest, and would present themselves at the kitchen together at mealtimes. Nonetheless, they constantly argued loudly and endlessly.

Outwardly they were perfect opposites. Gedalia was tall, husky, and broad-shouldered. His head was large, his hair curly, and his neck short. He was famous in the regiment as an expert machine gunner. He spoke calmly in a deep and pleasant baritone. He did not speak very much of his past. All that was known of him was that before the war he had been a student in a yeshiva.

One night some of his comrades tried to poke fun at his rabbinical background. Gedalia rose wordlessly and disappeared into the forest, not returning until dawn when the platoon had to take over the guarding of the camp.

His Jewish companions noticed that on Friday evenings when Gedalia was free, he would slip off into the woods—to snatch a few minutes for prayer, it was whispered.

On missions he would generally be in the first rank, his

machine gun on his shoulder. The company commander respected his bravery and more than once, upon the completion of a mission, expressed the company's gratitude at a solemn festive formation and recommended him for a citation of valor in the official battle report.

Gedalia loved singing. Evenings, at the campfire, his sweet baritone voice would spill out into the forest. At times, when he and his Jewish friends were alone, they would succeed in wheedling a *zemer'l* out of him—the sweet tones of a Hassidic melody would waft through the hut—or a Jewish folk song or a fragment of a prayer. But only rarely did Gedalia do as they asked. Usually he would stop their pleading with a Russian partisan song.

Asher was a completely different sort. Short and skinny with a small face, standing alongside Gedalia he looked like a student beside his teacher. His movements were nervous and jerky. He took tiny, quick steps, like a girl. His hair was smooth and thin. He was talkative by nature and often spoke of his village and family, of his childhood and his partisan exploits. At times he would forget what he had said before and would come out with a second, very different version. His friends, who generally preferred to tell jokes among themselves, loved to listen to Asher talk. He was a master storyteller. He especially excelled at describing, often humorously, life in his village. His listeners became wrapped up in his stories and laughed deeply, forgetting for the moment that all they were hearing were tales that couldn't be checked on. His Russian companions liked his stories even more. Unacquainted with Jewish life, they naïvely believed everything that came out of his mouth.

270

Before the war Asher had been a tailor, but in the partisan camp he took pains not to mention that fact. Whenever his comrades wanted to be insulting they would call him "the little tailor." Asher, deeply hurt, would lash out with abuse, but would quickly be appeased and go back to his tales and fabrications.

He was number two man to Gedalia, the machine gunner—that is to say, Asher carried the ammunition for Gedalia, trailing him like a shadow. Asher was not distinguished by his fighting spirit, but at a time of danger, he never stirred from Gedalia's side. More than once his friend's faithful help saved the machine gunner from death.

Of the Russian partisans, Shmulik was particularly fond of Alyoshka Hohol, a tall fellow whose bushy blond hair hung rakishly over his forehead down to his small pug nose.

Alyoshka had come to the camp from northern Russia. Actually he had been born near Leningrad, so that neither he nor his friends knew how he had gotten the name Hohol, meaning "Ukrainian."

Alyoshka was the live wire of the company. Lighthearted and bubbling with energy, he was always ready to lend his voice to a song and set his feet flying in dance. He played an accordion that he had picked up on a mission. On every march, even on taxing retreats from German search-and-destroy missions, which were rather frequent, he carried the accordion on his shoulder together with his rifle. Alyoshka belonged to Anatoli's platoon. He, too, was attached to the soft-spoken Gedalia and roomed with the two companions in the same hut.

One morning, when Shmulik's feet were better—

enough to enable him to walk—Anatoli came in, slapped him on the shoulder, and said, "Enough loafing, young man, your hour as arrived."

Shmulik leaped to his feet.

"Will I get a rifle, too?" He looked intently at Anatoli, his eyes aglow.

"Slow down, boy," the other laughed. "You don't get a rifle so quickly. You won't need a weapon. You've been assigned to the maintenance platoon. You'll go to the kitchen and help Gallia, the cook."

Shmulik's lips drooped. Downcast, he followed Anatoli out of the hut. Aware of his gloom, Anatoli tried to cheer him up.

"Don't worry, it's only a temporary arrangement, just until you're completely recovered. You're barefoot, too. First we have to get you boots." He pointed to Shmulik's feet, still wrapped in strips of tent canvas to keep out the melting snow.

Bombezhka

A few weeks passed with Shmulik working in the kitchen. He would gather dry twigs for the cooks, chop wood, and draw water; but most of the time he sat and peeled potatoes. He was in a dark mood. This was not the partisan life he had imagined.

"Just like Fedka's house," he would pour out bitterly to Alyoshka. In Anatoli's presence he was more restrained. He looked upon Anatoli as his commander and respected him, even kept somewhat at a distance.

One day Alyoshka appeared in the kitchen. Disregarding Gallia's scolding and shouting, he snatched a nice-sized chunk of meat from the pan and whispered into Shmulik's ear, "Tonight we're going on a *bombezhka,** kid. We'll take you along and get you some boots. Don't let anyone know I tipped you off."

All that day Shmulik walked about in a daze. He did not see Anatoli, so he couldn't be sure how true Alyoshka's report had been.

That night, when he came back to the hut, his patron suddenly appeared and called to him smiling, "Get ready, boy, we're leaving."

In the blink of an eye Shmulik was outside. At a run he followed Anatoli through two rows of huts that looked like huge dog kennels with their slanted roofs dripping melting snow. At the end of the camp there stood a wagon hitched to a team of horses. Lisa, the nurse, was already sitting in it. Her nursing supplies had run out; she was coming along to stock up on linen for bandages. Alongside her, sitting at his ease, was Alyoshka, driver for the night. Before and behind the cart strode a band of young men armed with rifles and submachine guns. Last

---

* Blow-up, in partisan terminology; a raid on a hostile village to stock up on foodstuffs and clothing.

came Gedalia, the machine gunner, and his right-hand man, Asher. Shmulik wanted to walk with the rest but was ordered onto the cart.

It was the end of winter. The roads were mucky and the wagon wheels at times sank into the slime.

They left the forest after midnight. The skies were cloudy and visibility was limited to thirty yards or so. After about an hour the band emerged onto a paved road, where the going was easier. Alyoshka slapped the horses and those walking quickened their pace.

Passing through the forest they had chatted and joked, but now they advanced in silence. No sound broke the stillness except for the creak of the wheels and the crunch of the partisans' boots.

"Where are we heading?" Shmulik whispered into Alyoshka's ears.

Alyoshka answered softly with the name of a small village.

Shmulik's heart was pounding wildly. The village was in the vicinity of Druzdai, whose farmers had taken part in the liquidation of Jews in the neighborhood. More than once they had lain in ambush for Jewish wanderers emerging from the forest in search of food, stripping them of their shoes and clothing, and handing them over to the Germans. The village was smaller than Druzdai, and its houses were farther apart and less defended.

Before morning the band arrived at one of the friendly villages, and there Anatoli decided to stop and wait until nightfall to continue their journey.

A watch was posted at the outskirts of the village and the partisans distributed themselves among the houses.

274

Anatoli, Alyoshka, and Shmulik headed for one of the first homes. They knocked on the window and waited. Soon a frightened voice from inside asked, "Who's here?"

"It's me—Alyoshka. Open up, *khozyaika.**"

The door creaked, and in the entrance stood a young farm woman.

"Welcome, commander," she turned to Anatoli. "And how are you, Alyoshka? Long time no see."

"Do we get pancakes," smiled Alyoshka, grabbing the peasant woman's hips, "and something to wet the lips with?"

"Sure, sure," laughed their hostess, freeing herself from his embrace. "I'll put up a fire in the oven right off and warm some up for you."

"Where is the *khozyain?*"

"At home. Where else should he be? He got up early this morning to take care of the horses."

"Could he fire up the bathhouse? We'd like to bathe and change underwear."

"Why not? My old man will be right here and fix up everything."

Obviously Alyoshka had enjoyed the family's hospitality more than once and felt himself thoroughly at home.

"Is this a partisan, too?" the peasant woman asked, looking somewhat disdainfully at Shmulik's wrapped-up legs.

Feeling left out, Shmulik tried to edge toward the corner and hide his feet beneath the table. Anatoli knew

* Mistress of the house.

275

very well that farmers respected the striking uniform and effective weapons of the partisans. In an effort to boost the morale of the rag-clad boy he said, "Never you mind, *khozyaika*. We'll stop by on our way back and you'll see what an elegant partisan we've brought you!"

After a hearty meal the young men followed the farmer to the bathhouse. For the longest time Shmulik had not had an opportunity to enjoy such an abundance of hot water and scrub himself with real soap. After they put on clean underwear he felt as though he had grown a new skin. True, the white flaxen shirt he got was patched and its sleeves were too long and wide, but who cared about such trifles?

When the first stars appeared in the sky the band continued on its journey. After the day's rest in the village Shmulik felt his strength renewed and was in fine spirits. For a long time they followed a forest track, which led them onto a main road. There Anatoli ordered them to halt. They turned the wagon and horses over to the young boy who had accompanied them from the friendly village, and advanced on foot. Shmulik saw at once how his comrades' expressions had become more serious. They walked on in dead silence, looking about on all sides. The procession was led by Anatoli, with Gedalia and Asher at his side. Shmulik felt a pain in his legs. His foot wrappings had soaked up some of the damp, and large clods of mud stuck to his heels. Anatoli, seeing that Shmulik was plodding on with difficulty, called a halt. They sat alongside the road, their legs propped up.

"*Nu*, young fellow, it's not so easy to be a partisan, eh?" smiled Anatoli.

276

Shmulik blushed in confusion.

Again they walked on a stretch and reached an open field. A short distance away they could make out on both sides the dark outline of the treetops. They turned off the road onto a narrow path, and then crossed a grove, emerging on the bank of a river.

"*Nu*, boys, let's warm up a little before our cold bath."

Anatoli took a canteen out of his pack and pressed it to his lips. The others drank after him. Asher had a second canteen in his pack, also full. After he took a swig he pressed it to Shmulik's lips. "Drink, boy, you won't make it without this."

Shmulik swallowed. A searing fire raced down his throat into his stomach. This was the crudest *samogon* he had ever tasted—bitter, impure, and foul-smelling.

The young men held their weapons over their heads and entered the water one by one. Shmulik hesitated a moment then jumped in after the rest. The water reached his thighs.

"Why can't I feel the ice?" Shmulik asked his companions. One of them looked him over in mock contempt. "Why? Dumbbell, don't you know a partisan's hide is tough as a dog's?"

They emerged onto black soil. On both sides lay huge pits full of foul-smelling water and rows of black birches.

They walked slowly and took care not to fall into one of the pits. Again they advanced along a road with woods on either side.

Alyoshka, who had gone in advance of the rest, returned to greet them. He whispered something into Anatoli's ears.

277

"Down," muttered the platoon commander.

The clatter of a wagon greeted their ears—a farmer driving a team of horses. Behind him walked two men armed with rifles. The cart rattled by, almost on top of them, and disappeared around a bend in the road.

"Ah, too bad," said Alyoshka, "two defenders.* We could have picked them off like nothing."

Shmulik realized why they had not shot: they were too close to the village. It might have wrecked the whole *bombezhka*.

Before long they were out of the forest. The black outline of the village houses loomed ahead. Anatoli ordered the group to lie down alongside the road and sent two fighters forward. They disappeared into the village lanes and very shortly they were back.

Anatoli gave last-minute instructions. "There's a small patrol about, there will probably be a brief exchange of fire. Don't let one person get away. Anyone who tries to escape—capture or kill."

They split up into three groups: Gedalia and Asher were sent to circle the village and take up a position on the other side. Anatoli stationed another machine gunner with two other men on the spot, and the rest distributed themselves among the houses. Shmulik accompanied Alyoshka and Anatoli.

Before entering the village it had seemed as if everyone was fast asleep, even the dogs. As they approached the first houses, however, the partisans heard fierce barking.

* Members of local civilian patrols armed by the Germans to combat the partisans. More often than not their victims were Jews who came to the villages in search of food.

278

The shadows of three armed men, two black dogs in front of them, separated themselves from the fences around the houses.

"Who goes?"

"Down!" Anatoli pressed on Shmulik's shoulder. "Circle to the left," he ordered.

Alyoshka and a few of the others sprang forward.

Whs-s-s, tr-r-r-r—shots split the night silence.

Shmulik, hardly aware of what he was doing, fell flat on his face by a tree.

Knives seemed to be slicing the air. *T-s-s-s!* With a shrill whistle, a bullet whizzed past him.

Shmulik lifted his head and found himself alone by the tree. The shots were still echoing, but farther off. He could still make out the rat-a-tat-tat of the machine gun.

Where were the rest? What was the situation in the village?

Light shone in the window of the house across the way. The courtyard filled with voices and footsteps. Immediately Shmulik recognized the juicy, full-bodied curses of Alyoshka.

Shmulik ran to the courtyard. By the garden gate he all but tripped over a body. He shrank back, then jumped over the corpse and raced toward the spot where Alyoshka's shouts had come from.

He found the partisan tugging at the tail of a fat hog, with two comrades pitching in, pounding at the animal with their fists. The pig squealed deafeningly.

Before the gate to the pigsty stood the farmer and his wife, the farmer holding his peace, but his wife wringing her hands and wailing plaintively.

"Hey, Shmulik," cried Alyoshka. "I looked out for you.

279

See this?" He waved a gleaming pair of boots before Shmulik's eyes. "When we're finished we'll measure you up."

Shmulik felt his head spin. The bleating and mooing of the animals being led out of the barns and the sheds mixed with the men's voices and the shrieking of the women and children; and all of it was accompanied by the laughter and cursing of the partisans.

The mission was completed speedily. Swiftly two wagons hitched to two teams of horses appeared on the street. Potatoes, sheep, and a few hogs were loaded onto them. Shmulik met Lisa standing by one of the wagons, trying to fit a good-sized bundle carefully between the other sacks so that it would not get dirty.

"It's you, Shmulik?" she smiled. "Healthy and in one piece? And not needing my help? Wonderful!"

Then Lisa looked him over and frowned. "But you're still the same rag as before. Didn't you get anything? This won't do. Come on, we'll fix you up." She pulled him after her.

Shmulik was awed by everything about the girl—her height and carriage, her uniform, her broad army belt with its case for a Russian pistol. Her mocking eyes, though, left him in a state of confusion. *To her, I'm still a kid*, he thought.

"Hey, open up!" Lisa kicked at the door of a nearby house. There was no answer.

"Playing dead, the skunks!" she cursed, partisan style.

"Hey, open up!" Again she lashed out with her boot, setting the panes of glass in the small window ringing.

In short order a dim light appeared in the window, and

the door was opened. A frightened farm woman appeared, dressed in a broad linen shirt. It looked as though she had just gotten out of bed.

"Turn the light on!" snapped Lisa. "Can't you see there are partisans in the village?"

"I see, friend, I see. Please don't get mad. . . ."

Swiftly a gas lamp was lit and set on the table.

From the corner came the whimpering of two children.

"My poor babies, they're sick," the peasant woman whined in an effort to soften the intruders' hearts, her eyes racing between Lisa and Shmulik.

"*Khozyaika*, get us boots for this partisan," ordered Lisa. "One-two, we don't have any time!"

"Boots! In wartime! What do you mean, friends?" she asked, pretending astonishment. "Are you joking with me? Where could I get boots from?"

"Stop jabbering, woman!" Lisa growled, whipping out her pistol.

"Ay, Jesus Maria, you're a woman too," the peasant wailed, noticing for the first time that it was a young girl standing before her. "Won't you have pity on my sick children? I have nothing. They've stripped us bare already. They took everything. Everything, down to our last shirt. This isn't the first time partisans have been here."

Shmulik and Lisa noticed a chest lying in a secluded corner at the end of the room, covered with a colorful rug. Lisa winked to Shmulik, indicating that he should get one of their companions.

As Shmulika was about to leave, the door opened and Anatoli, Alyoshka, and two other fighters came in.

"Come on, boy, try on the boots!" Alyoshka called.

281

"No need for that," Lisa smiled wryly. "Haven't you got eyes in your head? Both his legs would fit into one of them."

"*Khozyaika*," Anatoli addressed the peasant woman. "We need boots for this young man."

"My friend, my father!" The woman leaped at him, seeking to kiss his hand. "Have mercy!"

Anatoli freed his hand and was about to leave. Suddenly his eyes rested on the half-concealed chest.

"Boys," he ordered, "Open up that Noah's ark!"

The woman tried to block their path. Losing his patience, Alyoshka seized her arm and flung her aside. With one blow of an ax he shattered the lock and lifted the cover.

Anatoli drew near, looked in, and flushed red. The chest was crammed with Jewish spoil: tablecloths, sheets, pillowcases. . . . Sticking out like sword points were holy ritual objects: silver cups, spice boxes, Sabbath candlesticks.

"Boys," he gasped, saying no more than that. . . .

What happened next was carried out wordlessly. The peasant woman was silenced. Shmulik did not even notice how she and her children were "wafted" out of the house.

"Lisa," Anatoli turned to the nurse "take all these linens." He himself took a pillowcase and filled it with the holy objects. Shmulik took a pair of pants from the chest and put them on and also took a coat that fit him snugly. But he still lacked boots.

"We ought to look in the cellar," Alyoshka said.

He took a torch, lit it, removed a few boards from the floor, and at once discovered steps. Without delay he went

282

down them. Shmulik stood on the steps holding the torch.

"Boys, look! A regular treasure!" they heard him cry.

In the corner of the cellar the partisans found tanned hides, thick ones and thin ones, and even cut-out boots that had not yet been stitched together. Shouting for joy, they brought their find up.

"Now we'll sew you boots, first class!" cried Alyoshka, slapping Shmulik on the back.

Shmulik—a Fighting Partisan

By the spring Shmulik was a genuine partisan. He had forgotten the exact day when he first was handed a rifle. Very swiftly he came to know the gun, how to disassemble and assemble it perfectly. His weapon glistened. He always carried in his pack, along with his combat rations, a few crusts of black bread and a chunk of salted hog fat as well as a soft cloth to polish the rifle. He wore new boots well coated with resin, so that they would not be ruined by the wet.

The day after his first *bombezhka* Anatoli had summoned Shmulik and told him to go to Asher and Gedalia. Shmulik found them ready to travel.

"We're going to get bread for the platoon," Asher ex-

283

plained. "On the way we'll stop off at the families' camp and order boots for you. There's a cobbler there."

After a few hours they stopped to rest at a nearby village. At one of the farms they stocked up on bread, fresh out of the oven, and continued on toward the forest.

"Why were you sent to get bread instead of somebody from the quartermaster's platoon?" asked Shmulik in surprise. Generally fighters did not go out to get food supplies, particularly on their return from a mission.

The two friends smiled. "Wait, you'll see why we were asked to go."

They plunged into the thick depths of the forest. From the looks of things there was not a living soul in the area. Trees waved their bare branches, and the earth beneath the wagon wheels flung mud up into the riders' faces. There was no longer any path to follow. The cart stopped. Asher and Shmulik stayed with the wagon, and Gedalia disappeared among the trees.

After fifteen minutes Gedalia returned, accompanied by a woman and two men. Shmulik's heart was stirred to pity and loathing at the sight of the figures clothed in rags, their hair wild and shaggy, their faces filthy.

The party approached the wagon. Their eyes gaped wide at the sight of the bread. The face of the youngest contorted; he stretched a trembling hand toward the cart, seized a large chunk of bread, and hurriedly crammed it into his mouth. The other two hesitated a moment, then did exactly the same. Asher and Gedalia did not interfere. Silently they regarded the people's frenzied hunger. The furrows in Gedalia's forehead deepened and even talkative Asher said nothing.

284

"Let's go," Gedalia broke the silence. His soft voice sounded sharp and angry.

He took a few loaves off the wagon and piled them into the arms of the three.

If word of this gets out to the regiment, thought Shmulik, *they'll really be in a terrible fix.* His estimation of his two friends soared even higher.

"There's a little left here," the woman said, beginning to gather the crumbs from the wagon.

"Come on, Shmulik," said Gedalia.

Shmulik followed his comrade into the forest thicket, the woman in front of them.

After a short walk they came upon two hovels, one behind the other. These were not like partisan huts raised above ground level with chimneys sticking up and belching forth smoke. These looked more like pits covered with branches and dirt.

Gedalia slid into the dwelling with Shmulik behind him. A dim light filtered in through the opening, enough to let Shmulik make out the figure of a man sitting on a crudely made bench. The man was pale and his two large eyes expressed indifference, almost as if he were blind.

"Haim, I've brought guests," the woman said upon entering.

The man's lips moved almost imperceptibly and no sound came forth.

"Haim, we've got bread."

The woman drew near him and ripped off a chunk from the loaf.

"Ah, bread," he mumbled. "Ah . . . bread . . . here," he said jerkily.

285

Shmulik shuddered. It was Haim the shoemaker.

"Haim, don't you recognize me?" he asked in a trembling voice.

"No . . . yes . . . you're Shmulik, you stayed alive," he said in a dull monotone.

It seemed to Shmulik it did not matter to Haim who was talking to him.

"Haim, what happened to you?"

He wanted to ask more, but in the face of such awesome indifference, words escaped him.

"His feet froze when the Germans swept through the forest in the winter looking for partisans," the woman explained. "He can't walk."

"My feet, they froze, yes . . . no feet," the man muttered, the man once known as Haim the two-fisted.

"Haim, we brought you leather. Can you sew some boots for this boy?"

"Boots? Yes," he muttered, as though he had not comprehended the words. "My legs hurt," he added.

"Haim, we'll bring the nurse here."

Tears rolled from the cobbler's eyes and hung on the tip of his beard.

"Yes, the nurse, dear friend, he can't take it anymore," the woman spoke for him, rocking to the rhythm of her own speech as she wiped his face with a filthy rag.

Twice more Shmulik visited the hovel, together with Lisa. Her nursing helped Haim's condition. Although he had lost his two large toes, the wounds began to form scar tissue. Little by little his despair and horrible indifference diminished and his spirits slowly began to revive. After two weeks he took up the tools of his trade and

286

Shmulik received a pair of shining boots from his hand.

Asher told Shmulik that Haim had had an offer to join the partisans but turned it down. The regimental commander had set the condition that he obtain a rifle. Haim, not wishing to endanger himself, went to join one of the family camps, those groups of Jewish refugees—many women, children, and old people among them—who hid out in the forests and whose ranks were frequently reduced by the German sweeps, the freezing cold, and starvation.

"I had bad luck," he grumbled. "A guy with bad luck is better off not being born."

Shmulik was confused. Was Haim expressing bitterness over his, Shmulik's, good fortune? Shmulik thought back to the day when Haim had left him, alone and limping, in the forest. For a second he had a feeling of satisfaction, but then, embarrassed, he hurriedly said good-bye to the cobbler, leaving behind a few loaves of bread and a meaty lamb's rib as payment for his labors.

The days stretched out endlessly. Impatiently Shmulik waited for an opportunity to talk with his commanding officer, Ivan Petrovich. Whenever he came upon the man, however, his courage fled him and he dared not begin a conversation.

Ivan Petrovich was a Russian captain who had escaped from a German camp and had joined the partisan regiment in which Anatoli served as a platoon commander. Quickly he rose to the rank of company commander. The Jews in the regiment respected and loved him for his courage and his positive attitude toward them.

Within the company, Shmulik still was not taken along

on missions, but left behind to protect the camp. He would stand guard at night with one of the girls or with the old horseman, Andrei, the father of one of the partisans, his eyes peering sharply into the darkness, his ears alert for every movement. The first few nights, every rustle of a leaf sounded like the footsteps of an approaching enemy. After awhile, however, Shmulik learned to tell the difference between various night sounds in the forest, and standing watch a kilometer or two from camp no longer bothered him.

One day, coming back from his post, he ran into Ivan Petrovich and a few other fighters returning from a bold and successful mission; they had derailed a German train full of supplies and soldiers. Many Germans were blown to smithereens.

The captain was in high spirits. After a regal meal prepared for them by the camp cook, Gallia—red, pan-fried meat, fragrant and smothered in onions—the group broke up, returned to their huts dead tired, and collapsed onto their cots. The commander, however, stayed on by the campfire, sunk in thought. Anatoli and Shmulik stayed with him.

For a long time Shmulik had been begging Anatoli to speak to the commander on his behalf and ask that he be transferred to a fighting unit. Now he sensed that the time was ripe to renew his request. He tugged at Anatoli's sleeve.

"Ivan Petrovich," Anatoli addressed his superior. "Our Shmulik is fed up with sitting around the kitchen. He wants to fight."

288

Ivan Petrovich raised reflective eyes and a smile stretched across his face. "Fight? How old are you, young fellow?"

"Almost fifteen."

The Russian smiled again. "That is, still fourteen and something. A bit early. . . ."

"Comrade commander, in wartime you grow up quickly. It's been more than two years now I've had to look after myself; I've had lots of experience."

The commander's face grew somber.

"Yes, lad, we live in terrible times. Our children have no childhood. But what would you do in a combat platoon? Missions are no joking matter. You can lose your life at any minute. I wouldn't want to leave you behind here, with three years of the war past. It won't be long now, not long at all until liberation. . . ."

"Please, comrade commander, you yourself say that the war is coming to an end and I haven't taken revenge yet on one German," Shmulik continued to plead.

Ivan Petrovich smiled again. He put his right hand on Shmulik's shoulder and a sad tenderness enveloped his face.

"I have a son, too, your age, lad," he whispered. "Who knows if I'll find him alive."

"Comrade commander," interjected Anatoli, in an effort to aid Shmulik. "Your son is a Russian and we are Jews. It's not the——"

The captain scowled and his eyes flashed. "In the village where I was born the Germans didn't leave one soul alive."

Anatoli had intended to say more, but at the sight of his commander's angry face, he fell silent. *A Goy can never understand this—even the best of them,* he thought bitterly.

289

For a moment they were silent. Ivan Petrovich rose. "Put him in your platoon," he ordered curtly and turned to go.

Shmulik breathed easy. He knew that commanders of Russian platoons would not have wanted him.

A Comrade's Death

"Anatoli's been called to the commander's hut," Alyoshka announced upon entering.

All ears perked up. Impulsively Shmulik leaped outside.

He knew that platoon commanders were not summoned to the commander's hut for no good reason. No doubt a big plan was in the offing, one that Anatoli would be ordered to carry out.

His instinct proved right. Very shortly Anatoli returned and said that they had to prepare to set out that evening. One group would be under his command.

The objective was a dangerous one. They had to cross the main road, on which the German army was always moving, and destroy the railroad bridge spanning the river.

"Jews they send on missions like these," grumbled Asher. "They don't want to risk the Russians."

Gedalia glared at him. Asher fell silent.

290

They set out as the first stars appeared.

After marching through the night they spent the next day in a wooded area alongside the river and at sunset began advancing toward their destination.

The season was early summer. Grain that was still green stood tall in the fields, swaying and bowing gently in the wind.

The band turned off the road and crossed a cornfield. Upon reaching one of the tributaries of the river they crossed it and emerged upon a dusty village road.

"About face!" Anatoli's command was passed from mouth to ear.

The company stretched out into a long goose line and continued to advance, but walking backwards, to confuse any enemy troops that might try to track them.

Soon they reached a grove of pine trees. Tree stumps stood out among the young pines. They were low enough to give the marchers a view, through the gaunt topmost branches, of the winding river in the plain below. Here and there the moon flecked the dark gray waters with silver.

"Down!" shot the command along the line and all dropped.

Suddenly flares crackled through the skies, red and then green, dissolving in a shower of sparkles above their very heads.

Not far off they heard the steps and voices of Germans.

"Hit it!" The whispered command flashed down the line and bellies pressed against the earth.

One after another came the flare barrages in increasing frequency. All lay still and tense, their eyes staring into the darkness, their ears ringing from intense concentration.

Silence reigned. An acorn dropped. A night bird

shrieked. A shot rang out, then another. The men's hearts were pounding and they held their breath.

"Crawl back!" came the whispered command.

After half an hour they were in the forest again. There they were able to straighten out their aching backs. They marched half an hour more, then rested. They lay down alongside the road, their legs up.

It was obvious what had happened. The German guard by the bridge had been reinforced. Had they known of the partisans' coming? Had someone spotted them coming, then informed the authorities? What were they to do? Should they return to camp without fulfilling their objective?

Anatoli, leader of the mission, was furious. In his mind's eye he could already see the mocking eyes of Kolka, head of the second platoon in Ivan Petrovich's company. Kolka did not like Jews and rejoiced at their every defeat. He was also envious of Anatoli, a Jew, who had six blown-up trains to his credit, while Kolka had only four. Ivan Petrovich always chose Anatoli's platoon for the most dangerous missions, sometimes even accompanying them himself. How could Anatoli return now empty-handed?

"Comrade commander," Gedalia broke into his train of thought. "Let's cross the river and blow up the bridge on the other side."

The group came to life. What would Anatoli say? The job would be a dangerous one. The other side of the river was infested with another enemy, the White Poles—partisans who fought both the Russians and Germans, but competed with the Germans in the slaughter of Jews.

Anatoli said nothing.

"Comrade commander," Gedalia continued. "We don't need the whole platoon. I'll go with two others. It would be easier for a smaller group to get away. I'm familiar with the area."

Anatoli still said nothing. Was he listening at all? Shmulik wondered.

The stars were beginning to fade. The night was short. Very soon dawn would break and it would be impossible to move. Where could they spend the day? They had no place to rest. They could not stay in the forest for their food had run out. The fighters' eyes were glued to their leader, waiting for his decision.

"The three of us will go," said Alyoshka. "Gedalia, Asher, and me. Will you go with us?" he asked Number Two, jabbing Asher's ribs with his elbow.

"Get out of here, pasty-face," growled Asher. "Go on, go on. . . . Hurry!"

Everyone knew that wherever Gedalia went, Asher went, with Alyoshka right behind them.

"You know the area well, you say?" Anatoli raised thoughtful eyes toward Gedalia.

"My father spent a lot of time in these parts and he used to take me here during vacations."

"Is the river deep?"

"I know a place to cross it not far off."

"Let's go," Anatoli said, leaping to his feet.

"Soon it will be daybreak," someone muttered.

"No matter, the skies are darkening."

"It's going to rain."

"All the better."

Within moments the thunder began to roll, at first far off and then directly above their heads. The group

293

advanced swiftly. Flashes of lightning illumined the sky here and there. The trees groaned like wounded animals. The wind grew stronger, making it difficult to advance. Then a mighty rain swept upon them. By the time the partisans found shelter under the trees, they were completely soaked from their toes to their waists. Every thread of clothing was wet, even their boots were full of water. Their shoulders and backs were dry, though; the water had not yet gotten through their sheepskin coats.

"Noah's flood," grumbled Asher.

Weary and trembling from the cold, they reached the river's brink.

Gedalia lifted his machine gun over his head and stepped in first. The others followed in line.

The bank on the other side was high. Gedalia walked along the shore, the rest silently following after.

Worry gnawed at Shmulik. Were the explosives wet? Would they ignite?

They rounded one bend of the river, another—and the bridge came into view. The shadows of two men moved by at a set pace. The bridge guards were moving slowly along the track. They would proceed several yards and then return.

It was one hour before dawn. The sky above was black. Not one star shone amid the cloudy expanse.

"Lie down!" whispered Anatoli. He gave last-minute instructions and accompanied by Gedalia, Asher, and Alyoshka, began crawling toward the bridge.

"Comrade commander, take me, too," pleaded Shmulik.

"Okay, crawl!"

294

Gedalia and Asher set up their machine gun at the edge of the embankment opposite the bridge as Anatoli and Alyoshka set to work. Holding his breath, Shmulik followed Anatoli's nimble fingers. There were the TNT bricks like pieces of yellow soap and there was the fuse. Alyoshka tied the cord to the safety and stretched it over the embankment.

All slid below, withdrew a good distance, and pressed against the wet earth.

Long moments of waiting passed. The stillness of the night rang in their ears, the blood pounded in their temples.

"Pull!" ordered Anatoli with bated breath.

Silence. Again the cord was yanked. And again.

The bridge stood tall as ever, unmoved.

Anatoli sprang forward and raced to the spot where they had left the mine. Shmulik followed after. The fuse had slipped out, the mine had not gone off.

Alyoshka cursed a streak in Russian. The group could not stay there another minute. Shmulik's keen eyes had detected shadows moving along the track. The German detail guarding the bridge was returning.

Silently the partisans rolled down the embankment and crept a few yards further among the stumps of the trees beside the railroad tracks, trees cut down by the Germans for fear of the partisans. There they lay. In the east dawn was breaking.

Gedalia was in a black mood. He was determined not to return to camp in shame.

"Let's pass the night here and try again."

To spend the night in that small grove was dangerous.

295

All around lay hostile villages and the German garrison was not far off. Anatoli said nothing. It was hard to decide. He was responsible for the lives of thirteen people.

Petka, a Byelorussian youth who had not yet turned seventeen and was the platoon's second machine gunner, stared silently at the accursed bridge, then looked angrily at Shmulik.

"Why the hell did you come along? It's all your fault. ..."

Shmulik's eyes filled with tears. Anatoli smiled.

"Most of this detail is Jewish. For us, thirteen is a lucky number, Petka."

"With you Jews, everything is backwards," grumbled Pavel of the long mustache.

All during the journey Pavel had not concealed his dissatisfaction. Back at the camp he had tried to get out of going on the mission. Anatoli was unable to figure the man out. At times he displayed courage bordering on madness and at times, the cowardice of a child. Heaven knew what made him tick. He was an ace at drinking. He could pour a bottle of whiskey down his throat without batting an eyelash and walk off fully erect as though he had downed pure spring water.

"Pavel, Petka, should we stay here or go back?" Anatoli deliberately addressed himself to both men.

"You're the commander," Pavel shot back in irritation.

"We'll stay. Should we go back and get laughed at?" Petka responded, wiping with his sleeve the drops of water dripping onto his face and neck from his hair.

"And what will we eat?" asked Asher, always the practical partisan.

"Starlings' milk and field mice eggs," grumbled Pavel.

296

The rain had stopped. The clouds had blown away. A clean, red sun rose from among the treetops. The water drops glistened atop the grasses and the branches of the willow trees that grew along the river bank. By the time the group recrossed the river and entered the forest, the sun stood high in the sky. After they set up guard duty and sentries were posted, they stretched out on the ground and sank into deep sleep. Shmulik was ravenous. He bolted down the last of his bread and the chunk of fatty meat that he had in his bag and fell asleep. He awoke to the sound of a vigorous blow. At first it seemed a shot had been fired. Then he recognized the whack of an ax biting into a tree. All the men were alert, their weapons at the ready.

"We saw a peasant chopping wood," the sentry informed them. "We tried to stop him but he got away."

Shmulik was on the verge of asking why they had not shot him, when he realized that the noise would have brought a German patrol upon them.

Anatoli looked grim. The situation was extremely grave. The peasant could inform on them.

"Maybe we should turn back?" Asher asked offhandedly.

"Shut your mouth!" Alyoshka snapped.

Gedalia looked up. Night was drawing on.

"Comrade commander, waiting isn't worthwhile. Let's finish the job."

The sun was sinking behind the treetops and the river glowed red. Again they crawled toward the bridge. Their scout informed them that the German guard was not in sight. That seemed remarkable, but they had no time to delay.

297

Anatoli assembled the mine and stretched the cord out over the road's embankment. Shmulik followed him with glowing eyes.

On the opposite bank two figures appeared, two shadows silhouetted against the whiteness of the bridge. "Halt! Who goes?"

Ts-s-s-s, r-r-r-r—the machine gun rattled.

One figure pitched forward, the other dashed off toward the forest. "Pull!" cried Anatoli.

A thunderous boom shook the area. It seemed to Shmulik that the earth had opened up. A sharp stone slammed into his thigh as he lay flat on the ground, his face against the cold soil. A cloud of dust arose, thick stone fragments were flung about, huge masses of cement crumbled.

Shmulik was wounded in the thigh. His head spun, his eyes ached, his leg was on fire. He put his fingers on the wounded spot—it was moist and sticky.

The cloud of dust began to break up, and the booming ceased.

"Back! Run!" he heard Anatoli order. "Where are you all going? Back!"

Shmulik's eyes opened wide in amazement. Gedalia and Pavel were in the middle of the river, in the deep water, then on the opposite shore. They bent over the dead German, removing his weapon.

The bridge was no more. Fragments of stone, cement, iron girders, and wooden beams lay scattered on the road. The murky gray waters were still in a tumult. The bridge's foundations protruded from the water supporting a few swaying wood and steel fragments that looked like the last shreds of flesh on a skeleton. Fearfully Shmulik saw

298

that he was alone near the site of the explosion. Where had all the rest disappeared to?

Among the wild bushes along the shore a rifle barrel gleamed for an instant then disappeared. Shmulik began running along the shore and overtook the group. They moved on in silence, listening to the echoes of their own steps. Swiftly they were swallowed up by the night. All that remained was the crossing of the main road. Then the danger would diminish as they put the hostile villages behind them. The men were panting, drops of sweat glistened and rolled down their faces. They sat down to rest briefly. In one more hour they would really rest, when they would arrive in one of the villages to eat.

Half an hour more to go. The hunger was still bearable, but thirst was sapping their strength. The strip of road loomed white ahead of them. One after another they approached and waited.

A pistol and two grenades hung from Gedalia's belt. Pavel bore on his shoulder the submachine gun he had taken from the dead German. His face was spread over with contentment. Shmulik looked at his own rifle dissatisfied. He envied Pavel.

"Cross one at a time on the run," came the command, whispered down the line.

Gedalia and Asher rose first. They were showered with bullets from both sides of the road. A bullet whistled over Shmulik's head. Before him he saw Pavel's broad back, and the partisan's new submachine gun swaying on his shoulder. Suddenly Pavel disappeared. Where to? Shmulik ran on a few steps, stumbled over something and fell. He lifted his head. Under his legs was a body.

Shmulik did not look at the sprawled figure but rose

299

and kept running. He could not stay. He had to catch up with the rest.

Before him was Anatoli, down on one knee, Petka alongside him. Alyoshka and two others were lying on the ground returning fire. The shots of the Germans and the partisans intermingled and it was difficult to tell them apart.

They were running forward again. The shots were decreasing. Among the missing were Pavel, Gedalia, and Asher. Petka's face shone pale, even in the moonlight. He groaned with every step. A bullet had smashed into his right arm, but he still clutched to his chest his precious weapon, his machine gun.

The fighters returned to camp as mourners. The mission had cost them dear. In the morning two more men reached camp. Then more came. Pavel returned with a wounded hand. Finally, only Gedalia and Asher were still missing.

Shmulik entered an almost empty hut—only Alyoshka lay on his cot, his face hidden. The odor of *samogon* assailed Shmulik's nostrils.

"Alyoshka," Shmulik blurted, "they're not. . . ."

Alyoshka looked at him silently. A few hours later Shmulik saw him striding through the camp with his submachine gun on his shoulder. Shmulik did not dare to ask him anything.

Two days later Alyoshka came back. On his shoulders he bore the corpse of Asher, and Gedalia, wounded, was leaning on his arm. Alyoshka related how he had found Gedalia not far from the road, crawling, pulling Asher's body behind him.

It was days before the partisans could get the details

of the disaster from Gedalia. He had been wounded first. Asher had rushed to his side, but he had not been aware of that immediately. When Asher had noticed that the whole platoon had crossed the road and Gedalia was not with them, he retraced his steps and dashed under a hail of fire to his friend. He found Gedalia alongside the road, bent over his machine gun raining fire on the enemy and covering the platoon's retreat. Asher saw at once that Gedalia's right arm was wounded. He pulled the wounded man aside and took his place at the machine gun. Slowly they too began to retreat. The shots died down, almost completely. Gedalia was on the brink of fainting.

"Asher, the machine gun," he whispered with his last remaining strength.

"To hell with the machine gun," muttered Number Two between his teeth, hiking the wounded man onto his back and plunging into the bushes. They had gone only a few steps when they were sprayed with another hail of bullets. Gedalia must have been hit a second time and fainted.

When he regained consciousness he found himself stretched out on the ground among bushes, alongside him the cold body of Asher.

The grave was dug on a small hill between two young fir trees. The burial ceremony was brief—a few shots, a mound of black earth. Heads bowed, the partisans went back to their tasks. Only a group of Jews and Alyoshka remained by the grave. Shmulik wept openly. No one tried to calm him.

Gedalia's shattered arm hung in a sling. He said nothing, his eyes fixed on the mound. The last rays of the sun vanished, leaving them to the silence of the night.

Anatoli straightened up first.

"Come on, Gedalia," he held out his hand to the wounded man. "Soon we'll be as peaceful as he is."

"The wolves will munch on his bones," said Alyoshka, his face pale.

Gedalia did not move. With a sudden motion he thrust his good hand into his pants pocket, took out a small skullcap and placed it on his head. The others looked on in wonderment.

"*El malei rahamim,* Father of mercies. . . ." The mournful chant spilled out into the void of night. Tears streamed from Gedalia's eyes as he intoned the prayer. The others joined in—the whispered lament of Jews in the forest alone and bereaved, weeping over their brother's grave. . . .

The wounded men's plight grew more and more critical. Pavel's hand swelled and his pains increased. Gedalia was in serious condition. The fragments in his body tormented him and his fever rose ever higher. A doctor from the next platoon realized that an operation was necessary. That, however, required sterile dressings and injections that they did not have. Lisa the nurse was beside herself.

During his every spare moment Shmulik sat by Gedalia's bed. He knew that the latter's life hung in the balance if the medicines were not procured.

That evening he approached Anatoli. "Comrade commander, let me go to the city. Maybe I'll manage to get the medicine."

Anatoli shook his head in disapproval. He knew that the supplies they needed were not sold in drugstores.

Shmulik's eyes filled with tears. Was Gedalia doomed? Anatoli rose and left the hut. After an hour he returned and summoned Shmulik. "Shmulik, do you know Vilna?" "No."

"Damn! . . . Well, would you want to come with me anyway?"

"To the city! Sure!" Shmulik jumped up enthusiastically.

Anatoli had decided to meet with Dr. Kwiatkowski, the physician who had tended him during his illness, and through his aid obtain the vital injections.

Shula on a Mission

Shula heard Shmulik's tale, and tears shone in her eyes.

"Shula, can you help us? You work in a hospital, and we haven't been able to meet with Dr. Kwiatkowski."

"I'll try to get to his apartment. Let's meet here tomorrow the same time."

Shula had forgotten completely how late it was, so good had it felt being with her dear friends. She did not stop asking them questions and telling them of her own adventures. Painfully she related how Rivka Wilensky had changed her name in a convent to Biruté Magdalena and despised Jews.

Shmulik's eyes blazed.

"I've got to see her! It couldn't be! Maybe you made a mistake?"

It was decided that Shula would try to coax Biruté Magdalena to come into the yard the next night and that Shmulik would come to the convent gate.

By the time Shula arrived at the convent it was almost midnight. The gatekeeper eyed her suspiciously. Upon entering her sleeping quarters she met Sister Felicia.

"Where have you been so late?"

"At the hospital. One of my patients is doing very poorly, so I sat by his bed," she answered softly.

Sister Felicia searched Shula's face and walked off with no comment.

All the other girls in the hall were asleep. Shula looked at her neighbor's bed. Rivka was lying with her eyes closed, but Shula thought she noticed her eyelids move.

She's just pretending to be asleep, the thought crossed her mind. Shula went over and shook her arm.

"Rivka, listen, I met Shmulik in the street today."

The girl shook, her eyes opened wide, and once again Shula saw in them the terror of a hunted animal.

For a moment they looked at each other. Rivka flushed and turned pale alternately. She sat up in bed and said in an angry, tear-choked voice, "What are you tormenting me for? What have I done to you? I don't know any Shmuliks, I don't know any Yids. If you don't leave me alone I'll complain to the mother superior. I'll tell her you go around with Jews at night. I. . . ."

This time Shula felt that she had the upper hand.

304

Biruté Magdalena no longer spoke with the same certainty that had been hers in the beginning. Now her voice was quavering.

"Rivka, listen, the war will be over soon. You won't have to disguise yourself anymore. Don't be afraid. Shmulik wants to see you very badly. Tomorrow at ten o'clock go to the courtyard. Just up to the gate."

"No, no! I don't want to see any Yids. I hate them! Leave me alone. I'm a good Catholic and I want to stay a nun." She turned her back on Shula and pulled the blanket up over her head.

The next day, on her way home from work, Shula turned into a side street where Dr. Kwiatkowski lived. The sign had been taken down, however, and new tenants occupied the apartment. *This will be bad news for Shmulik and Anatoli*, thought Shula. *How can I get the injections we need?* Shula knew she could not get them from her hospital, for they were in the possession of the surgeon and the head nurse. Moreover, they could not be bought on the market.

The three friends struggled to arrive at a solution together. Then Shula remembered how once, when cleaning a cabinet in the convent's main infirmary, she had seen the necessary injections. That room, however, was kept locked. Rivka had a key to the students' infirmary. The question was, would it unlock the main infirmary?

The next morning, as the girls were about to leave for work, Shula took a knife and nicked her thumb. Holding out the finger dripping blood, she approached Rivka and asked her for iodine and a bandage.

"Just when we're hurrying to work," Rivka grumbled. "Get it yourself. I don't want to be late because of you."

"Where's the key?"

Rivka tossed it to her and left.

Shula turned toward the large infirmary. The room was empty. In the corner stood the closet with the precious medications. Trembling, she poked the key into the lock. A slight exertion of pressure and it opened.

The precious injections lay before her. Swiftly she hid them in the pockets of her gown and left.

Her eyes shone when she placed her treasure in Anatoli's hands later. Proudly she told how she had got them. Her account of Rivka's remarks, however, infuriated Shmulik.

"It can't be that Rivka Wilensky would say things like that," he insisted. "There must be some mistake. I've got to see the girl. How can we arrange it?"

"Wait for us in the street," Shula suggested. "On our way back from work in the evening you'll see her."

"Nothing doing," objected Anatoli. "We've got to hurry back to camp and bring Gedalia the medicine. Every day counts."

"Go back alone and let me stay on," pleaded Shmulik. Momentarily he forgot that he was standing before his partisan commander and saw in him only his Jewish friend. Anatoli left them after a prolonged handshake. He no longer embraced or kissed Shula as he had first done. This was not Onyté. Shula had grown a great deal; her face, no longer a child's, showed sobriety and maturity.

The two of them stood looking at each other. Shula's cheeks were flushed. Anatoli seemed so manly and handsome to her. His face was tan and his large, long-lashed eyes shone with integrity and intelligence.

One more glance, one more handshake, and Anatoli had vanished into the night.

As the girls walked home from their hospital jobs at dusk, the city streets were overflowing with pedestrians. Workers were heading home, lines snaked outside food stores, and women pushed carriages along the sidewalks and on the lawns.

A light breeze relieved the heavy heat of day and gently rustled the thin skirts of the women. Despite the heavy flow of traffic the street seemed weary and lifeless. Here and there an elegantly dressed woman would pass by in the company of a uniformed escort.

Biruté Magdalena walked slowly at Shula's side, dragging her legs sluggishly along. Shula's eyes raced from one sidewalk to the next. Would Shmulik come? Or had he been found out as a Jew? Or captured?

A sooty-faced chimney sweep emerged from a side alley and advanced toward them. On his back he bore a ladder and a pail; a broom and rope swung from his arm.

"Passing a chimney sweep means bad luck," huffed Rivka, glowering at Shula.

Shula did not answer. She tried to maintain a calm front.

They crossed the main road and turned toward the side street leading to the convent. The houses seemed closed in, guarding the life that was within. There were few stores and no lines. On either side of the street lay gardens and chestnut trees gently waving their broad-leafed branches. A barefoot boy stood by the window of a small toy shop looking at wooden horses and dolls on display. As the girls drew close he turned his face toward them.

"Biruté, look at that boy. Recognize him?" Shula tugged at her companion's hand and riveted her eyes upon her.

A tremor passed across Biruté Magdalena's face but quickly she recovered her mask of indifference and replied, "What's so special about him? A barefoot peasant boy!"

Disappointment and a burning grief raced through Shula but she clearly saw that Rivka had recognized Shmulik. She resolved to break through the girl's stubbornness.

"Biruté, that's Shmulik. Don't you recognize him?"

Rivka's face reddened and her eyes grew watery. "Pestering me again! If you don't leave me alone I'll tell everyone, today, that you sneak around with Yids. I know you run to him at night. You lied to Sister Felicia; you're a Jewgirl."

The flood of abuse pouring out of her companion's mouth threw Shula into a ferment. Rivka, however, no longer able to hold back her tears, suddenly dashed off toward the convent.

She just could tell on me, thought Shula fearfully.

But there was no doubt about the matter any longer; the girl was Rivka Wilensky. Shmulik had recognized her at once.

"I'll come to the convent gate tonight," he whispered to Shula as he slipped by her.

"Are you hungry?" Shula asked.

"Yes."

308

"I'll bring you something."

Shmulik turned toward the ruins, hunger oppressing him. The food he had brought from the forest had run out. Impatiently he awaited the agreed-upon hour.

Why didn't you ask Shula to give you a piece of bread right now, you jackass? he scolded himself inwardly. *And why should I roam around the streets risking my neck? What have I got to worry about Rivka for, the lying traitor?*

The more thought he gave to that question, though, the clearer it became that Rivka was not his only reason for staying. He certainly could do nothing for her, conditions being what they were. On the contrary, it would be best for her to remain in the convent for the time being.

The image of Shula arose before his mind's eye just as he had seen her, her long gray nun's habit falling down over her ankles, her rebellious curls slipping from beneath her headpiece to hang down to her gray eyes.

Images from his happy childhood years floated up at the sight of Shula. How good it would feel to grasp her warm hand and gaze into her clear tender eyes.

Sunk in thought Shmulik threaded his way toward the ruins, which he had been haunting for two days.

It was seven o'clock. He had a long wait before the rendezvous—three full agonizing hours in those ruins, hungry and tired as he was. If only he could lie down a little, close his eyes and go to sleep. *Maybe I'll meander to the city park and lie down under one of the trees,* he thought.

He had decided to head for the street leading to that woody area when his eyes met the bold, piercing gaze of

309

a young boy. Shmulik stopped in the opening of one of the courtyards and saw that the boy, too, stopped.

Trailing me, he realized, fearful that at any minute the stranger would head right for him yelling, "A Yid, catch him!"

Shmulik quickened his pace toward the ruins but was aware that the other boy was doing likewise.

Beads of sweat glistened on his brow. He felt their salt taste on his lips. *If I can't lose him I'll shoot him*, he resolved, fingering the pistol in his pants' pocket.

Suddenly an idea flashed through Shmulik's mind. He stopped, looked about as though searching for something, and darted into a half-ruined house. Behind him he heard the panting of his shadow, who began to yell in Lithuanian, "Hey, you, stop! I'll call the Shauliai."

Swiftly Shmulik unzipped his pants as though preparing to urinate.

"You won't get away from me, damn Jew bastard," he heard the other's voice again. The youth's head appeared in the doorway.

"Why ain't there toilets in this damn city?" Shmulik said in Byelorussian, with a thick peasant accent. The question stunned his pursuer.

"You from out of town, too, looking for a place to go?" Shmulik went on amiably.

"Ah, go to hell, you animal!" cursed the youth. He spat at Shmulik and left.

Rivka Wilensky

For the longest time Rivka Wilensky tossed about on her bed. She had recognized Shmulik, Shmulik from Mapu Street. His eyes glowed in the darkness at once full of pity, rebuke, and curiosity. Again she remembered the courtyard in Mapu Street in Kovno, her parents' home, and her brother David who had hung around with Shmulik. It had been so nice gathering by the birch tree in the garden to play or talk or argue!

Nothing remained of those blessed days. The outbreak of war had ushered in wandering and flight to a village in the suburbs of Vilna, to a Pole's farm.

She still experienced vividly the horrors of the day when the Shauliai appeared on the farm and took off her mother and father. Now she knew why they had seized them and that only she, Rivka, had been saved. Her parents had not agreed to pray to Jesus and the Holy Mother. Their host's wife had pleaded with them morning and night to convert but they stubbornly had refused. God had punished them for their stiffnecked resistance—so Jadviga, the mistress of the house, had explained to her. And Rivka was very afraid. She did not want to be killed.

David they had killed on the spot, in the court. Struggling to get loose, he had kicked the Lithuanian who had been holding him. Then he lay sprawled out beneath the cherry tree and Rivka could hear the groans. He was still

311

alive—only badly wounded. The Shauliai shot him again and he died. She began to weep aloud and shout, "Duvid'l!" But Jadviga had clapped her hand over the child's mouth and dragged her to the cellar. There she draped a chain with a small bronze cross around her neck and ordered her to pray.

Rivka was determined to stay alive. She was scrupulously religious, observing all the rituals and praying daily to Mary.

Jadviga had tearfully bemoaned the fate of Rivka's mother and father, declaring how it pained her that she had been unable to help them.

Many were the tears Rivka shed when she was left alone. For two days she tasted no food.

Sunday came. Rivka saw that Jadviga had put on her mother's silk dress and her shoes. Rivka's father had been led off by the Shauliai barefoot. Why, she had wondered then, had her father taken off his boots?

The worm of doubt began gnawing at her. That same evening she had seen Janek, Jadviga's oldest boy, trying on her father's new boots, the very boots her father had put on before he had been taken away from her.

She, Rivka, was afraid. No one dare know that she was Jewish. She wanted to live. She would be a nun. Now she was called by the lovely name of Biruté Magdalena. But Shmulik? Why had he come there? And Shula—she would not leave her alone. Shula told her how Shmulik was risking his life for her sake. He was going to come that night to the gates of the convent to see her. No, she would not go out. Not under any circumstances! She did not want to die. She tried to pull the blanket over her head and fall asleep. It was hot and suffocating.

Shula was not in her bed, Rivka noticed. No doubt she had gone out to Shmulik. Shmulik was waiting for Rivka alongside the gate. If they caught him they would do to him what they did to David. Shmulik had come from the forest, where he had been safe. Who had asked him? Let him leave her be, live her own life. What had Shula said to her on the way home—that she, Rivka, had betrayed her father and mother, butchered by the "good" Nazis. Lies! Good Christians could not be murderers. But doubt still gnawed at her. How had Janek gotten hold of her father's boots the same evening of that miserable day? Why had her father been led off barefoot? And Jadviga had worn Rivka's mother's dress. Jadviga had polished the boots of Rivka's father with a brush. But Jadviga was very religious, she prayed every day.

Rivka trembled beneath the blanket. Why was she so cold? It was July already. Shula had said that their rescue was not far off. Shula knew everything. But Rivka was afraid of what Shula said. The night before Shula had told her that the Russians were already nearby. The nurses in the hospital were talking about it, too. Some were getting ready to leave Vilna and flee toward the west. "When the Bolsheviks come they'll fix us like we fixed the Jews."

Minsk had fallen, the Russians were drawing close to the borders of Lithuania. Rivka had seen vehicles loaded with furniture and luggage in the streets.

"Then we'll be free and we won't have to hide in the convent anymore," Shula had whispered into her ears, eyes radiant. But Biruté Magdalena had no desire to leave the convent. And in the meantime Shmulik could be killed. . . . She would go down for a minute. She would only tell Shmulik to get out and go back to the forest. She would only go down for a minute.

Rivka slipped out of bed and glanced about her; all the girls were sleeping. In the dark hallway she could see only the small oil lamp flickering beneath the portrait of the Holy Mother. Rivka descended the stairways barefoot in order not to raise any echoes.

The cursed door would have to squeak; she winced. She stopped and waited. No one had heard. Rivka ran to the gate.

"Ouch!" she cried as her foot hit a sharp rock. Pain shot through her. A long shadow fell over the courtyard's paving stones.

"Who's there?"

The tall, gaunt figure of Sister Felicia towered over her, her arms folded across her chest, the very statue of a goddess of vengeance.

"Where are you going?"

Rivka said nothing. She was very frightened of Sister Felicia.

"Where are you going at this hour?" Sister Felicia raised her voice.

Rivka trembled in silence.

Sister Felicia seized her by the arm. The nun's bony fingers sank into her flesh.

"Just to the gate . . . I. . . ."

The nun fixed her watery eyes on the stammering child. "What have you to do at the gate? A date with a boy? At night, in a convent?"

Rivka was at an utter loss for words. Her lips quivered.

"Come along, show me who he is."

314

Felicia walked on in front, pulling the quaking girl behind her.

The gate was closed, the guard was dozing on his bench. All around was silence. No one was there. Rivka sighed in relief.

The nun looked at her in amazement.

"Why did you go to the gate?"

"I couldn't sleep."

"You lie! Go to your room and wait until I return."

Sister Felicia went up to the girls' dormitory. Had she been mistaken? Onyté was peacefully asleep in her bed.

The nun noticed that for a few nights the girl had been absent from the convent, returning at a very late hour. That very day, Sister Felicia had inquired after her in the hospital and had been told that Onyté had finished working at the usual hour and had left. Strangely enough, though, the nun had been in the room only a half-hour ago and had found the girl's bed empty.

The nun's pale cheeks reddened with anger. The impudent Jewess was making a fool of her, and of the entire convent! She would teach her a lesson!

At the appointed hour Shmulik had arrived at the convent hoping that Rivka would come down to speak to him. He found Shula waiting for him as planned.

"Shmulik, I brought you bread."

Shmulik climbed on the fence and was about to jump inside when the angry voice of Sister Felicia and the whimpering of Rivka reached their ears.

"Shmulik, run," whispered Shula.

Shmulik jumped down and vanished into the night.

Shula slipped off her shoes, dashed across the length of the courtyard, and slipped into the dormitory. Without undressing she lay down in bed and curled up snugly in her blankets.

From beneath the edge of her blanket she saw Sister Felicia enter the room, with Rivka behind her.

When the two girls came back from work the next evening they were ordered to go at once to the room of Mother Beatta.

Shula's throat was dry. She sensed trouble. Her first thought was to flee. But where to? Where maintain herself for one more week or maybe even a few days?

She saw with her own eyes how frightened the Lithuanians had become. They were streaming out of Vilna, which had become an army camp. Shmulik had told her that he was heading back to the forest to join his regiment and take part in the liberation of the city. What did Sister Felicia want of her? What had she found out?

Mother Beatta fixed her with cold, angry eyes. Sister Felicia's face was very long and the nun was not even looking at her.

Rivka was crying. *What a disgusting girl, that Shula,* she thought. *I never should have gotten mixed up with her.* Why did Shmulik risk his life for her? It was all Shula's fault. *She mixed him up and me too. . . .*

"Where do you disappear to at nights?" she heard Mother Beatta demand.

"I was in the hospital."

"You're lying! Sister Felicia asked after you there!" Shula paled.

"A few days ago valuable injections disappeared from the infirmary cabinet. Where is the Pentathol? The Coramine?"

Shula's legs shook.

"I don't know," she said weakly.

"You know very well. If you don't tell who took them, I'll call the Gestapo. Now."

Shula said nothing. Rivka sobbed.

"Biruté Magdalena, you are responsible for the drugs. Your key fits the infirmary's cabinet. Did you give Onyté the key?"

Rivka hung her head.

"Lock Biruté Magdalena up until we decide what's to be done with her."

For a moment the mother superior paused, reflecting.

"Biruté Magdalena, are you a Jewess, too?"

Mother Beatta knew nothing of Rivka's Jewish origins. She had been transferred there along with the other girls from the closed down convent and no information had been given concerning her.

The question terrified Rivka.

"No, n-n-o!" she stammered.

"Onyté! Do you know Biruté Magdalena from before? Tell me the truth. Is she a Jewgirl like you?"

Shula straightened up and answered, "No. Biruté Magdalena is not a Jewess. She's a Christian. Mother Beatta, she is not guilty. I took the key myself."

"So. And the injections, too?"

"Yes."

"Why? You sold them? You made some money?"

"No. I gave them to someone who was wounded."

"A Jew, eh?"

"Yes."

The old nun rose from her seat breathing heavily, her eyes ablaze. It seemed to Shula that any second she would leap upon her—and strangle her. But Mother Beatta controlled herself. She did not yell or strike out. She only pointed at Shula and hissed, "This one . . . lock up. Give her nothing."

Liberation

For a week Vilna rang with shooting. Clouds of dust swirled above the railroad office, the tallest building in the city. Then all was silence, followed by the rumble of trucks and tanks, and the dusty faces of soldiers dead tired but drunk with victory. From time to time a lone shot would shriek through the air.

Group after group of partisans strode through the liberated streets. Occasionally a forest fighter could be seen crossing himself as he took up guard duty.

The Jewish partisans were not exultant over the liberation; their eyes did not sparkle for joy. Dumbstruck mourners, they wandered about the huge cemetery, the caved-in houses, the dead alleys that only shortly before had been the Vilna Ghetto. Here and there a lone skeleton of a door frame leaned askew. Amid piles of embers they could see fragments of chairs and tables that had not yet burned up completely. A contemptuous wind swept through the dead ghetto's gutted alleys, rolling fragments of books and scrolls along the filthy pavement. Shadows of human beings scratched and poked about in the heaped-up dust and rubbish, in hopes of finding some remains of what had formerly been their homes.

There was nothing. Dust and ashes, stones and trash. . . .

The stifling air drove the Jewish partisans out toward the streets that were still inhabited. Those streets too, however, seemed wasted. There, too, Jews had once lived, but no longer. . . .

From time to time a sanitation truck would cross the street with a screech.

Shiny, red-cheeked apples were swaying on the trees. Eyes peered through the windows of the hospital, resting momentarily on the juicy fruits outside and then closing. Many were never to reopen. The fortunate patients would go home to their families, to their fathers and mothers, to the arms of faithful wives. Only the wounded Jews were devoid of hope. The first wild flush of victory had swiftly passed, leaving a cold emptiness in its place. *Why did I stay alive? Who needs me?*

On one of the beds in a small side room lay Shmulik. He had been hit by a bullet while pursuing a platoon of Lithuanian Shauliai who had barricaded themselves in the convent.

Shmulik looked at the window. The light hurt his eyes.

319

Half his head and one eye were bandaged. Shula said he was lucky not to have been killed.

Shmulik went over in his mind the happenings of the last few days. Shula had proved to be a real nurse. It was she who took care of him. In addition, Anatoli visited him frequently, sitting alongside his bed, speaking of shared memories and planning ahead.

Anatoli had taken him off the street. A good fellow, Anatoli. And Shula. . . .

Shmulik had returned to the forest angry at his commander—what gave him the right to smile that way at Shula and squeeze her hand? Now, longing took the place of irritation. Shmulik was still young. He was not yet fifteen.

When he opened his eyes at night he would see Anatoli and Shula bent over his bed, Shula's small hand in Anatoli's rough palm.

Shmulik had thought he was going to die. Upon regaining consciousness he had whispered, "Anatoli, I have a little sister . . . Hanna. . . . When I die, be a brother to her. Take her . . . to the Land of Israel. . . ."

The sinking August sun smiled through the window. Soon Shmulik would be visited by Rivka Wilensky. She always came at the same time. She still wore a cross around her neck, but by now she concealed it beneath her habit. She still lived in the convent. She was prepared to leave if someone from her family would come. The girl was all alone and very frightened.

Shmulik was very anxious to see her shed the identity of Biruté Magdalena. After all, she was a fine girl and of the Jewish people.

Again he recalled Shula's story. When the nuns had taken her down into the cellar she thought her time had come. She was sure they meant to turn her over to the Germans. But days passed and no one came except for the nun who once a day brought her bread and water. Her cell was always gloomy. Its one tiny window projected only halfway above the floor of the courtyard's back porch. Through the window she was able to see only the fence and a part of the wall of one building. The room contained a narrow iron bed with a straw mattress and on the wall a picture of Jesus crucified, before which a small oil lamp burned.

"Pray to Jesus to save your sinful soul," said the nun who brought her the bread and water.

So five days passed. On the sixth even the nun did not appear. Had they forgotten her? From the courtyard came the sound of men's voices and the clatter of swift footsteps on the yard's paving stones.

What was all the fuss, why were so many trucks rumbling about? The small window looked like a black patch on the gray cellar wall. The flame in the oil lamp flickered. Long shadows danced across the floor. The day had been stiflingly hot, but now a cool breeze blew in through the window.

Shula was so hungry and thirsty she wanted to cry. If only she could squeeze through the window into the yard. But she could not. Her way was blocked by two iron grids. She tried to squeeze her head between the bars but could not. Was she doomed to die of hunger and thirst? That couldn't be! If the nuns wanted to kill her they would have handed her over to the enemy one-two-three, she reasoned.

321

Shula tried as hard as she could to move the grids but was too weak. Her eyes filled with tears. She did not want to cry but the tears flowed of themselves. Someone was crossing the yard, softly. Was it a cat?

Shula's heart pounded. "I'm here, I. . . ."

By the light of the small oil lamp Shula made out a young face pressed against the window's bars.

"It's me—Rivka. Don't be scared."

Shula sobbed brokenly.

"I brought you food. . . . I hid my portion. . . . Don't cry, Shula, sh-h-h. They might hear us."

"Rivka, it's you?"

"It's me, Shulinka."

"What are they planning to do with me?"

"I don't know. Everything's topsy-turvy in the convent. They're packing things. Three truckloads left today. They must be emptying out the convent. The students have been told to be ready to travel."

"All the nuns are leaving?"

"No. Mother Beatta and a few others are staying."

"And you? Will you go, too?"

"Me?" For a moment there was silence. The question had taken Rivka by surprise. "I don't know anymore."

"Don't go away, Rivka. Don't go to the Germans. Stay here. You're Jewish."

"Yes, Shula. But I'm scared. I could never be like you."

"Don't be scared. Go into hiding. Soon we'll be free."

Two days later Shula was taken out of the cellar by Anatoli and the men of his platoon. Rivka Wilensky had shown them the way.

Epilogue

The end of summer 1945. Spider webs were borne aloft with every breeze, glistening in the light like silver woven on the looms of night elves.

The webs had enmeshed the ruins of German Street and Rodnizki Street, and the Jewish alley, the wretched haunts of the city of Vilna, formerly a thriving city of the Jewish people.

Alongside the house of the Jewish Committee, which had been organized after the liberation, sat a group of Jewish partisans on a pile of stones. Not all of them had taken off their forest clothes. The struggles they had undergone were still engraved on their faces.

Where to now? That was the question. Not all of them had clear answers.

Tulik Rubinstein—formerly Anatoli Hakim—rose tall among them. At his side was Shula Weiss. Not yet seventeen, the tall, slender girl looked much older. Her face showed refinement and tenderness, stubbornness and courage. She and Anatoli were wearing traveling clothes and their baggage was in their hands.

Where to? Theirs was to be a long journey, their destination clear: the Land of Israel. Shula and Anatoli were heading for the border. In the company of other partisans they were setting out for Poland and from there would cross lands and seas, pushing ever onward.

323

Shmulik accompanied them to the station. He had recovered completely but he had to stay behind. He meant to seek out his sister, Hanna.

He had already visited the Girius farm. There he found neither Stasé nor Hanna. The Giriuses would reveal nothing as to Hanna's whereabouts. They claimed that they had given the girl to another family and did not know where she was.

Shmulik realized that Stasé did not want to part with Hanna. But he would find her. Not for nothing had he been a fighting partisan, and the recipient of a medal as well.

The truck beeped its horn. Again hands pressed together and everyone embraced.

Rivka and her mother arrived. Mrs. Wilensky had returned from a concentration camp. Upon liberation she had immediately set out to find her daughter.

Rivka was blessed with good fortune—she had a mother. No longer was she an abandoned waif. She had removed her convent uniform. However, upon her chest, beneath her dress, lay the small bronze crucifix.

Another handshake and a last embrace. The vehicle began to move. Shula and Anatoli were looking out the window. Shula was waving her hand, with tears in her eyes. Anatoli's arm circled her narrow shoulders.

Shmulik knew that they would be happy. The day would come when they would build their home in the new homeland. And he would come join them, with Hanna. Then they would forget the torments of the past.

Would they ever really forget?